BE WARNED:

From the moment you meet beautiful Diana Stewart and the bizarre stranger who has invaded her life, you will be entangled in a medical thriller that brings suspenseful storytelling to a new state-of-the-art of shock. Superbly crafted, this taut and terrifying novel will have you suspended in a state of fear with each page, as it turns a lovely young woman's dream of happiness into a nightmare—and as New York's Upper East Side, with its most elegant brownstones, becomes the spine-chilling world of the hunter and the hunted. . . .

ENTANGLED

"GOOD HORROR . . . A FAST MANHATTAN SHREIKER!"

—*Kirkus Reviews*

"A FAST-PACED MEDICAL THRILLER!"

—*Publishers Weekly*

More Bestsellers from SIGNET

Entangled

by PAUL JASON and JEFFREY SAGER

A SIGNET BOOK

NEW AMERICAN LIBRARY

TIMES MIRROR

PUBLISHER'S NOTE

This novel is a work of fiction. Names, characters, places, and incidents are either the product of the author's imagination or are used fictitiously, and any resemblance to actual persons, living or dead, events, or locales is entirely coincidental.

Copyright © 1982 by Pro Media S.A.

All rights reserved.

A hardcover edition of *Entangled* was published simultaneously by The New American Library, Inc., and The New American Library of Canada.

 SIGNET TRADEMARK REG. U.S. PAT. OFF. AND FOREIGN COUNTRIES
REGISTERED TRADEMARK—MARCA REGISTRADA
HECHO EN CHICAGO, U.S.A.

SIGNET, SIGNET CLASSICS, MENTOR, PLUME, MERIDIAN AND NAL BOOKS are published by The New American Library, Inc., 1633 Broadway, New York, New York 10019

First Signet Printing, April, 1983

1 2 3 4 5 6 7 8 9

PRINTED IN THE UNITED STATES OF AMERICA

For Ellen

The dogs were howling again.

It wasn't even light out, for Chrissake, it was still dark, and the dogs were howling.

The retardo dogs.

Waking her up.

Making her face everything again, one more time, just like yesterday.

Dragging her out of the dream in which she was one of them TV Angels, with long dark hair and beautiful legs.

Two of them.

Like everybody else.

She kicked the covers off, letting her dirty yellow nightie slide back across her thigh, and raised her right leg high in the air, muscles tensed, toes pointed down, like the ballerinas she studied in the magazine pictures. She squinted along its exquisite length to the end of her big toe like a sniper with a telescopic sight. She pushed the thick, dank hair out of her eyes to do it better.

An absolutely perfect leg. She knew that. Lord knows, she should. She had looked at the magazine ads long enough and she had never seen any that looked better than her own. Long and full and rounded in the thigh, tapering down to the slender, subtly muscled calf, which narrowed to the small, delicately turned ankle and the immaculately proportioned foot.

Perfect.

Beautiful, sexy, functional.

Maybe the best leg she had ever seen in a lifetime of looking at legs.

Too bad she didn't have another one.

The alarm kept ringing. The alarm had woken the dogs, and the dogs had woken her. Angrily she groped around in the dark, sideswiping the clock, knocking it to the floor, silencing it immediately. She fumbled around on the night table until her fingers touched the thick stem of her black plastic eyeglasses. She put them on and peered down at the clock. 4:30. Jesus!

She was awake now, awake and fully conscious in a world she hated completely. She hated the animals, and she hated the filth, but most of all she hated the thing leaning against the wall, its metallic smile gleaming at her in the dark. Mocking her. Reading her mind. Every morning, when she woke in the darkness to the cries of the animals, it was there to greet her, shining in its polished malevolence, its plastic and leather complication, its technological assurance. Thigh-high, perfect in form, functional. Artificial. Fake. A cheat. Her left leg. Her fucking spare part. The leg she owned to replace the leg she never had. And her own was so beautiful.

Thrusting the covers off the bed, she sat up with a start, planting her foot on the floor with an audible smack. She flung herself upright and, with the expertise of life-long practice, hobbled across the room and grabbed the prosthesis like a naughty child. She strapped it on, her mumbled curses mingling with the insistent baying of the dogs waiting to be fed. She stamped down hard, securing her thigh into its leather socket. "Get in there, dumb Funkus!" she muttered.

Thump went the leg.

"Fat Trunkus!" snarled the girl.

Thump went the leg.

Sweating now, her mood a thing of muddied colors, she moved out into the narrow corridor, her awkward gait angling her body slightly to the right. She paused for a moment to peer into Joel's room. He was still asleep, as usual, snoring with his mouth open, leaving her to feed the goddamned animals. Good. That was still better than dealing with him and his needs. He always talked about his needs like they were living things, living things demanding attention and care. Her attention. Her care. Well, there was no way she was going to deal with Joel and his needs when it wasn't even light out, for Chrissake. She walked on past his cubicle.

When she went into the cage room, it was the stink that hit her first. It made her want to gag. It made her want to kill the animals. Maybe this morning she would kill one of 'em. One of them cats. Or maybe a rabbit . . . better yet, one of them dogs. She despised the dogs most of all.

She ripped open a large sack of feed and flung fistfuls of brown meal across the floor. Unlatching the cages, she watched in disgust as the beasts scrambled out and fought for the food. Then, for maybe the ten-thousandth time, she set about cleaning the cages, pulling the excrement-smeared newspapers from the wire floors of the pens, replacing each with a fresh sheet of newsprint from the stack by the door. Some mornings she would spit on every clean page, just so she'd be the first to foul it, before the little beasts let loose with their own torrent of waste. This morning she contented herself with a well-placed kick at those animals that had left the biggest mess for her to clean.

She had gotten as far as the cage belonging to the wire-haired terrier with the broken snout when something from the newspaper caught her eye. At first she wasn't even sure what it was.

The page stared up at her. The New York Times. Society section. Weddings and engagement announcements. A gray blur of print, three scattered pictures. It was the picture in the lower right-hand corner. . . .

3

She pulled out the page and held it close to her face. She felt her heart skip. Her fingers tightened around the edges of the paper. It was such an amazing picture that she scooted into the bathroom, where she could look at it in private. She turned on the light and locked the door.

Then she looked at the picture again.

Her forehead wrinkled in a puzzled way.

The picture was of a girl with long dark hair and smiling eyes. A girl who was thinking of something happy.

She held the picture up close to her eyes until the photograph was merely a collection of black and white dots one next to the other. She moved the photograph away to arm's length. The girl in the picture was well groomed, neat.

Her lips moved hesitantly as she mouthed the headline above the photo. "Diana Stewart and Thomas L. Johnson Announce Their Engagement, Bla, Bla, Bla."

Suddenly her eyes opened wide in recognition. She held the photo next to her cheek and stared into the mirror. The girl's face was like her own! Tentatively, she pushed the hair away from her forehead. It wasn't a mistake. Nose for nose, ear for ear, the girl had her face. In-fucking-credible!

Her eyes darted back and forth from the newspaper to the mirror, from photograph to reflection.

Glossy hair; ratty hair.

Smiling eyes; red-rimmed eyes.

Gleaming teeth; dirty teeth.

An open, glowing, joyful look; a pinched, wary look.

Except for those things, she and this girl could almost be the same person.

Except for those things, and the fact that this rich bitch Diana Stewart had both her goddamn legs, or else this Thomas L. Johnson, whoever he was, wouldn't be marrying her.

It was unfair, that's what it was.

1

Diana Stewart walked down Greenwich Avenue with the smooth, sure stride of a dancer. A striking girl, as much because of a glow of good health and good fortune as because of any unusual turn of feature.

A great deal of that good fortune had to do with the handsome young man who walked hand in hand beside her. His name was Thomas Leland Johnson and, at twenty-eight years old, he possessed all the self-assurance that comes from having an extremely fine job with a Wall Street investment bank, a job that had been arranged by an extremely wealthy father.

On this steamy summer afternoon, when most of the young men walking down Greenwich Avenue wore work shirts and cut-off jeans with little individual dashes of flair to announce their uniqueness to the world, Thomas Johnson's clothes shouted Princeton right back at them. His custom-made blue linen jacket, cuffed white poplin pants, and red checked Brooks Brothers shirt said to everyone who passed, in no uncertain terms, that Exeter '66, Princeton '70, was *just visiting*. While there were a lot of things in the last ten years that Tom had considered doing to show his parents that he was his own man, living in Greenwich Village wasn't one of them. He'd never do that. He didn't believe there was a laundry south of Murray Hill that would do his shirts the way he wanted them.

Tom was indulging himself in one of his favorite minor recreations. He was watching the guys in work shirts and cut-offs turn around on the street to stare at his fiancée's legs. Heaven knew they were certainly worth staring at: ballerina's legs, long and sensual and lean in the thigh, stretching down to the extended arc of her tightly sculpted calves. Absolutely remarkable. But what was really interesting to Tom was the way the guys carried it off.

The method was expressive of personality. Some just turned around and ogled, as open as you please. Others went through a whole elaborate ritual, stopping dead, snapping their fingers or slapping their foreheads as if they had forgotten something terribly important, then turning around with a great sense of purpose, pretending to look past her toward the horizon. All to catch that exquisite peek. What Tom liked best about it, of course, was knowing that each of those guys ached like hell to be in his place, walking hand in hand down the street with a girl who looked like Diana Stewart. The knowledge gave him a feeling of well-being and superiority, like cruising Park Avenue in a Rolls Royce.

A man in a hurry brushed by Tom and murmured an apology.

Tom didn't answer him, but instead checked for his wallet. "You have to watch out for pickpockets around here," he warned Diana.

"Oh, look Tom! I didn't think they'd be open Saturday."

Suddenly Tom wasn't walking with his fiancée anymore. Diana had slipped her hand free of his and run over to stare into a store window. Tom didn't even have to look to know what kind of store it was.

A pet shop, naturally. Asking Diana to pass a window with puppies in it was like asking Diana's dog Taffy to pass any tree still left unfouled on Manhattan Island. Diana was the biggest sucker for animals since Noah, and like Noah, she would happily have taken two of everything, if Tom had let her. She didn't realize that the happy little balls of fur scratching against the glass were deliberately bred for adorableness, designed to steal your heart and separate you from your wallet. She didn't understand that in only three months they would mutate into full-grown beasts that made on the rug and slobbered on your guests.

Diana's fondness for animals was only the first of her two obsessions that confounded Tom no end. The other was her love for dance. She was always running off to dance practice. He knew that was what kept her body in sensational shape, so he didn't mind too much, but it did take up a lot of her time. And his, when she dragged him off to see a ballet with her. Diana knew the names of everyone in Balanchine's company the way that sports nuts knew the entire Yankee lineup for the '27 World Series.

Often Tom thought that the perfect present for Diana, combining her two great passions, would be a dancing bear. But she'd probably be so taken with the damned thing that she'd end up hibernating with it for the winter.

Without looking at her, Tom said, in a slightly louder tone than was absolutely necessary, "I win again."

Diana was too absorbed with her furry friends to pay any attention to him.

"What did you say?" she asked absently.

Reluctantly Tom walked over to stand beside her in front of the puppy-laden window.

"I said, 'I win again,' " he repeated. "I just bet myself a dollar you couldn't pass this place without looking in." He had, in fact, done no such thing, but he would have, if he'd thought of it, and it seemed as good a way as any of making his point.

"Different strokes," Diana said cheerfully. "You like bankers, I like puppies."

"I never thought of it that way."

"Sure. It's all a matter of upbringing. Your house was always full of bankers, mine was always full of puppies."

"In my house," Tom replied, "they grew up to be rich and prominent. In yours they grew up to bite strangers on the leg."

Diana chose to ignore that, mostly because a heart-breaking little furball had just caught her attention. "Look there," she said, pointing. "The little guy with the black patch on his eye. Isn't he adorable?"

"He's cute enough." Tom didn't think it was safe to be any more enthusiastic.

But that was enough enthusiasm for Diana. "He likes you, too," she said. "Look at the way he's staring at you."

"He's not staring at me. He's eyeing that hydrant over there."

They were playing a game now, a game that Diana enjoyed more than Tom. "How can you say that?" she demanded. "Look at his eyes. Like a war orphan. He adores you! It's written all over him."

"The only thing that's written all over him is 'Buy Me,'" Tom replied. "You said the one last week adored me, too. You said that one had eyes like a Keane painting."

"Well, he did." Diana turned to face Tom, trying her best to appear as wistful to him as the puppy did to her. "Can we go in and look at him, just for a minute?"

"I can see him fine from right here."

Sometimes, Diana thought, her future husband lacked poetry. If these sweet little furry things were columns of profit and loss figures, he'd be happy enough to stare at them for hours. She took hold of Tom's hand again and looked into his eyes, giving it everything she had.

"I want to hold him, Tom."

"Honey," Tom said, in the manner of someone attempting to explain a complicated sequence of events to a small child, "if you hold him, you'll want to buy him, and we can't buy him, because in less than two months we're going away for our honeymoon, and I refuse to take any animal, no matter how cute, on our honeymoon. Besides, you already have a puppy."

"Now that sounds to me," Diana pouted, "like I have to decide between you or my puppy."

Tom put his arms around his fiancée in a gesture at once both affectionate and possessive.

"Better take me, sweetheart," he said, "you've already got me housebroken."

◆◆◆

"Don't give me that, Stewart," Sarah Cooper said, watching Diana spin around triumphantly in the intricate white wedding gown. "You love it. He doesn't even want to share you with a dog."

"What love can do, that dares love attempt," Diana answered.

"*Romeo and Juliet*, Act II, English 104," Sarah jumped in knowingly.

"Junior year, Professor Nicolov, B+." Diana smiled back. "I deserved an A."

Standing there next to the dress racks on the fourth floor of Bergdorf Goodman, looking at herself in the store's three-way mirror, Diana was radiant. Few brides look as stunning on their wedding day as she did right then.

Sarah had insisted on being present at the final fitting of Diana's gown. Seeing the dress before Tom did reconfirmed her special place in Diana's life, their unspoken pact of sisterhood.

"Best friends" was an understatement, yet theirs was a friendship that didn't stand out. It had simply always been there. Never questioned and thus never doubted. Diana's remaining link with the simplicity of her youth, when life's most important problems were whether one's breasts were too big or too small and whether, through some act of God or Clearasil, the zit on your chin would disappear before Saturday night's date.

9

From high school through Smith College they had known all the details of all the boys and men in each other's lives: the first time Robby Youngstein tried sneaking a hand under Sarah's dress, the size of Jonathan Boyd's tongue, and the unexpected news that Arnold Abbott didn't wear underwear. They were each other's history. And from hairdos to husbands, they passed continuous and uninhibited judgment on each other's existence.

"You look absolutely incredible," Sarah said. It was a statement of fact, without envy or flattery. "It's practically obscene. When Tom sees you in that, he's going to throw you under the nearest pew and have you right there in church."

Diana just smiled, accepting, and continued to stare at herself in the mirror. Sarah twiddled nervously with the long curls of her bright-red hair. In deference to the occasion she had worn her nicest suit, a brown gabardine Evan Picone, whose loose fit didn't quite manage to hide the soft bulge of an ever-nagging weight problem.

Just when Sarah was getting ready to ask if the future Mrs. Johnson had decided to become a complete narcissist and stand there staring at herself forever, Diana said softly, "I wish my parents could have seen me in this. Especially Mom."

Sarah was unexpectedly touched by the remark and reached for Diana's hand, "It doesn't do any good to think about the accident. You're supposed to be happy."

"I am happy," Diana replied, trying to sound convincing. "I'm just sad that they can't be happy with me, that's all."

Emotion welled up inside her, and she fought to hold back the tears. She was sure her parents' absence was going to be the one thing she would always remember most about the wedding ceremony, and she didn't want it to be that way. Life goes on, as Tom had told her so many times, and even though it was a cliché, she knew it was true. If there was one thing in the world of which she was absolutely positive, it was that nothing she could do would bring back her parents. There was no reason to keep thinking about their death and letting it cast a pall over what was supposed to be the happiest day of her life. But she couldn't stop thinking about it. They were her parents, and even though they were gone, they wouldn't go away.

Her musings were interrupted by a young salesgirl, all smiles and resolute charm. "It's perfect, isn't it?"

Diana shook herself back to the present. "I love it. You'll be extra careful putting it in the box, won't you?"

"You'll never know it was folded," the salesgirl reassured her.

Diana found herself wondering how many times the girl had been asked the same question and had given the same answer. It was like that at the book store, too. Everybody thought they were the only ones asking for the new fad-diet book. Everybody thought they were the only ones getting married.

Everybody thought they were the only ones whose parents died.

Sarah's six-year-old, curly-topped daughter, Nina, crawled up next to Diana's feet.

"Diana, will you name your baby Taffy, too?" the little girl asked. She was referring to Diana's constant companion, the small cocker spaniel that was the bane of Tom's existence and that was just now trying to find his way under the hem of his mistress' wedding gown.

Diana laughed, thinking of what her future husband would say if he heard that suggestion.

"Maybe the third one," she kidded. "I'm going to name the first two Rover and Spot."

Sarah smiled down at her daughter. "Honey, why would she name her baby after her dog?"

Nina reached for the little spaniel's ears. "Because she loves him," she said, as if that settled the whole thing.

And perhaps it did, but the naive certainty of Nina's

response brought all those nagging questions bubbling up in Diana's mind again. Impulsively she threw her arms around her best friend and spoke with a sudden intensity. "Sarah, you've been through all this already and you're my best friend, so tell me for the tenth time that I'm doing the right thing."

Sarah looked at her friend's troubled face and decided that what she was hearing was an absolutely serious, deeply important request. It was true she had her reservations about Tom—she had once told her husband, Jack, that Tom Johnson sent his shirts out to be stuffed—but she had spoken her mind on that score before.

"Look," she said, "Tom's from a good family, right?"

"Too good," Diana answered grimly.

"He likes the same things you do, right?"

Diana smiled. "Almost never."

Sarah turned the knife one more time. "And you're crazy about his friends, right?"

"Wrong," Diana answered.

"Honey," Sarah said, spreading her arms, "it's gonna be a terrific marriage. You guys will have plenty to talk about. No matter what anyone tells you, that's the key to connubial bliss."

Diana burst out laughing and embraced her friend again. "Sarah, you're terrific. Promise me we'll stay best friends." Her voice turned slightly wistful. "Sometimes when people get married, they drift apart."

"Only from the person they're married to," Sarah replied.

She didn't look as though she was joking.

But Diana wasn't going to let that bother her. She was determined to resist the dark view of marriage that so many women she knew seemed to share. She wasn't like most of her friends, who looked upon marriage not as an opportunity for emotional growth but as the cancellation of all possibilities: no more good times, no more exciting men. One acquaintance of hers had described marriage as twenty years without parole.

Diana had long since stopped arguing with people who expressed that opinion. Besides, what could she say? All she knew was that she was in love with someone who loved her and told her so every chance that he got. If that wasn't enough to make a marriage work, Diana couldn't begin to guess what was.

Sarah watched the emotions flow across her best friend's face, saw the stubborn determination there, and felt guilty that she had been so blunt on this of all days. But damn it, a friend is supposed to tell you those things, even when they're not what you want to hear. She retreated from her guilt, hiding in practicality. "Mrs. Johnson!" she said in a gruff, comic-opera voice, tapping the crystal of her wristwatch.

For an instant Diana was uncomprehending. Then she looked startled. "Oh, lord, you're right!" She checked her own watch. "Fifteen after. If I don't get back in three and a half seconds, this wedding'll take me right down to the unemployment office. Mr. Russell isn't exactly noted for his tolerance of employees who take two-and-a-half-hour lunch breaks." Diana hoisted the hem of her wedding gown and scurried back toward the dressing cubicles behind the showroom. "I'll be ready in a sec."

"Four-minute limit," Sarah called after her, grabbing for Nina, who was grabbing for Taffy, who was trying to follow Diana. The salesgirl put on a longsuffering look.

Diana had left her clothes in the third cubicle. Or was it the fourth? She tried the third door and found it locked. A muffled grunting sound came from behind it. "Sorry," she offered, trying the next door and stepping inside.

Slipping out of the exquisite gown, she hung it carefully on its padded hanger, smoothing away some imaginary wrinkles. She studied her near-naked body in the dressing-room mirror. Prime meat, she thought; men had gone to war for less.

Quickly she bent down to the chair to retrieve the dark blue pantyhose she had taken off for the fitting. But they weren't on the chair, they were on the floor, balled up in a corner of the cubicle. Jesus, had she really left them on the floor like that? She slid her left foot in and pulled them up.

Something didn't feel right.

The pantyhose didn't fit at all anymore. They were gullied with runs, droopy at the knee, and stretched out shapelessly at the foot. They looked as if someone had jammed their leg into them with a shoe still on. But that was crazy. People simply didn't go around sneaking into dressing rooms in fine department stores, sticking their feet into other people's underwear. Or did they? For all she knew, maybe it happened all the time in a store this big and in a city so full of weirdos. Hastily Diana peeled off the pantyhose, feeling as if she'd just sat down on a still-warm toilet seat.

She threw on her dress and slipped her right foot into her shoe. Now, where was the other shoe? Damn it, this was getting ridiculous. She was late enough already, without . . . Then out of the corner of her eye she suddenly saw it!

On the back of the door, maybe five feet off the floor the shoe was pressed flat up against the mahogany paneling, as if suspended in midair. It looked like it had been nailed to the wall.

Diana let out a long, slow breath. She reached for the shoe, her fingers trembling slightly. What the hell was going on here, anyway? She took hold of the rubber heel and slowly pulled it toward her. The shoe had not been nailed. It was held in place by a huge wad of wet pink bubblegum. As Diana pulled, the gum stretched a full foot, glistening like some obscene pink umbilical cord. Then it snapped with an audible pop.

She glanced at her watch again, and in a moment all that was on her mind was whether it would be faster to walk back to work or take a cab through the midtown traffic.

"For God's sake!" The words had tumbled out of Diana's mouth.

2

Diana stood back and observed her work, a hand on her hip, her head cocked to one side. She was building a display pyramid out of copies of the latest diet cookbook, ten copies wide at the base, ten rows high at its peak. At this point she had five rows in place, each book positioned with care. Her work could not have been more meticulous had she been handling delicate Limoges figurines. And in truth she felt that way, for she loved everything about books. First of all, she loved what they contained. Knowledge and information, emotion and style. An author's sweat and blood. But she also liked the books as objects. A gold-edged, leatherbound rare edition was a beautiful thing. But no less beautiful was a brand-new book with the aroma of fresh paper and ink still on it, that unmistakable smell you got whenever you opened up a crate of new books straight from the publisher's warehouse. She liked to look at them, to feel them, to arrange and display them as she was doing now.

She considered herself fortunate indeed to be working in such an elegant and well-known bookstore as Scribner's, with its big old windows looking out on Fifth Avenue, the most exciting street in the world. Whenever she looked at the big black door she couldn't help but think of all the great authors who had passed through it. Hemingway had walked through that doorway. So had Lardner and Wolfe and, of course, Fitzgerald.

In fact, it had struck Diana how Thomas Leland Johnson himself could have popped right out of Fitzgerald's

This Side of Paradise, with his Princeton friends and non-chalant grace. Even the way he turned a phrase had the ring of Fitzgerald. "Better take me, sweetheart, you've already got me housebroken." Could Jay Gatsby have said it with more charm or conviction?

It occurred to Diana that Tom would have delighted in the comparison, for he saw himself, unconsciously perhaps, as one of Fitzgerald's worldly, well-bred, reasonable men somehow caught in the thrall of a madcap. And "madcap" was exactly the word Tom would have used. It evoked Carole Lombard tossing an expensive chapeau over the side of the *Ile de France* in mid-Atlantic. Madcaps were enchanting, but they dragged you to your doom.

Tom had been much impressed—mesmerized, Diana thought—by an English professor of his, who, in discussing Zelda Fitzgerald's fabled charm, had used the expression "the spindrift of madness." What he had meant was that her charm was like the white filigree on top of a powerful wave that would eventually suck you under. It pleased Tom to think of his madcap Diana as equally dangerous, with her ballet lessons and stray puppies. He expected his friends to envy him and feel sorry for him simultaneously.

Diana saw a different truth. She wasn't that carefree ingenue, even if she sometimes played the role to please Tom. Indeed, in recent months even Diana's most spontaneous moments of gaiety and ebullience were not without their twinge of guilt. That was normal—to be expected—at least according to everything she had read and everyone to whom she had talked. How many times had she been told, "You're not responsible, Diana. The accident wasn't your fault." But still she felt the guilt.

Sometimes, when she lay in a half-sleep, when the rhythm of Tom's breathing was the only sound in the room, she would hear the phone ringing and remember the midnight conversation.

"Is this Diana Stewart?"

"Yes. Who is this?" she had mumbled, chasing the sleep from her voice.

"I'm terribly sorry to bother you at this late hour, miss. May I ask if you're alone?"

Her first thought had been, "It's an obscene phone call. Next he'll want to know what I'm wearing." But there was something about the voice. . . . She sat up in bed.

"Who is this, please? What do you want?"

"This is Sergeant Morton, Miss Stewart, down at the Sixth Precinct. I'm, uh, afraid I've got some really bad news for you."

Diana's heart skipped a beat.

"It's your parents, ma'am."

The receiver almost slipped out of her suddenly clammy hand.

"What's wrong with them?"

The cop had trouble getting the words out. "Your parents were in an accident on Route 128, and I'm afraid they didn't make it."

All she could say, in a thin, quiet voice, was, "Not both of them."

"I'm sorry to say, miss, your father was driving, and we think he blew a tire or something." The policeman's voice was coming to her through a distant fog. "One thing we're sure of, Miss Stewart. They died on impact. They didn't have any pain."

Diana had often wondered what Sergeant Morton looked like. She thought it strange that she would never see the person whose phone call had made her an orphan. Why had he asked her if she was alone? Tom thought maybe some people had heart attacks or something. The cops didn't want to get sued.

This had all happened more than six months previously. Yet as her marriage drew nearer, Diana found the memory of that grim night replaying itself in her head over and over again. Not only the crash, but a conversation held earlier on the same day, when her father had called from his office. They'd be driving up at nine, he'd said, his voice a little too jovial. Looking forward to meeting their future son-in-law. Diana remembered nodding into the phone as he'd talked. She knew they were coming up, it had been planned for weeks. Why was he reiterating it now?

Then, with his voice still too casual, too cheerful, he had said, "Listen, honey, I want to talk to you when we get there. Alone."

"Okay," she'd said. "What about?"

"Something personal," he'd answered. "Something I, uh, think you should know about. Hell, if you're old enough to get married and have kids, then it's time we sat down. And, honey, it's just between you and me for now—okay? Not for Mom. Okay?"

She had agreed, vaguely uneasy. Was it her father's health? Her mother's? Visions of cancer had raced through her mind.

But that conversation had never been held, her questions never answered. Not those nagging questions, nor the most important one of all: What would her parents have thought of Tom?

Diana had met Tom in a most pedestrian fashion almost two years before. He had walked into Scribner's looking for a book. Diana had recently been promoted to assistant store manager and was no longer required to chase down books on the selling floor. Yet this time she was quick to help; Tom intrigued her. Even in as stylish a town as New York he stood out. He had a youthful handsomeness that was strangely at odds with a graceful, worldly manner. Perfect, Diana had concluded, even before he had uttered a word—right down to one slightly crooked tooth.

He had been looking for an analytical book on economic theory, every bit as precise as he was. When Diana found the book wasn't in stock and suggested another store nearby, Tom was so obviously determined to maintain their conversation that he continued to purchase book after book until he had finally talked her into having coffee with him. Many books and many coffees later, she was living with him.

She had never thought she was the kind of person who could be swept off her feet like that. But he had an element of boyishness, of sudden enthusiasms, which endeared him to Diana, touched her in ways no other man had.

Accustomed to managing for herself, Diana was at first apprehensive, then pleased by the way Tom took charge. Tom made the decisions; Tom planned their lives. He did this in accordance with his volatile and confused feelings toward two powerful but unseen entities called My Parents, whom he invoked and cursed in the same manner island priests invoked the gods and demons of the volcanos.

Diana had never met these creatures. She and Tom had lived together for almost a year, and during that time Mr. and Mrs. Johnson had not once visited the apartment or even phoned. And Tom had never volunteered to take Diana to visit them. She was certain it wasn't that he was ashamed of her. Tom was better than that. But he liked to sail his taut craft on the sea of life making as few ripples as possible. So while Diana knew that his parents' disapproval of her was assurance to Tom of his independence, she was also aware of how carefully he kept that disapproval straitjacketed. Very simply, it was an adolescent rebellion, and Tom was too old for it. It had worried Diana.

Then her parents died so swiftly, in such a random, idiotic way, that for days the only thing that made any shred of sense to her was her relationship with Tom. And he was a rock through it all.

He helped with the funeral arrangements and, she was sure, lied to her about the bills. In every possible way he cared for her. He never complained. He never grumbled at her sullenness, her preoccupation, her lack of responsiveness. He made her feel like a person of infinite value for whom it was a privilege to do all the things he was doing. He waited patiently for her to become herself again.

Which was why, standing now in Scribner's, looking at her half-built pyramid of books, Diana felt secretly ashamed of the strange and confusing thought that had just crossed her mind: that Tom Johnson might not be the best person to have in your corner in a crisis. She was ashamed of the thought, but it wouldn't go away. She guessed it had something to do with the fact that in the twenty-two months they had known each other, Tom had never lost his temper with her. In the inevitable ups and downs of a close relationship, it intrigued her that anyone could be so stubborn in avoiding confrontation.

Quickly she shoved the doubts into the cellar of her mind. "Enough," she almost muttered aloud. Prenuptial jitters. She was going to have a wonderful marriage to a wonderful man who loved her, and that was that! With none of her usual reverence and care, she stuck another book onto the pyramid of bestsellers.

✦✦✦

"GET OUT OF MY HOUSE AND TAKE YOUR PIG DOG WITH YOU."

The words had been sitting on the tip of her tongue all afternoon, and now she couldn't hold them back anymore.

"I KNOW WHERE YOU HIDE HIS WORM AND IT SMELLS LIKE FISH IN THERE."

She stood mumbling at the Fifth Avenue bus stop opposite Scribner's, but she wasn't waiting for any bus. She was staring at that rich girl working in the bookstore across the street.

"I'LL BE WAITING UNDER THE BED, YOU BITCH."

People crowded around her, jostling and bumping her as the bus approached, angry at her for being in their way. She battled back with a repertoire of small, well-hidden punches and kicks aimed at anyone who tried to move in front of her.

What she really wanted to do was rip off their ears. They'd knock over a poor one-legged cripple just to get a seat on the goddamned bus. Well, they could shove it up their kunkus.

And the bus drivers, they weren't any better. They thought it was okay to drive their machines right up in front of her to pick up the retardos who were pushing and squeezing just to get to work. Never caring that they were blocking her view.

She couldn't believe it! Some fat bag lady was going to walk right in front of her. No way, Fatso! Maybe she couldn't stop the buses, but Fatso didn't have four wheels.

Her elbow shot into the bag lady's ribcage, sending odds and ends from a thousand sidewalk garbage cans spewing into the street. Next time I'll rip your head off, Fatso.

It was a free country, wasn't it? At least, that's what they said on the TV all the time, even though she'd never gotten anything for free in her whole stinking life. You always had to pay for it one way or the other, even if it was only the insults of the men who ran out of their stores and tried to chase you away, when all you were doing was standing on the street watching the TV that they put in their windows.

But now she didn't care about that, because she'd found something better to watch than any old TV show—that girl across the street. That girl whose picture she'd seen in the newspaper, the one she had followed from the house on Eighty-second Street, the one who looked like her. Like she should look. But that girl wasn't so smart, that was for sure. That girl spent all her time piling books up on tables. Or handing them to people. What kind of a thing was that to do, for Chrissake? If she looked like that girl, she'd find better things to do with her time, you could bet on that.

Hell, she had something better to do right now. And she was doing it.

That girl who had occupied her every waking moment. She had found her.

✦✦✦

Dance class. If there was anything Diana liked better than being at the bookstore, it was this. Dance class was art, discipline, exercise, and self-expression all at once. After a long day on the floor at Scribner's it was a chance to clear her head and allow her body to take over, letting the moves burrow their way down into the nerves and muscles until she did them automatically, smoothly, without thinking about them. And the wonderful part was that Tom never dared to object, not about the time and not about the cost, because he knew it was this, more than anything else, that kept her body lean and supple, able to do the things they still didn't dare speak about out loud, not even to one another, able to excite him every time he looked at her.

Twice a week after work Diana trooped off to dance class—Jazz, Modern, and Classical Ballet—taught by a chunky, middle-aged lady named Madame Margot, who had a large, loftlike practice room in the rabbit warrens above Carnegie Hall.

As the students all knew, Madame Margot taught dance because she loved it and was not good enough to be a ballerina. That didn't bother any of them. No one there expected to turn into Maria Tallchief or dance *pas de*

23

deux with Baryshnikov. But they reveled in their dance and they knew that Madame Margot did, too, and they valued her devotion and craft and attention to detail.

Today the class was dancing to an old Duke Ellington record, "Things Ain't What They Used to Be," chosen for its rock-steady beat. Twelve young women in leotards executed the steps, while Madame Margot, implacable as a drill instructor, counted cadence in the background: "One, two, three, four, five, six, seven, and One, two, three, four . . ."

Diana caught a quick flash of herself and the other women in the mirror that took up most of the wall behind her. What she saw was a scene surprising in its intense eroticism. Formal and precise, and twice as erotic for being so. Twelve young bodies in different colored leotards—red and yellow and blue and purple and black, looking like the crayons she used to carry in her pencil box when she was a child—bending and flexing in unison to Ellington's old rhythm, twelve bodies displaying their beauty and function and potential, all at the same time. Trim waists, tethered breasts, supple calves, voluptuous thighs, all made neuter and geometrical by the impersonality of the mirror, like some trick shot in an old Busby Berkeley movie. Diana thought that she and her classmates were the sexiest thing she had ever seen, and the idea both shocked and pleased her.

If there was any true eroticism to the tableau, Madame Margot was either oblivious to it or ignored it. She continued to sound like a drill instructor. "All right, ladies," she said, at the end of the exercise. "It's getting better. In fact, quite respectable. Diana, you're getting a little more supple. Mary, you're finally managing to keep the beat. I'm very proud of you."

The two complimented dancers smiled happily at one another. Madame Margot was as sparing with her praise as a pro football coach. It was her way of spurring the ladies on in the quest for excellence.

"Gelsey Kirkland doesn't have to worry," she continued, possibly because she saw the look exchanged by Diana and Mary and didn't want self-satisfaction to lead to laxness. "You girls still have a lot of work to do, if you want to look like dancers. Now, in this next number," she said, as she selected a new record, "I want you all to work on using every part of your body."

"That's what my husband says," Mary murmured, and the class broke out laughing.

+++

Diana gave herself the luxury of an extra-long, extra-hot shower after class, letting the heat soothe her sore leg muscles. She was the last one out of the building and emerged to find it raining so hard that she could barely see the street. Shadowy blurs, hunched over, passed on the sidewalk. Larger forms plowed cautiously down the street itself, creating bow-waves on the drowned pavement. As usual, when you really needed one, there wasn't a taxi in sight. Diana had nearly resigned herself to having to backstroke to the subway when the distinctive *bleep-bleep* of Tom's car-horn cut through the roar of the rain. Sure enough, the little green MGB convertible was sitting at the curb, hubcap-deep in water. Tom blinked the lights and waved for her to join him. She waved back, took a deep breath, and sprinted down the steps and across the sidewalk, holding her purse over her head like an umbrella, yet knowing the gesture was futile. At just the right moment Tom opened the door for her, and she wiggled herself into the tiny car, slamming the door as quickly as she could.

"Hi, gorgeous," Tom yelled over the bass-drum noise of the downpour pounding on the car's fabric roof. "Need a lift?"

"More like a rescue," she yelled back, matching his light tone but unable to keep the puzzlement out of her voice. Tom seldom picked her up after class, and never this cheerfully. "What's the occasion?"

"True love, that's all."

She nodded, charmed with his unexpected playfulness. "Did you foreclose on an aged widow this morning?"

"Close enough. Let's just say it was a good day at the bank and that your future husband closed a big deal." He started the engine, adding to the noise, and grinned at her. "A deal so big it deserves—no, demands—celebration!" He put on a mock-stern face and consulted his Rolex. "You have exactly five seconds to name a restaurant at the corner of Sixty-fifth and Third Avenue. Four, three, two—"

"The Sign of the Dove," she squealed, delighted. She leaned over and kissed him on the cheek. "I hope it's as good as the book."

"Who knows," he replied smartly, not even minding that her hair was dripping on his blazer. "You've never been to the restaurant, and I've never read the book." He put the car in gear.

Outside, a gray smear lurched in front of the car, haloed eerily by the headlights. An unopened umbrella hung limply at its side.

Tom's mood shifted instantly to annoyance. He leaned on his horn. "Damned bums."

The apparition stood its ground, a weird figure with wide, staring eyes and flapping arms, alternately appearing and disappearing to the beat of the windshield wipers. Tom banged the horn and cranked down his window slightly, letting in bursts of hard-driven rain. "Get out from in front of my car," he yelled. "Move it, buddy!"

And the figure moved. It leapt and landed spread-eagled on the hood. Its fingers clawed at the windshield wipers, tearing one off from the driver's side. Diana heard herself screaming uncontrollably, and Tom reacted to her panicked call, pushing her back in the bucket seat. The figure on the hood banged furiously on the windshield, using its fists to pummel the glass. Muffled, garbled shouts came spewing from its mouth.

"Okay, asshole," Tom yelled back. "That's it! That does it!" He reached for the door handle, but a second too late. With a quick, crablike movement the figure on the hood reared back, the black umbrella held high like a spear. Then savagely it lunged forward and down, driving the umbrella's metal point through the car's fabric roof. Tom stared in mute horror as the needlelike spike plunged deep into the leather upholstery next to his head.

"Jesus Christ!" Tom shouted, the fear almost choking him. "He's trying to kill us!"

His hand shot out to grab the weapon, but it was yanked upward and out before he could reach it. A river of water poured down through the gaping hole hacked into the car's canvas top. Diana forced her eyes to look up, only to see the black harpoon boring in on *her* this time. With an agonized shriek she propelled herself forward as the blade hurtled inside, puncturing the plastic armrest next to her.

"Oh, God, Tom," she cried, writhing away from the wicked steel tip. "Get us out of here! GET US OUT!"

The figure on the hood moved with the intensity of a jackhammer—jabbing, thrusting, seeking its prey. Suddenly the sportscar had become a frenzied hellhole, its occupants easy targets at point-blank range. Diana wanted to open the door, escape from the death trap, but her body was limp and refused to obey her.

Tom reached for the gear shift in desperate need, but the cold steel came again, plunging down with the force of a javelin. Instinctively he jerked his hand back an instant before it would have been impaled. Water flooded in, making it impossible to see anything.

And then, somehow, Tom had the car in gear. He gunned the engine and sent the MGB careening out into the street. For a heartbeat the figure was thrown face-first against the windshield directly in front of Diana. She peered into a tortured face, blurred by rain. Demented, hate-burned eyes stared straight into Diana's own. Then the car surged forward, and the assailant slid off, clawing frantically at the smooth surface of the car's hood. Through all the howl of sound, through the engine and the rain and her own terrified wails, Diana could still hear a strange, flat, metallic thud as the body hit the street.

But it was a fleeting sound and lost in the rising whine of the car's engine as Tom accelerated blindly into the rainstorm.

❖❖❖

With a screeching of brakes Tom pulled up before a reconditioned brownstone on East Eighty-second Street.

"Damn, damn, damn," he muttered, smacking the steering wheel with his palm, more in resignation than anger. He was cursing the latest injustice of this harrowing night. First there was the madman's attack, spoiling his victory at the bank, not to mention his convertible top. Then there was the thief at the service station who had recognized their desperation and charged seventy-five bucks to patch the cartop with some kind of hideous silver tape. Only to be followed by what seemed like an endless ride home, both of them chilled to the bone on one of the hottest nights of the summer. And now this!

Diana sat next to him in the car, afraid to move or comment. Motor idling, the MGB waited in the middle of the street directly in front of their brownstone apartment. Tom's parking space—he thought of it as his space—was there but unusable. A Cadillac and a Mercedes crowded into it from either end, their bumpers encroaching on the allotted spot.

Diana saw the look in Tom's eye and knew what he was thinking. "Why don't you park around the corner by the fire hydrant?" she chanced. "It'll be quicker that way."

"Not tonight, I'm not." He eased the car forward, dead set on parking his own car in front of his own house, by God, or knowing the reason why not. "How much room do I have in back?"

"An eighth of an inch."

"Good." Tom grunted, readying himself for combat.

He gunned the car into reverse, twisting the steering wheel further than he should. The car leapt backward, jerked to a stop, then sprang forward and stopped again. His entire concentration focused on the task, Tom proceeded to see-saw his way noisily into the minuscule parking spot, until he had finally shoehorned the MGB in there, snug as a bug. He turned to Diana and flashed her a look of fierce satisfaction.

"There!" he declared emphatically.

"Are you happy now?" Diana blurted out.

Then, seeing how near the edge she was, he took her hand gently. "Easy, kiddo. It's going to be okay."

"It's not okay! I'm not okay! We both could have been killed."

"It's over now, Diana," Tom answered firmly.

"But that maniac wanted something in our car. I know he did. He was trying to get in."

"Diana, if he wanted to get in, he would have tried opening the door. Don't look for logic where there is none. Now it's over. We're home now."

They got out of the car, their wet clothes making a funny squishing noise as they unstuck themselves from the seats. Diana waited for Tom to lock the car and was truly grateful when he came over and put his arm snugly around her waist. He must have sensed how much she needed him then. They climbed the front steps of their brownstone, and without letting go of each other, squeezed through the front door.

3

It was a scorching Sunday afternoon, and they were all at the Club. They were all, in fact, at one of several places that Tom called the Club. There was the Union Club and the Racquet Club and the Princeton Club and several exclusive Wall Street luncheon clubs his father belonged to; and this one, also exclusive, the Wild Acre Country Club of Westchester County. Diana was saved from confusion by the fact that the country club was the only one she was permitted to enter. So if Tom said, "I'm going to the Club," she didn't much care which of them it was. If, on the other hand, as had happened this morning, he said, "We're going to the Club," she knew that he meant the country club, so she knew how to dress and what to expect.

New York was suffering through one of its celebrated August heat waves; this was the fifth straight day the mercury had broken ninety degrees. If you couldn't get out of the city sometimes, you'd go crazy. Today, though, Diana was almost comfortable as thoughts of last week's savagery had already slipped from her mind. She lounged lazily by the pool with Tom, Sarah and her husband Jack, Greg, and—what was this one's name?— Lisa. At least Diana thought it was Lisa. Lisa sounded right.

Greg was Tom's roommate from Princeton and the only one in the group not wearing a bathing suit. He was dressed in gleaming tennis whites from head to toe. White Addidas, white tank socks, white shorts, a white

LaCoste shirt, and a white towel draped casually around his neck.

But tennis was the furthest thing from his mind.

For as long as Diana had known him, Greg had always had a truly amazing facility for finding spectacular-looking girls. Not just ordinarily beautiful girls, but one-of-a-kind, break-the-mold jobs who seemed to have stepped right out of the pages of the higher-class men's magazines, as if Greg had the magical ability to scatter dust on those pictures and make them come to life. None of them ever had much in the way of conversation. They didn't need it. Their mere presence was an assault on a man's nervous system. Diana wondered whether any of these girls had ever learned how to say anything more complicated than "I want." Greg seemed to prefer them that way. In fact, Diana often thought that if he could figure out a way around the social stigma, Greg would be just as happy with an inflatable rubber doll.

This new one, Lisa, was quite something, even for Greg. Wearing the very smallest string bikini, she stretched her awesome, silky length on a lounger, her glistening golden head cradled in her arms, while Greg rubbed suntan oil into a tanned back and legs that obviously did not need it. With the intense, monomaniacal absorption of someone building a model ship out of toothpicks, Greg rubbed and rubbed, obviously willing to spend months at the task, if need be.

Diana could see what Greg was doing. He wasn't trying to keep his date from getting a sunburn; he was trying to arouse her. His hand kept slipping down between her thighs, where the sun would never shine. His eyes gleamed with excitement as his fingers kneaded the already glistening flesh.

Lisa looked up with annoyance. She opened her full, lush mouth and in a small, piping, prepubescent voice said, "Don't do it that hard. You hurt when you do it that hard."

Greg leaned down, put his lips close to her ear, and purred, in his most seductive tone, "I'm trying to make sure it gets into all your pores, sweetness."

"That doesn't mean you have to push like you're sanding a table," she protested. "Don't you know you have to have a touch, for Chrissake?"

Greg looked around to see if any of his friends had heard. "Don't swear, darling, there's a child present," he whispered.

"Well, God knows I don't want to embarrass you." Her tone indicated that she and Greg played out this scene with a fair degree of frequency. "I think I'll take a dip and get this crud off," she said a bit too loudly.

She stood up in one lithe, supple motion, displaying an almost sinfully voluptuous figure. Several heads turned. She stretched. Several more heads turned. She found something wrong with the placement of her teensy bikini top and adjusted it. Anyone who hadn't been staring before was staring now.

Then she began her progress to the pool with one of the most amazing motions anyone there had ever seen. She moved, like a one-girl parade, with a modified cheerleader's strut, as though there were a whole marching band behind her. Her high, firm buttocks kept time, as if on ball bearings. When she finally dove in, clean and sharp as a knife in the water, the exhalation of breath could be heard around the pool.

Greg stood up and reached for his tennis racket.

"I promised one of Dad's friends I'd meet him for doubles," he said to no one in particular. Then, turning to Tom, he added, "Tell Lisa I'll be back in a while, will you, sport?"

And he walked off toward the tennis courts, with as much dignity as he could muster, swinging his racket with casual abandon.

Sarah waited until Greg was well out of earshot before

collapsing in giggles. "God, what a cute couple. Where did Greg find that one?"

"At the Princeton Institute," Diana said, "doing work in experimental physics."

"Trying to figure out a way to keep those things up, no doubt," Sarah said, still watching the pool.

Just then, Nina came toddling up to her mother. "Can I go swimming now, Mommy? I'm hot."

"*She's* hot," Jack mumbled under his breath.

Sarah patted Nina affectionately on her behind.

"Not just yet, sweetie-pie. It's too soon after lunch." Nina plopped herself down in the shade of her mother's beach chair as all eyes were drawn again to the big girl in the small bikini doing gymnastics in the pool.

"Actually, I think she's sort of fun to have around," Tom murmured, taking in Lisa's every move.

"Around what?" Sarah smirked.

"Well, we'd all better get used to her," Tom said, turning to Diana, "because I bet Greg's bringing her up for Labor Day weekend."

Diana's eyes opened wide with disbelief. "He's really inviting that girl to stay at his parents' house?"

"Darling," Tom replied, "Greg's coming with us to Amagansett."

Nina picked that moment to intrude on the conversation.

"Mommy, can't I go swimming now?"

"I'll take you in, cutie," Diana said. She stood up swiftly, with none of the extra rotary motion Lisa put into every move, but several eyes around the pool turned anyway. Hooking her thumbs under the seat of her bikini trunks, Diana gave them a measured tug until only the bottom two inches of the thin pink scar on her right hip peeked out from under her swimsuit. She held out her hand to Tom, giving him a you-better-come-along roll of the eyes. "Come on, pal, let's get wet."

Tom got out of his beach chair reluctantly and took one of Nina's hands, while Diana took the other. The three of them started toward the pool.

"You didn't tell me Greg was spending Labor Day weekend with us," Diana began tentatively.

Tom gave a shrug. "He really wanted to come along, so what's the big deal."

Diana tried to cover the hurt in her voice. "The big deal is that it's my only three-day weekend all summer, and I thought you wanted to spend it with me."

"I figure it this way. We'll be up there for seventy-two hours and at most we'll be with Greg and Lisa—what—a total of twelve hours? That's less than twenty percent."

"Twenty percent compounded daily," Diana frowned. "I can hardly wait."

The three of them reached the shallow end of the pool and sat down on the edge, dangling their feet in the coolness of the water.

"Look, Diana," Tom demanded, "what do you have against Greg? You never liked the guy, so why can't you just say it?"

" 'Cause he's your best friend, damn it, and I wanted to try to like him."

"Well, maybe you didn't try hard enough."

"Maybe I didn't," she countered. "He hasn't exactly been Mr. Warmth with me, either."

Tom shook his head. "It's not his fault. He only knows how to relate to women in one way."

"That's the whole point, Tom," Diana insisted. "I'm never going to relate to Greg *that way*, so why do you always force him on me?"

Tom kicked at the water, his voice sharp. "All right, I should have asked you first. I admit it. I was wrong. But it's too late, so let's just forget it." Both their faces were set now. Neither of them wanted to create a scene, but neither wanted to back down.

"If you're so buddy-buddy with Greg," Diana said,

half-teasing, "why can't you just tell him you want to spend a romantic weekend alone with your nagging, possessive fiancée?"

Tom sighed deeply. "Diana, whether I'm buddy-buddy with him or not, I'm not going to be rude to the guy."

Diana swallowed. She had to be honest with him. "If you want to know the truth, I don't understand why you're friends with him to begin with."

Tom pondered it a moment, then eased out his answer. "Maybe there's a part of me that's like him. I'm not sure. But even if I can't explain it, why can't you just accept it?"

"I'm trying to accept it, but I want to understand you."

"Do you think I always understand you, Diana? There's a lot of things you do that puzzle me."

"Then why don't you ever ask me about them?"

"Because people shouldn't have to justify their feelings. I give you the benefit of the doubt."

Diana sat very still, watching his face. Was it really that he gave her the benefit of the doubt, she wondered, or was it that he just didn't want to deal with what he found difficult to categorize and control? She reached out and placed a hand on Tom's naked shoulder. His skin was warm and it felt like the warmth was coming from within.

Nina's voice cut through her musings. "Is it time to go swimming now?"

"You can play in the shallow end, but only up to your waist," Diana cautioned. She let Nina down into the water as the little girl squealed with excitement. Diana could see people watching them, assuming Nina was their daughter, thinking what a handsome young family they were. The idea pleased her more than she would have believed possible. Maybe she was getting more domesticated than she thought.

Keeping an eye on Nina, she walked with Tom to the other end of the pool. One after the other they dove to the bottom. Their bodies slid smoothly against each other, the water between them. Diana grabbed Tom in her arms. They stayed down as long as they could.

✦✦✦

The big night had finally arrived. Diana had awakened that morning with a feeling of dread. In fact, she had been dreading it for days. Not the wedding—she was nervous and excited about that. But the final, unavoidable preliminary. The event she had come to think of as the weigh-in before the big bout. Dinner with Tom's parents.

She knew she was foolish to be so apprehensive over the thought of sitting down to eat a meal with a couple of middle-aged people, but she couldn't help herself. They loomed so large in Tom's thoughts and actions that they had taken on an almost supernatural aura in her eyes. The givers, and, if they so chose, the takers away. She even wondered what would happen if her husband-to-be's parents flat-out hated her, thought she was too unsuitable to try to whip into shape. Diana refused to let herself speculate. That was one test she didn't want to see Tom put through. She decided that things would never get that far out of hand; not if, beginning right now, she would just turn it on and charm Tom's parents. She would charm the socks off them.

But it wasn't going to be easy. Not if she hoped to make it clear that Diana Lynn Stewart intended to maintain an identity beyond that of Mrs. Thomas Johnson. Diana couldn't remember a night with Tom she had looked forward to less than this one.

She wondered if her nerves were showing. The surroundings themselves were enough to intimidate her. She had spent one hundred and seventy-five dollars in a little boutique off Lexington Avenue for what she thought was an appropriately fashionable cocktail dress, but the twenty-two room apartment she was sitting in suddenly

36

made her bare shoulders appear vulgar and the strapless yellow chiffon dress seem gaudily out of place.

The sunken living room, certainly the most elegant Diana had ever seen, suggested a cross between a men's club and a museum. No fold-out couches in this place. Even the doorman downstairs looked as though he had been on duty since before the turn of the century. Everything was very staid and very rich. Mr. and Mrs. Henry Johnson, standing in the corner mixing drinks, also looked very staid and very rich. Maybe they were going over their exam questions. One thing Diana was sure of, this was an examination, and dinner was merely a pretext for it. The first question might be naming the people in the portraits on the wall. They were surely Tom's forebears, but they looked more like obscure, now forgotten, vice-presidents of the United States. For all Diana knew, they were both.

As the elder Johnsons conferred, a uniformed butler, looking like something out of an old English movie, served delicate hors d'oeuvres from a heavy silver tray that bore, in engraved script, a large, imposing initial J. When the butler was out of earshot, Diana whispered nervously to Tom, "I think that tray cost as much as my entire college education."

Tom put a reassuring hand on her knee.

"That's just the way my family tries to intimidate people."

"It's working," she answered.

Diana was going to say something more, but suddenly Mrs. Johnson was hovering over her like an avenging angel, holding another silver tray, this one bearing drinks. Mr. Johnson stood beside her. They looked slim and elegant, perfectly dressed, both with distinguished gray hair, like Norman Rockwell's idea of an old moneyed family. Diana wondered if they had looked as much like one another when they met as they did now. She had heard that of couples, that they grow to look like one another, but she had never believed it until right then.

Mrs. Johnson promptly set the tray down on a coffee table that looked as though a hundred slaves had spent their entire lives polishing it, sat down opposite Diana, and began her attack without preamble. Her voice was soft and cracked and insistent, like old money.

"Diana," she said, "I was chatting with Mrs. Samuel Porter the other day, and we would both be most pleased if you would join us on the fundraising committee of the Schofield School for the Blind. We meet on Tuesday afternoons at the Colony Club and we really do need some enthusiastic young people."

To her horror, something that she hadn't remembered for years sprang into Diana's head, blocking out all other thoughts. It was a school cheer invented by one of her favorite authors, Ring Lardner, for a little nonsense play he had written. At the time, she had thought it so marvelously irreverent that she had committed it to memory, and occasionally she recited it at parties. Now she could think of nothing else.

> We are always there on time!
> We are the Wilmerding School for the Blind!
> Better backfield, better line!
> We are the Wilmerding School for the Blind!
> Yea!

Diana had the not entirely disconcerting thought that if she were to stand up right now in this plush, forbidding living room and deliver the Wilmerding yell with appropriate cheerleader motions and enthusiasm, she could effectively and with utter finality alter the course of the rest of her life.

She decided she didn't have the guts and instead looked nervously at Tom, focusing on his immaculate white

French cuff, as if she would find the answer to Mrs. Johnson's question written there in a tiny scrawl.

Then Tom jumped in to save her with a firmness that surprised her. "Mother, we've talked about this before. Diana works on Tuesday afternoons."

Mrs. Johnson's expression told everything there was to know about her opinion of women who had to work on Tuesday afternoons. Or any other day, for that matter. And of sons who spoke up for them.

"I'm sure Diana can speak for herself, dear," she admonished, as if to say, You're not the one being questioned here. "All I'm trying to suggest is that after you're married, it might be wise if Diana became involved in some charitable organizations, rather than staying on at that bookstore." She fixed her most things-are-self-evident smile on her future daughter-in-law and added, "Now, is that such a bad idea, Diana?"

Well, Diana thought, here is a lady who doesn't mess around. She puts one foot in the door and starts to cart off your furniture. But Diana didn't want to argue. She was determined to bob and weave through fifteen rounds without throwing a punch—for Tom's sake.

Mrs. Johnson rang a silver bell to signal for more hors d'oeuvres, and Diana came out of her corner. She spoke in a calm, quiet voice. "I love books, Mrs. Johnson, and I love spending my day around them. I've never thought of quitting."

A trace of disapproval played across Mrs. Johnson's eyes.

"Then perhaps you might consider working part-time, dear. That way you might have time for everything."

"It's a fortunate person indeed who has a job that they can be so enthusiastic about," Mr. Johnson interjected. "And I understand Diana's been very successful at what she does."

Well, well, Diana thought. Was Mr. Johnson taking

her side, or pouring oil on the waters? Or maybe just sticking his oar in to see which way the boat would rock? Unexpectedly she found herself liking the old pirate. She gave him a polite nod and turned her attention back to Tom's mother.

"I tried working part-time at Scribner's for a year and a half," Diana explained. "When I was finally offered the assistant manager position, I jumped at the chance. It was something that I had set out to do. If I worked part-time, I would have to go back to being a clerk again."

Mrs. Johnson's smile was gone instantly. She looked as if someone had slapped her in the face with a large wet fish. She was not accustomed to being disagreed with, especially not by people who wanted something that belonged to her—in this case, her son. She moved to what she thought was a safer area of the ring and rushed in again, with the smile back on her lips.

"I have good news, children," she said. "I managed to get Henry to forgo his golf game yesterday—not an easy thing to do, I assure you—and we broke the back of the guest list. Even with family, friends, and Henry's business acquaintances, we ought to be able to keep the wedding quite manageable—a bit under four hundred people, I should think."

This time the look Diana shot Tom was tinged with more than alarm. Later, he would tell her that it reminded him of the old joke about, "Who do you have to screw to get out of this movie?"

So again he answered for her, afraid of what she might say if left to her own devices. "Mother, we discussed this before," he said firmly, "Diana and I decided that it might be more meaningful if we kept the wedding list to just family and a few close friends—say about two dozen people."

Mr. Johnson chuckled. Diana thought she had heard that chuckle before. Old English actors chuckled like that in Dickens movies, when they were doing things like explaining to Oliver Twist why he couldn't have any more gruel. It was a complacent, condescending chuckle, and no one chuckled like that unless he knew he held all the cards.

"Tom, my boy," Mr. Johnson said, "there are two dozen people at the bank alone who'd be terribly hurt if they weren't invited. You certainly don't want to start on your new road in life offending people."

Which told Diana a good deal about her future father-in-law. He let his wife do most of the talking, but when he came in, it was for the kill. There was no answer to his statement as he had framed it, except, perhaps, "Yes, I do want to start on my new road in life offending people."

Mrs. Johnson jumped in to carry away the corpse. "And that doesn't even begin to take in our friends from out of state, and our friends from the Hamptons."

"Mother," Tom said, much louder now, "I promised Diana the wedding would be small, and it will be small."

Diana could tell by the noticeable flicker of shock on Mrs. Johnson's face that her son had probably never addressed her in that tone of voice before. This could be dangerous, even more dangerous than getting up and giving old Ring Lardner's cheer. Quickly Diana spoke up in an effort to defuse the situation. "Tom doesn't mean to get so upset, Mrs. Johnson, it's just . . ."

Mrs. Johnson cut in, addressing her son as if the young woman in front of her did not exist. "I'm sorry you made that promise, Thomas, but really, this has very little to do with you."

Nothing to do with him? *Nothing to do with us*? Diana felt the rage rising within her as she thought of all the possible answers to that statement, each of which would undoubtedly result in a speedy invitation to leave the Johnson home forthwith and for good. At the moment she didn't much care. But before she could say any

41

of what was on her mind, Mr. Johnson spoke up again calmly, taking charge, smiling at her, and for an instant Diana really believed that the old man was on her side and indeed wanted her for a daughter-in-law and was trying to save her from anything irrevocable.

"Diana," Mr. Johnson said, "in the normal course of events your parents would be taking care of the wedding. But God has left it for us to do. I don't begrudge it, mind you, and the Lord knows we can certainly afford it. But what we can't afford is to slap our friends—your friends—in the face. No one's sorrier than I am about the tragedy that befell your parents and that they can't be here among us. But it's fallen to us to do this thing, and I'm sure you understand that we want to do it as we see fit."

"Father," the younger Johnson began, almost before the older man had stopped speaking, "neither of us . . ."

"Tom," Diana pleaded, feeling she might scream if this sanctimonious shredding of their wedding plans continued another instant, "it's not that important. Really it isn't."

"Of course it is," Tom replied. "To both of us."

Diana blinked. The silence from Tom's parents was deafening. Then slowly a warmth suffused her. It wasn't so much that Tom was finally standing up to his parents, it was that he was doing it for her. His quiet assurance wasn't the same buttered steel that his father employed. But it certainly was genuine. She wondered if Tom could catch the hint of a smile that was crossing her lips.

Tom turned to his mother. "We do understand your concern, Mother. Family image and commitments and all. And we're not trying to be difficult about it. But we feel—both of us—that our wedding would be more special, more meaningful to us personally, if we celebrated it surrounded by people who really mean something to us."

"We can invite them too, dear," Mrs. Johnson replied lightly before Mr. Johnson zeroed in again.

"Are you telling us, son, that none of this family's obligations mean anything to you anymore?"

But Tom didn't rise to the bait. "Of course not, Father. I meant nothing of the sort. But it should be obvious that I have additional obligations now, which are equally important. I'm sure you can understand that."

If the elder Johnson was nonplussed by Tom's defiance, he was too professional to let it show.

Mrs. Johnson made one of those practiced, feminine moves, some smoothing business with her skirt, which finishing schools teach as a method of unobtrusively getting everyone's attention. "Well," she said briskly, "we certainly don't have to make any definite decisions this evening." Her tone implied that everything was settled for the moment, shoved under the rug. The other three sat staring at her in silence. And they hadn't even finished cocktails.

The meal turned out to be the longest Diana had ever eaten. She tried to remember everything she had ever read about etiquette. Small fork for salad, big one for meat. Don't bring your mouth to your food, bring your food to your mouth. Leave your spoon on your saucer, not in your cup.

She was absolutely sure that she would grow old and die before she finished dessert. Not because of the food: hot salmon pâté in brioches, inch-thick prime rib in a white mushroom sauce, asparagus tips au gratin, endive salad, and strawberry tart. Indeed, the food was superb, as she had expected it would be. But either the Johnsons had decided to steer clear of any further minefields or else they had a rule, as many families did, that nothing of any real importance should be discussed at the dinner table. Instead they filled the evening with table talk. For Mr. Johnson, this had to do with money. Money was how he made his living—stocks and bonds and mutual funds and other investments—and he found money an infinitely varied and fascinating topic of conversation.

To Diana, who thought of money only as something you should have in your pocket if you wanted to buy groceries or something, this was a puzzling attitude. But not to Mr. Johnson. He could obviously see his money in his mind's eye as he spoke about it, arranged in neat, green piles down in a cool, guarded vault somewhere, and he could see the piles growing as he did some shrewd, subtle thing with them, involving splits and debentures and interest rates and other arcana that left Diana completely bewildered—and Tom clearly delighted. The enthusiasm and knowledge Tom brought to the conversation was a side of his personality Diana had never seen. Of course, he had talked about the bank with her, but it was in the way all couples talk about their day-to-day affairs. What she saw at the table was totally different: two men sharing a love of the same profession as equals, or nearly so. Diana felt a moment's sadness, wondering why this camaraderie between father and son did not extend past their work.

For her part, Mrs. Johnson seemed unfazed by all the financial chatter. What mattered to her was what you did with money in the amounts her husband possessed. What you mostly did, apparently, was have lunch with it, in the company of other ladies of approximately your age whose husbands had roughly the same amount of money as yours did. She kept asking Diana if she had ever had lunch in any of those places, and of course Diana hadn't. They all had French names like La Côte Basque and Le Veau D'Or, which Diana couldn't understand, let alone afford to eat at.

And throughout the meal Mrs. Johnson kept finding sly, seemingly unimportant questions to ask, which were about as innocent as those a shrewd detective might ask of the person he suspects is responsible for the corpse on the rug. Tom learned a great deal about his fiancée that night that he had never thought about before, in matters he had always taken for granted. Diana had never had a coming out, had never had a governess, and had never seen Rome's Trevi Fountain, but had spent a weekend in Las Vegas for her parents' twentieth anniversary.

And throughout the evening Mrs. Johnson never lost her charm or her smile.

Finally, after what seemed to Diana like a hundred and fifty years, they were saying their good nights. Mrs. Johnson tendered her a strained peck on the cheek and told her how lovely she was. The doorman brought Tom's little MGB around, and soon they were away from Park Avenue, zipping up the East Side with the top down and the hot night air blowing through their hair. Diana leaned her head back on the seat and looked up at the stars, watching the tops of the buildings slide away.

After several blocks Tom broke the silence. "Pretty bad, wasn't it?"

"It could have been worse," Diana said in a small voice. She curled around in the bucket seat and laid her head on his shoulder, watching him as he drove. "I did get the distinct impression, despite all the graceful hospitality, that whatever your mother had in mind for you, it didn't look or sound like Diana Stewart."

"My parents are stubborn, high-handed snobs. It has nothing to do with you personally."

"You know, I hate to admit it," Diana said, "but with all that, I still liked them."

"Well, you shouldn't, damn it! They don't deserve it."

"Maybe. But they're probably the only two people who love you half as much as I do."

Tom careened into a nearly deserted side street, virtually taking the turn on two wheels, his driving—usually as cautious as everything else about him—betraying what he felt.

"Let's elope!" he said suddenly.

Diana had pondered this herself, but considered it too outrageous to even suggest.

"I mean it, Diana. To hell with a big wedding. To hell with everything. Let's just elope. I'm twenty-eight years old and capable of leading my own life."

But was he, Diana thought? Could a man who had never ironed his own shirt, never lived on a budget, never even bought a suit off the rack—could such a man cope with the loss of all those things, all the perquisites that came with having chosen his parents wisely? No, she didn't think so. And eventually, probably sooner than not, he would blame her for his misery. They had too much going for them to let that happen.

"We can't elope," she answered brightly. "Besides, your parents did decide we could have a small honeymoon—only two hundred people."

For a moment, it didn't register. Then Tom guffawed. Then suddenly they were both laughing uncontrollably, subsiding into giggles only when Tom nearly sideswiped an oncoming taxi, whose driver leaned out and cursed them in Spanish. Tom returned his eyes to the road, and Diana squeezed his thigh seductively. She felt a surge of affection for him. Here was this immensely reasonable man, her future husband, willing to throw his family and fortune to the winds with what was probably the most adventurous thing he had ever thought of.

She leaned very close to him. "Don't worry about me. I love you," she breathed into his ear. "Let your mother have her wedding. We'll have the rest of our lives."

Tom jammed the pedal to the floor and sped through a red light.

4

By the time they got home Tom's anger had dissipated, helped in no small measure by Diana's playful seduction. Having exchanged the unspoken promise of a night of lovemaking, they were feeling like a pair of high school sweethearts racing to the consummation of a prom-night date.

Climbing the brownstone steps with Tom made Diana think of something that hadn't occurred to her until just now. The Johnsons had shown remarkable tact. Although they were well aware of it, neither of them had remarked on the fact that she and their son were living together. The situation must certainly be a thorn in their side; it didn't take much imagination for Diana to figure out what Mrs. Johnson's attitude must be toward "that kind of girl." And Mr. Johnson, what about him? Being a male, he would probably be more tolerant. Indulgent. He would understand why his son might want a live-in girlfriend, and perhaps even secretly admire the young man for his sowing the proverbial wild oats. But actually to marry such a girl was—what was that expression Greg once used?—"letting your small head rule your large one."

No sooner had Tom opened the door to their apartment than, as if on cue, a small bundle of canine fur came scampering joyfully across the room to lick Diana's shoes. It was an everyday ritual that celebrated her return, a welcome reminder that this was her home.

Diana loved her apartment. It was Tom's apartment,

actually, but in the forty-nine weeks and four days since she had moved into his bachelor digs, she had put too much of herself into the four rooms to think of the place as only Tom's. It was a lot of little things, but they had made all the difference. Like painting those awful green walls in bright, cheery Latex colors, reupholstering the two beat-up armchairs in white Haitian cotton, and replacing the cold chrome-and-glass dining table with a beautiful mahogany table her great-grandfather had built one hundred and thirty years before. Yet more than the walls and furnishings, it was all the happy moments she had spent there that made 159 East Eighty-second Street so special to her.

The apartment itself was on the ground floor of a beautifully reconditioned old brownstone in one of the more fashionable sections of New York. The layout was open and airy. With all the rooms facing south, the apartment always had plenty of sunlight. Straight ahead off the small foyer was a wonderfully high-ceilinged living room, while to the right lay a narrow L-shaped kitchen with a window at the end of it. A small hallway to the left of the foyer led to a commodious bedroom and a modern bathroom. But best of all was the garden out back. It was the garden that had become Diana's favorite hideaway.

From the bedroom one could look out at it from six-feet-high windows, while in the living room one had only to open the tall glass garden doors to walk right into one's own backyard retreat. True, it was small, rather more a courtyard than a garden, with a high brick wall all around it. But it was quiet and it was green. It was perfect for the dog and wonderful for her. When the city got to be too obtrusive, too uncaring, when the sheer volume of noise and crush of people got to be too much to take, the garden was a peaceful oasis where she could be by herself to think her own thoughts and put herself back together.

In the Cloisters, the magnificent uptown museum of medieval art, Diana had seen a famous tapestry that depicted a captured unicorn, a delicate white creature, resting peacefully inside a circular fence. The tapestry had been reproduced all over the world, probably almost as much as Wyeth's *Christina's World*, but Diana thought it was special to her. Sometimes, when she was sitting alone out back, surrounded by the high brick wall, she thought of herself as the unicorn in the garden. A rare creature, unknown even to herself.

At the cocker spaniel puppy's barking insistence Diana finally scooped him up, talking to him in the most sincere tones of affection.

"Taffy!" she cried. "What a good little boy you are. Look how clean Taffy kept the apartment, Tom. Isn't he the best?"

"Your dog's getting so good, Diana, he doesn't make on the newspaper, he reads it."

"You missed me, didn't you, you little devil?" Diana cooed to the dog. "Well, I missed you, too."

She set the puppy down on the floor. "Come on, fella, let's see if you need some fresh water." She walked off toward the kitchen, the puppy following happily behind her.

Tom always tried to be busy when these little displays of affection were going on. He and Diana usually treated her inordinate love of animals as a joke, but it wasn't a joke to him. He felt that people, especially girls, who lavished affection on animals, usually did so because they were unable to give the same affection to other people. He was particularly suspicious of the kind of young women who lived in Greenwich Village and decorated their apartments with paintings of rearing stallions. He didn't think it took a headshrinker to figure out what that meant. Thank God, Diana had never gone that far. She had settled for those good old Metropolitan Museum posters of Degas dancers.

In Diana's case he hoped that what he considered to be her animal fixation was only the manifestation of a very warm heart and the sublimation of a strong maternal instinct that would find its proper outlet once she began to have all the babies they both wanted.

Then, maybe, that goddamned little dog wouldn't be underfoot all the time.

With Diana out of the room, Tom took a small, carefully wrapped package out of his blazer pocket and put it on a coffee table, where she would be sure to notice it. Then he pressed the Play button on his large chrome-plated tape machine and filled the room with the romantic saxophone of Gato Barbieri. Good music for setting the mood.

He loosened his tie. The room was stuffy as hell. New York in the summertime was one enormous oven. It was already ten o'clock and it was still at least eighty-five degrees. He walked over to the airconditioning unit and turned on the starter.

Nothing.

He clicked it back and forth angrily. Still nothing.

"Diana!" Tom called out.

He yanked open the glass door to the garden, letting in night air that was nearly as hot and stifling as the air in the apartment.

Diana was still in the kitchen with Taffy, who was jumping around her legs in anticipation of being fed.

Absently she reached down into the large bag of Purina dog biscuits she kept on the kitchen floor near Taffy's bowl. All she came up with was a fistful of air.

That was odd. She had bought the bag only the other day. Taffy had been given maybe six biscuits from it. It should have been full. If Taffy had gotten into it, he was going to be one sorry dog.

Diana reached down further, all the way to the bottom of the sack. It was absolutely empty. She picked it up and peered into it. It contained not a single biscuit.

Even if Taffy had gotten into the bag, he could not possibly have eaten five pounds of dog biscuits. And if he had, Diana would certainly have known—hell, the contents of the animal's stomach would be all over the apartment, and here the dog was bouncing around as hungry as could be.

She felt a slight shiver run through her body, when it occurred to her that maybe Tom had been feeding the dog. That was something he usually stayed clear of unless specifically requested. She walked into the living room to ask him about it. Taffy spied the open glass doors and scampered out into the garden.

"Tom, did you give the dog anything to eat?"

"No," he answered brusquely. "Did you call the superintendent today about fixing the air conditioning?"

"Damn," Diana said, which meant she hadn't.

"Come on, honey." A hint of exasperation crept into Tom's voice. "I reminded you at breakfast. It's been two days."

"I was thinking about it this morning, but then I got busy and just forgot again." Diana felt terrible. A good wife would have remembered.

"We're going to roast again tonight," Tom said. "You know, I was wondering this morning whether you were going to remember."

"Well, then, why didn't you call me?"

"I was testing you," Tom replied, absolutely serious.

"Testing me for what? Landlord?" Diana asked.

Tom smiled. He had a maddeningly exact sense, Diana thought, of how far to let a little squabble go before nipping it in the bud. Moderation in all things.

"Tomorrow," he said, "I'm going to tie a string around your finger."

"Bondage. Now you're talking. Sounds like fun."

Then the red wrapping of the lovely little package on the table caught her eye. Diana reached for it in anticipation. "What's this?"

"What's what?" Tom answered, all bland innocence.

"This package here, dummy."

"Never saw it before in my life."

"I bet," Diana said, smiling. This was the other side of him. The little surprises, the spontaneous gifts for no reason at all. "Can I open it?"

"Sure," he said, "but first I want to tell you what it's for."

"Don't tell me, let me guess. For almost repairing the air conditioning?"

"You're warm."

"For getting up in the morning and almost having breakfast ready for you?"

"Getting warmer . . ."

"For almost making it to your New York Bankers' Association dinner last week?"

"Wrong again, and you only get three guesses."

"Then tell me," she said, dying to unwrap the little red package.

"It's because you put up with me."

Diana's face dropped. "Now I feel horrible. I never give you anything for putting up with me."

"Okay, then give it back," Tom deadpanned.

"How come you always know when to call my bluff, you bastard?" Diana squealed, ripping the package open as quickly as she could.

When she saw what was inside, she glowed. It was an exquisitely crafted porcelain ballerina, gracefully perched on one leg, the other stretched out flawlessly behind her, her flesh tones exact, her tutu a delicate light-blue, a lovely little white crown in her hair.

"Oh, Tom, she's the best one yet!" Diana said excitedly. "She even looks like me."

"You never looked that good," he teased.

She gave him a playful swat and walked over to the fireplace. On the mantel above it were about a dozen similar porcelain and china ballerinas. Carefully she studied the assemblage of figurines, trying to decide where the new addition would best fit in. Making her decision, she set the figure down and stepped back to admire the result. For a moment she was lost in the picture they made, almost as though she could actually see them move.

When she spoke, she wasn't really talking to Tom. "I wish I could do that, instead of just playing around with it. Wouldn't it be something to be able to dance like that?"

Diana leaped exuberantly across the room, landed on her right foot, and twirled. The *tour jété* was the first combination she had learned and she had it down pat.

Then she stood motionless, her eyes locking with Tom's. Slowly she raised her left leg straight out to the side and upward toward the ceiling until it wouldn't go any further on its own. She took it in her hands and pulled it up still further toward her head, wanting just once to do the most difficult position in ballet, the celebrated *jambe à la main*. Never had she been able to overcome the pain, to fully open the arc, to point her toes straight up at the ceiling.

The strain was too great; another inch, and she felt as though her whole limb was going to rip right off. She let her leg drop, the disappointment crowding into her eyes.

"You're getting better," Tom encouraged her.

"No, it's not good enough. I have to practice more."

"You'll get it."

"Sometimes I think that it's beyond practice. You either have it or you don't."

"Not true," Tom retorted playfully. "Now it's back to the rack until you get it right."

A short time later, having combed her hair, Diana stood before the bathroom mirror in bra and panties, brushing her teeth and feeling far more conscious of her body than she would have liked. It hurt. Whenever

Diana got out of a session with Madame Margot, she hurt in places she normally didn't think about from one year to the next.

She had read about runners, who were getting so much publicity right now with their Spartan endurance and their sports podiatrists and their "running through the pain." Runners didn't know what pain was. Put them in there with Madame Margot for a couple of hours, boy, and let's see how long it is before they feel up to doing another marathon.

Well, at least if she was going to suffer, she wasn't going to suffer in silence. She called to Tom, who was sitting up in bed reading what was surely another investment report. "You know, every time I get out of that ballet class, I'm sore for two days. All kinds of muscles that even you haven't managed to find."

"Just don't get too brawny," Tom said, in a tone that indicated he was paying at least some attention.

"I want to look like Nureyev," Diana replied.

"Great ass," Tom told her.

"Who, Nureyev or me?"

"Nureyev," he answered, which shut her up. She reached behind the bathroom door for her nightgown. She would put it on and go into the bedroom and show him who had a great ass.

Her hand came away empty.

She pulled the door forward and looked down at the floor, where the nightgown must have fallen. It wasn't there.

This was stupid. Every morning when she dressed to go to work, she hung her nightgown on the hook behind the door, and every night when she got ready for bed, she took the nightgown down from the hook and put it on. It was one of those things she did without thinking, like brushing her teeth. If you stopped to think about brushing your teeth, you couldn't do it. Too many hundreds of little motor responses involved. Taking the toothbrush down from its holder, taking the tube of toothpaste out of the medicine chest, removing the cap from the toothpaste, spreading the toothpaste on the brush, putting the cap back on, replacing the tube in the medicine chest, closing the chest, turning on the water, putting the brush under the water, putting the brush in your mouth . . .

Lord, if you thought about all that stuff, you'd never be able to do it, not without a PhD in physics and another in anatomy. You just did it, that's all . . . just as you hung your nightgown up on the hook behind the bathroom door.

Except that the nightgown wasn't there.

She called out to Tom again. "Have you seen my blue nightgown anywhere?"

"Last time I saw it, it was on you," he said in that same unconcerned tone of voice. "Looked very nice, as I recall. Almost as good as on Nureyev."

She didn't even bother to answer that one. She was too busy worrying about the nightgown. This was one of those little things that bothered her, that she could really get compulsive about. Like when she couldn't find a book. She would be reading a review in the *Times*, and it would talk about a particular early story of Cheever, say, and she would vaguely remember the story and think it was in an old collection she had—*The Brigadier and the Golf Widow*—and she would go over to the shelf, and the book wouldn't be there. And she would start thinking, had she loaned it to a friend, had she sold it when she left college, had it been part of that stack she had given away when she moved in with Tom? Then she would pull down all the books from the shelf to see if it had fallen behind the bookcase, and hours later she'd be standing there surrounded by piles of books, but no *Brigadier*, and the next day she'd run over to the main library on Forty-second and Fifth and check out a copy.

Only this time it was a missing blue nightgown she wanted to find. She walked into the bedroom to look around. Under the pillow. Under the bed. In the bed. She even made Tom get out of bed while she stripped off the top sheet, but didn't find the nightgown, and made the bed up again. Then she looked in the closet, finally getting down on her knees and groping with her hand into the darkest, most recessed parts. No nightgown.

"How can a person lose a nightgown?" she said to the world at large. "Really, Tom, I know I hung it up in the bathroom."

"Then I guess that's where it is," he said. He was all for any course of action that would get Diana out of his immediate area as she continued on what was rapidly becoming The Great Nightgown Search.

Diana went back into the bathroom. The only remaining place it could possibly be was in the clothes hamper, even though she knew it wasn't time for the nightgown to be washed. She opened the hamper. Of course it wasn't there. Angry now, her adrenalin pumping, the whole ridiculous Nightgown Episode blown all out of proportion in her mind, she scooped up all the dirty laundry and spread it on the bathroom floor, her brassieres and shirts, Tom's socks and underwear. . . . Damn! Still no blue nightgown.

Furiously she gathered up all the laundry, put it back in the hamper again, and slammed down the lid.

There was one other remote possibility. Once in a great while she left something in the bathtub to soak. She was positive she hadn't done that this morning, but there was nowhere else to look.

She pulled back the shower curtain.

And gasped.

And looked again to make sure she wasn't seeing things.

The bathtub was filled with a dark, dirty, brackish water. There were little slimy things floating on top. She couldn't bear to look at it.

"Tom," she shouted, "did you wash something in the bathtub?"

"No," the bored voice came back at her. "Why?"

"It's just gross," she said, and her voice mirrored her disgust. "It's all full of filthy water. It looks like the Okefenokee swamp in here."

"The drain probably backed up. That's another thing to call the super about in the morning. Have him get the plumber."

That was Tom, she thought. Nothing if not practical. A person's nightgown was missing. A person's clean bathtub suddenly took on all the aspects of a proving ground for strange forms of tropical larvae. Well, far be it for Tom to get concerned about something like that. Just call and get it fixed. Or better yet, detail somebody else to call and get it fixed. In this case, herself.

She couldn't blame him, though. If you were brought up to believe that the whole world was on the other end of a telephone, waiting to do what you told it to do, then you acted accordingly. As he was doing now.

"I wish you'd come and see this," she insisted, and then held her breath as she bent down to take a closer look.

She could hardly bear it. It was dark. And it was foul and it smelled. It was as if some rancid, alien presence had come scrambling up the pipes like a sewer rat to befoul her neat, clean apartment. She felt invaded, violated, all out of proportion to the incident. She didn't want Tom to know how upset she was, but what in hell was in the bathtub anyway?

"Tom, I really think you ought to look at this a minute," she suggested impatiently. "It smells like a dead animal's been in here."

"Please, honey," came the annoyed response, "just drain it. If it's that disgusting, I'll take your word for it."

"Well, you're a great help," Diana replied, before sticking her arm deep into the brown, murky water. Her fingers found the clogged drain and pushed what felt like a soft squishy substance through the narrow opening. She jerked her hand out of the tub and watched the small brown whirlpool suck away the water.

Diana couldn't get into bed before she and the bathtub were scrubbed thoroughly clean. Then she lay between the sheets still wearing her cotton panties, because she absolutely refused to get another nightgown out and was feeling sufficiently estranged from Tom not to want to lie naked beside him. It was immature, it was arbitrary, it was not an attitude she would have cared to defend, but that was the way she felt. Tom, in silent retaliation for what he considered her rejection, lay on his back, his legs crossed and his arms folded across his chest, staring at the ceiling of the darkened room. Their bodies were an inch apart, but it might as well have been a mile. Each was determined to out-suffer the other, if they had to lie there all night. But the day's exhaustion would not be denied, and they were gradually carried toward a needed sleep.

Diana had almost managed it, consciousness slipping away from her, one nagging thought after another erasing itself from her brain, when she remembered: She hadn't seen the dog.

There she had been, tossing clothes all over the place, down on her hands and knees scrounging around on the floor in a manner that Taffy would certainly have regarded as an invitation to play, and she hadn't seen him. In fact she couldn't remember, through the overlay of banal routine, if they hadn't by mistake locked the dog out in the garden.

"Tom?" she said softly. Even though she knew he was awake, something in the circumstances made her feel formal enough to inquire.

Tom grunted, a nonverbal signal that said: I am awake, but I would just as soon not be awake, and I would certainly just as soon not be bothered unless it's something of the utmost importance, such as a nuclear attack on the Upper East Side.

"Where's Taffy?" Diana asked.

"In the living room," he answered, in a patently false I-am-only-half-conscious voice.

"He never sleeps in there." Just one more little thing off-kilter, gone wrong.

"He's sulking behind the sofa," Tom told her.

"Why? What's wrong with Taffy?"

"I don't know. We didn't discuss it."

"Very funny." Diana knew she'd never get to sleep now.

"Taffy!" she called out into the dark room.

Normally that would have been the signal for a swift scuttling across the floor, tiny claws scraping across the wood, and a warm, furry ball plummeting into her arms looking for love and affection.

But this time, the fur ball didn't hurtle into her arms, and she didn't hear the scuttling of tiny claws. Instead she heard something else. Something indefinable. She didn't know what it was, she couldn't put a name to it, the sound was simply something that should not have been there.

It sounded as though it had come from the garden.

Diana sat straight up in bed, tense, alert, completely awake.

"Listen!" she whispered. "I heard something. Someone's out in the garden, Tom."

The bored monotone answered, "I didn't hear anything."

"Well, I did." Her voice was louder and more perturbed than she would have liked. She sounded almost as if she were insisting on her own sanity.

The tone reached Tom. He got out of bed, walked over to the window, and looked out into the garden.

Exasperated, he turned back to Diana. "Are you sure? What did you hear? Voices?"

"No, I heard noises," she answered, in absolute certainty.

He sighed wearily, a man much put-upon. "Where's the flashlight?"

"In the kitchen cabinet, bottom drawer." And then, because she was worried, and he was up and out of bed and trying to do something about it, she added, "Be careful."

Tom put on his robe and slippers and stumbled through the dark apartment into the kitchen. He groped his way to the kitchen cabinet, found the bottom drawer, opened it, and stuck one hand in like a blind man, fumbling around until he found the thick, tubular, metallic surface that was obviously the flashlight. Only then did he ask himself why he simply hadn't turned on the light and walked through the house. Diana was obviously infecting him with her crisis mentality. Well, okay. If she wanted tension and mystery, he'd give her tension and mystery.

He switched on the flashlight and walked back into the living room, spreading the beam around, feeling like a fool.

Then the light caught the dog, and he didn't feel like a fool anymore.

The cocker spaniel pup squatted on the floor at one end of the living room, tense, ready to spring, eyes wide open, feral, staring balefully out at the garden, looking far more like a jungle animal than a frisky little pet.

Tom felt uncomfortable at the sight of the small dog and he turned away. He went to the floor-length glass doors that fronted on the garden, opened them, and shot the beam into the darkness outside.

"Who's there?" he asked. He had trouble getting his voice out.

He shined the light carefully around the garden area, being just as careful not to step outside. As long as he was standing on his own living room floor, he felt safe. You couldn't have paid him to go into the garden.

He threw the light around the dark some more, still saw nothing, and turned it off. He closed the doors, locked them carefully, and walked back into the bedroom.

"It's probably just that cat you're always giving milk to," he told Diana.

She stared at him, sensing he wanted to say something more.

No way was he going to tell her about the dog. Tom removed his robe and slippers, then almost casually allowed his pajama bottoms to fall to the floor. He got into bed again, letting his thigh touch hers tentatively, almost as an afterthought. For a moment she stiffened. He thought she was going to move away. But she didn't. She lay still, and after a time Tom felt an almost imperceptible increase of contact, a strangely shy return of pressure. Encouraged and even surprised by her response, he rolled onto his side, facing her. She was a smooth, pearlescent milkiness in the shadowy room. Her large nipples were dark smudges on the mounds of her breasts. A tremor passed through her, though she showed no other sign of being aware of him.

Gently, cautiously, he reached out and lightly traced the curve of her breast. "Darling," he murmured.

"Don't talk," she whispered back fiercely. But her nipple stiffened beneath his fingers, and he felt himself get rigid.

He moved his hand, like a glider over warm fields, softly down the length of her ribcage, over the swell of her belly. In the darkness he could hear Diana's breathing grow rapid, as if she were taking little nips out of the warm air. He brushed his fingertips lightly across the surface of her cotton panties, as if testing the weight they would bear. Heat rose from her slightly parted thighs, and he could feel her wetness through the thin cotton cloth.

His hand creased her lips before sweeping down the

silkiness of her leg, resting on her kneecap, and traveling back up the outside of her thigh. His fingertips were almost electric now, inching along the pencil-thin scar on her hip, caressing it, as though it were an object of devotion or veneration. Then more assertively to the top of her panties, lifting their upper edge questioningly.

For a heartbeat, nothing. Then, sensuously, in surrender, she raised her hips and let him slide the panties slowly down her buttocks. Now she lay wanton, arms akimbo over her head, her face dreamy, her hair fanned out loosely on the pillows. One long leg stretched out, the foot caressing Tom's calf. The other leg drawn up, the knee high and pressed across herself half-concealing, half-revealing the dark triangle between her thighs. She writhed slowly, feline, watching him from beneath lowered eyelids. Slowly, smoothly, she drew the other leg up until her thighs were pressed against her breasts. Then she parted her knees wide and wider still, opening herself for him like some erotic flower. With something between a cry of delight and a moan Tom bent forward and placed his face against the pungent wetness of her, burying himself in her taste and aroma, using his teeth and tongue and lips until she convulsed and spasmed.

She rolled her hips from side to side, the waves of heat moving up her belly as Tom's tongue roughened her clitoris. She felt herself tearing at his hair, but couldn't remove her fingers—they wouldn't obey her, but instead urged him on, demanding, begging, forcing his head down. "Jesus," she moaned softly. Her pelvis heaved high, the pleasure burning her from deep inside. Then her entire body shook with a magnificent eruption.

Tom rolled away to lie on his back beside her, smiling quietly, his breathing fast and happy, letting her peak and subside, letting the aftershocks run through her sweat-sheened body. She was never as lovely, never so feminine, as during lovemaking. Whatever their problems, they had none in bed.

Soon, as he knew she would, as their ritual prescribed, she drew a languorous breath, stretched, and eeled her long body down the bed, her tongue tracing his ribs, his side, his belly, teasing his pelvis. Laying her cheek against his manhood, she let her hair dangle and tickle him. The strong man-odor of him came to her, exciting her as it always did. She turned her head and in a single quick motion she swallowed him into her mouth as far as she could, feeling him blunt and insistent against the back of her throat. She felt the thrill—half fear, half delight—as he cried out and thrust savagely against her.

Bringing him to the raw edge of explosion, she backed away, then brought him to it again. And again removed her lips. It was their best game, to see how close she could bring him to his climax. His body was slick with perspiration, taut with need. He wrapped both arms tightly around her buttocks, rolling her ferociously onto her back. With the deliberation of some powerful animal, Tom lowered his weight onto her. Diana reacted with small gasps of pleasure. She lifted her thighs further, welcoming, yearning. Her sweet breath caressed his neck. "Now," she whispered, and a moment later he was inside her.

From the garden she could see them doing it to each other. They looked like dogs, like the time she put Rinkus and the snot-nosed terrier in the same cage. Humping, straining their backs. Breathing getting louder. She could hear it. They seemed to really want it. Not like when Joel fell on her and did his pushups and got so big inside her and then so tiny and then fell away from her to sleep for hours. There was something else going on be-tween those two, something that didn't happen when Joel came to her and mumbled about his needs and grinded his hips up and down against her.

In the darkened room the girl's left leg stuck straight up like a flag, trim, gorgeous, splendid in silhouette, rigid with something he had done to her. Then it circled back down like a python, smooth and supple, to twine itself around his back and draw him in, closer, deeper.

Maybe that was it. That girl had both legs. Maybe if that rich bitch had only one leg, she wouldn't be able to feel like that.

She shut her eyes, pressed the blue nightgown to her face, and listened to the sounds coming out of the bedroom. She imagined having that lovely left leg for her own, so that she could move it around and feel like that girl did.

She itched inside with the excitement of it. Her missing leg itched too, as it hadn't in years. She wanted the itching to stop. She stuck her finger far up inside herself, and in a moment her hand was wet and she was exhausted, and she didn't know why.

Feelings raced through her body like a runaway subway, the emotions passing in a blur of confusion: curiosity, frustration, jealousy, hurt, and, finally, the end of the line . . . hate.

5

Three days later it seemed the heat wave had broken. The afternoon was brisk, almost like spring. There was even a breeze. Diana stood on a midtown street corner, holding Nina's hand. A long-avoided appointment of Sarah's had coincided with an afternoon off for Diana, and she had volunteered to take little Nina to the Central Park Zoo. This was one favor Diana had looked forward to doing. Afternoons with Nina were always fun, and besides, Diana regarded their time together as a warmup for when she'd be having kids of her own.

"I've been putting this off for six months," Sarah was saying. "I hate going to the dentist's."

Just then the light they had been waiting for changed, and the three of them started across the street.

"I don't have any cavities, do I, Mommy?" Nina asked.

"No," said Sarah, "but you will if you don't brush your teeth." She turned to Diana. "If she gives you any trouble and you see an empty cage, you know what to do." Sarah looked down at her small daughter, who acted as if she hadn't heard. Nina was too smart and secure a child to be frightened by a remark like that. "By the way," Sarah said, remembering. "Don't let her have any sweet stuff. I have a big dinner for her tonight."

"What's the fun of being a kid, if you can't gorge yourself on junk food," Diana laughed. "All I can promise is that I'll bring her back in one piece."

They reached the opposite curb, and Sarah bent down to hug her daughter.

"Now you be a good girl," she said. "And no nonsense."

Nina watched as her mother walked away.

"Mommy takes all the fun out of being a kid," the little girl complained.

Diana burst out laughing. "Nina Cooper, you're a little smartass, you know that?"

The elegant store windows of Gucci and Saks were already showing their tweedy fall fashions, and the two girls strolled happily up Fifth Avenue, pointing out their favorite outfits. On the corner of Fifty-seventh Street, opposite Tiffany's, a thin, middle-aged man with greased-down black hair and a dirty chalk-striped suit had staked out a few square feet of sidewalk and was loudly and busily haranguing passersby. It seemed to Diana that street crazies were proliferating these days. Bag ladies, winos, religious freaks, and garbage pickers. You really had to watch yourself. Taking Nina's hand, Diana moved to the edge of the curb, executing a wide arc around the man.

"Now you've done it, lady!" the man shouted. "That little move is gonna cost you plenty! I hope you have a good lawyer."

Diana knew that the thing to do was to go right on walking, to keep her eyes straight ahead, to mind her own business.

The man's demented outburst made her recall the strange noises that she had heard in her own apartment just the other night. What if some crazy nut like this one was prowling around out there in her garden? If somebody like that got a fix on you, you didn't have a chance. There was nothing you could do. All you had to be was in the wrong place at the wrong time. In their orbit.

Diana couldn't resist a sidelong glance. It was the wrong thing to do.

"Stop!" the man shouted, moving in her direction.

"Let's talk about it, for goodness sake! I can get you off the hook!"

Diana felt a nervous tug on her arm. It was Nina, looking up at her. Diana quickened her pace, pulling the little girl after her.

At the edge of his imaginary territory, the crazy man stopped abruptly. He stood there, hands on hips, calling after her. "Now you've had it, lady. I'll be seeing you later."

"Do you know that man?" Nina asked Diana.

"No, darling, he's just a crazy person."

But it made her shudder, and they hurried on toward the Zoo.

If there had ever been an argument about junk food, it was all over by the time they reached the seal pool. Nina was walking along hugging an enormous bag of popcorn, taking handfuls of the stuff and jamming it into her mouth. She pulled Diana over to the open polar bear area, where most of the big white beasts were in the water. The elusive briskness of the afternoon had disappeared as quickly as it had come, and now the atmosphere was again that same hot, muggy oppressiveness that had hung over the city for days. The polar bears, like most other New Yorkers, were simply doing whatever they could to keep cool.

Nina paused between mouthfuls of popcorn to ask a question. "How come bears swim?"

That was why Diana liked kids so much. They didn't ask, What is the meaning of life? or, Am I wrong in repressing my hostility? They just asked straightforward stuff like, How come bears swim?

"They're polar bears," Diana answered. "They're from the North Pole, so they're used to cold weather. They don't like the heat."

"Can they go swimming without their parents?"

Diana tried to keep from smiling. She wondered if she

67

would be able to answer questions like that if she got them all day, every day.

"If they're old enough and have permission," she told Nina.

The polar bears went into the caves where Nina couldn't see them and the little girl started to get bored.

"Can we go see the lions now?" she asked.

"They'll be inside, in this heat," Diana said.

"Then can we go inside? *Pleassse?*"

"It's not going to smell very nice." The thought of the hot, stuffy lion house on a muggy day like this was not Diana's idea of a good time. Even when the big beasts were outside, their odor was often overpowering. But Nina was not to be dissuaded.

"I want to see the lions," the little girl said. And then she looked up, with her best lost-waif expression. "*Pleaassse*, Diana?"

So of course they went to the lion house.

Diana had to use both hands to swing open the heavy metal door. They had been out in the bright sunlight so long that it took a couple of minutes for their eyes to adjust to the dimness. Diana couldn't see anything, but she had been absolutely right about the smell. Slowly she began to make out dark shapes moving along both sides of the long, narrow enclosure, and a moment later the shapes became recognizable as lions and tigers pacing their cages.

"Are there any jaguars in here?" Nina piped up. Diana looked around. She didn't think she even knew what a jaguar looked like.

"I don't know about jaguars, but there's a lion," Diana said, pointing further down the row of cages.

The king of the jungle certainly didn't look like one. Its mane resembled the flea-bitten furs hanging outside the secondhand shops down on Twenty-third Street.

Diana and Nina were the only people in the lion house, and the beasts seemed to sense the presence of humans in the building. They didn't like it. Perhaps they valued their privacy, too.

The two girls stepped tentatively toward the center of the animal house. The monkeys in the enclosure picked up the nervousness of the big cats. They began letting out little squeals, chattering and jabbering, running up and down the length of their wire cages. This irritated the large beasts even more.

It was a chain reaction. One minute, everything had been quiet; the next moment, pandemonium. The big cats threw themselves against the bars of their cages and roared in rage, terrifying the monkeys, who leaped and squealed even more wildly. Suddenly, the enclosure was a madhouse—a dark, dangerous place full of rabid, screaming animals.

Nina clung to Diana's arm, terrified. The zoo had stopped being fun.

Then there was a sudden loud, clanging noise behind them. Nina let out a shriek and wrapped her arms around Diana's knee. The big door, which Diana had left slightly ajar, had swung shut, pitching the narrow room into near darkness.

Diana felt something pinch at her rear! She whirled around. The long arm of an orangutan protruding through the bars reached out to grab her. Diana slapped at the hairy limb and Nina let out a doleful wail. Gripping Nina's hand tightly, Diana made off for the exit at the opposite end of the building. The little girl lurched forward, her tiny legs scrambling to keep their balance. She needed three strides to Diana's one, and for a brief moment her feet kept Diana's frantic pace. But then she faltered, fear numbing her reflexes, and she sprawled flailing to the floor in a tangled heap. Diana pulled the child to her feet and half dragged her the rest of the way.

When they finally reached the big door, Diana gave it a yank. It wouldn't move! Diana tried to remember whether the other door had opened in or out.

She pushed, then tugged. The door wouldn't budge!

The big cats hurled themselves again and again against the bars of their cages. The noise was deafening. For an instant Diana felt blind, unreasoning panic. Visions flashed through her head of herself and the little girl trapped in there for hours. The Zoo was so old. How long could those bars hold up under such unremitting pressure?

Then through the cacophony of animal shrieks and howls came another sound. Unintelligible, a kind of weird gibber. Diana squinted into the darkness at the other end of the building, feeling the terror surging up in her throat. Something—something on two legs—was hunkering down the floor toward them! Her first thought—and she knew it was irrational even as she had it—was that the orangutan had somehow gotten out of his cage. But she could see him, still behind his bars. He was backed against the wall, his eyes turned on the blurred thing in the darkness. His fangs were bared, and the coarse red hair on his body was standing up.

"Momma! I'm scared!" The words tore out of Nina's mouth in a high-pitched scream.

And they were answered, answered from the darkness by an eerie, screeching mimicry. "I'm scared! I'm scared!" But there was no fear in the voice. Only hatred and madness.

The thing shuffled toward them. Diana pulled frantically at the door.

And then, mercifully, her efforts were rewarded. The heavy iron door opened a grudging inch, squealing in protest, then swung free, flooding Diana's eyes with a blinding dazzle of sunlight. Instinctively she looked back into the building, seeking a glimpse of what had threatened them. But her haloed vision revealed only a ragged outline of something plodding toward them, something oddly postured, moving almost upright. And eyes. Two fierce, demented eyes boring straight into her own.

Diana scooped Nina into her arms and ran, not stopping until she had put the building far behind them. When she finally slowed and set Nina down, her mind was still spinning. What—or who—was that thing back there? Did it have some connection with the street crazy they'd encountered earlier? Had that weirdo followed them to the Zoo? Maybe he was some pervert who liked little girls.

She bent down to examine Nina's arm. The child was close to tears, her elbow scraped raw. Damn, Diana cursed to herself, Sarah would be so upset. Taking a Kleenex from her purse, she cleaned the skinned elbow as best she could. Then, promising the child the most tremendous chocolate sundae, she set off toward Fifth Avenue with Nina in tow, their pace just a little quicker than usual.

✦✦✦

Diana was still only warming up, but Madame Margot had already put on Bach's "Musical Offering." Bach brought out Madame Margot's urge for excellence like nothing else. Today's ballet class would be formal and precise.

"Come on, ladies," Madame Margot barked, "support your elbows. This isn't Arthur Murray's."

The students held onto the bar, concentrating on their *pliés* and *petits battements* in preparation for the upcoming lesson. Today, though, Diana had no use for the five classical ballet positions. Today she wanted to stretch, to attempt those positions—the *arabesque penchée*, the *grand écarté*, and, of course, the *jambe à la main*—that Madame Margot always claimed would be impossible for her to ever achieve. Diana's body had been too mature, too old, when she had started ballet. And now, her ligaments were too tight and her muscles too short.

Diana balanced herself on the tips of her toes and then, bending her torso forward, slowly extended one leg straight back. Her head touched her knee: the *arabesque penchée*. It hurt like hell, but at least she could make it look respectable.

"Diana," Madame Margot commented, "if you insist on these exercises, let me at least see those elbows tucked in. Come on, now, back to the bar."

But Diana didn't move. She was determined to try the *jambe à la main*—just once. If she didn't practice it, she knew she'd never get it. She lifted her right leg straight out to the side, then high in the air. Reaching with one hand to grab hold of her calf, she strained with all her might to pull her leg up still further toward the ceiling, as high and as taut as it would go. But today it wasn't high enough or taut enough. It probably never would be.

From a window in the building across the alley she could watch the dancers jumping around in there like a bunch of hungry gerbils. Fourteen assholes on twenty-eight legs, flexing and bending and doing things she couldn't do. Legs, calves, thighs, in all shapes and sizes; thick ones, tight ones, black ones, flabby ones, and of course . . .

The one she liked best. It belonged in a magazine, in the advertisements. That's how nice it was. And it was getting stronger.

A gruff voice intruded on her fun. "Excuse me, miss, are you waiting for someone?"

She whirled around to stare into the face of a young man in a uniform.

Cop.

"Shave your head, Kojak," she snarled.

The cop was polite. "I'm sorry, but if you're waiting for someone, you'll have to wait outside. It's seven o'clock. I have to close up the building."

She let out a belch.

"Please, lady, don't give me a hard time. Move it along, will you?"

"No problem." She stepped down hard on the cop's foot with her phony leg, the heavy one.

The cop yelled out in pain.

"Stick it up your ear, Kojak," she growled, and clumped down the hall.

After a twelve-minute adagio and a set of simple *relevés* Madame Margot dismissed the class. "All right, ladies, we still have a lot of work to do. See you all next week."

The girls broke into applause as Madame Margot turned to walk to her office. Just in time, Diana thought. If she had had to do that last step one more time, she would have keeled over dead, right there on the floor.

Diana felt as though she could have spent all evening under the hot shower. The smells of liberated womanhood permeated the locker room—Right Guard, Charlie, Ben-Gay—but they couldn't drown out the unmistakable stench of sweat. By the time she was ready to leave, only one girl, Jeannie, a marketing executive with Avon, was still there.

"If you had a gun, I'd ask you to shoot me and put me out of my misery," Jeannie said, buttoning up her blouse.

Diana smiled. "I wouldn't have enough strength to pull the trigger."

"You seemed to be doing pretty well out there today."

"I've been running around the reservoir every morning," said Diana, proud that someone had noticed her progress.

"You're kidding, that's the worst thing for you."

"Who told you that?"

"Did you ever see Baryshnikov out there jogging?"

"No. But I bet you he doesn't have to be at work by nine o'clock, either."

"You can ask Madame Margot. Running builds the wrong muscles. It takes away from your coordination. Makes you bulky."

"I can't believe it. I've been torturing myself for six weeks to build the wrong muscles. Two-hundred-pound monster thighs, that's all I need."

Jeannie giggled. "C'mon, I'll buy you a drink at The Sherry."

"Can't," replied Diana, "I've got to get over to a butcher on Lex before he closes. He's saving me a roast."

"Okay, see you next week."

Jeannie walked out the door, and Diana was alone in the locker room. Quickly she threw on her skirt and blouse, grabbed her purse, and walked into the hallway. She hurried down the long, dimly lit flight of stairs, unable to explain the sudden feeling of apprehension that had come over her.

She didn't see the girl on the floor above, limping her way down the stairs in a slow, agonized silence, holding onto the handrail, peering over the side.

The girl made her way down to the landing, and instead of following Diana further, walked along the hall to the ballet practice room. She tried the door. It was open. She went inside and took off her raincoat. The ballet practice bar beckoned her forward, daring her to try. She walked over, placed both hands on the smooth wooden bar, and squeezed hard. She looked at herself in the huge mirror. She didn't like what she saw and closed her eyes.

Standing on her artificial limb, she slowly raised her good leg off the ground as high as she could. It was painful, it was difficult, she was losing her balance, her hands were slick with sweat, she was slipping off . . . She hit the floor with a sickening thud that shook every bone in her body.

With excruciating tenacity, she picked herself up, took hold of the practice bar again, and tried once more to do the step she had seen so easily executed only minutes before.

Behind her the door to the practice room opened. An

elderly man wearing a gray security-guard's uniform entered the room. He had heard the sound of something falling and had come to check what was the matter.

He saw a strange, ragged girl, jerking with an awkwardness that was almost comic, attempting to do some kind of ballet step.

"What's going on in here, miss?"

Either the girl was so involved in what she was doing or else she simply chose to ignore him. In any case, she didn't answer.

The guard spoke again, louder this time. "Miss, did you hear me? I said, 'What's going on in here?'"

The girl at the bar put her leg down and turned to him. The expression on her face was one of total fury. It was the most enraged face the guard had ever seen.

"Ballet practice, jerkus!" the girl croaked in a harsh voice. "Don't you know ballet practice when you see it? This is a ballet practice room, and I'm practicing ballet!"

"Not any more, you're not," the guard shot back. "The class is over."

"The lady said I could stay."

The guard shook his head. "She didn't say nothing to me. What's her name?"

"Doris Day."

Jesus, the guard thought. A nut. A man looks for a nice, quiet job, something that will bring in a couple of extra bucks in the evening, and he gets stuck with a nut.

He sighed wearily and approached the girl. "Come on," he said. "Time to go home."

"Shut your snout!" the girl growled, with terrible intensity. "I'm going to stay until I learn how!" And then she swung her leg at the wall-length mirror as hard as she could, shattering it into thousands of jagged pieces that fell to the floor. With a shock the guard realized that the leg was artificial.

"All right," he yelled, "that's destruction of property! You'll have to come with me."

He walked toward the girl, who simply stood there, swinging her prosthetic leg back and forth like a club. But he kept on coming. He just wanted her out. This crazy girl could cost him his job.

Then he screamed. A sharp, painful, terrified scream. The girl had sprung forward and smashed him in the shin with her artificial limb. He thought that it was at least four times as hard as any ordinary kick.

He bent over to clutch his leg. It had splintered. He could feel the bone. The crazy had broken his leg. Then he screamed again as she smashed him hard in the other leg. He toppled over onto the floor and lay on his back like a turtle, knees tucked close to his stomach.

Any hesitation he might have had about striking a young girl was long gone, but it was far too late for that. The girl stood over him, beating him with her weapon. Helplessly he watched her in horror until his eyes were filled with blood.

Then all he could hear was a strange incantation coming from the girl. Words he'd never heard before and didn't understand. Like some kind of religious nut, she kept chanting to herself:

Break the trunkus, eat the bone,
Food for three and then go home.

And then the guard heard nothing, because the pain was too great and he was unconscious. The beating stopped.

The girl looked down at him as though unsure of where, or if, she'd ever seen him before.

"Sorry, Kojak," she snapped, and drove her metal leg down hard between his eyes, squashing his skull as if it were a grape.

6

It was Sunday night and it wasn't all that late, but Diana and Tom were in bed, asleep. What was left of Diana's roast sat on the table in the living room. It had been a very successful dinner and a very successful evening. They had eaten, watched *The Way We Were* on Home Box Office, and then made love on the couch. It had been a good Sunday evening, the kind that fortified them for the week ahead. Now they slept, their faces peaceful and innocent.

In the dim, pearly gray light coming into the living room from the garden, a shadow glided across the high glass doors. A minute later there was the faintest of squeaks, softly repeated at intervals. The sound came from a screw turning in the kitchen window-fan, the ventilation unit encased in the window to suck cooking odors out of the apartment. The screw inched its way out of the unit with such an even rotation that it appeared to be trying to spin itself free of its own socket.

Finally it came loose and dropped to the floor with a small ping. Shortly afterward another dropped, then the remaining two. The fan jerked forward, easing into the kitchen. A pale, hairless hand gripped it tightly from behind, lowering it quietly to the Formica countertop. The arm behind the hand snaked in from the garden and through the hole created by the dislodged fan. Five slender fingers burrowed around molelike in the gloom until they found the brass latch and clicked it open. Then the window rose slowly, gliding upward on well-greased chains.

In she came through the now-open window with surprising agility, the artificial leg not seeming to hinder her. Clutching her black umbrella, she let herself down from the sill and placed the fan back in its hole. Then, only then, did she stand and survey the kitchen, a childish and malicious smile spreading on her face. It was like another world, this apartment. A person could have fun in here. Shit, why hadn't she thought of visiting them other girls. They were pretty, too—just like the new one was—long black hair, green eyes, two legs. Except that this new one was different. Prettier for one, and she liked the same stuff—dressing up, walking around, buying things in the stores. Not like that tight-assed waitress she had followed around for four fucking days just watching her serve burgers. Just burger this and burger that. No fun, no car, no nice shoes, no Blondie to peg. Nothing you'd ever want for your own.

Then she saw it. She couldn't believe her eyes. The rich bitch's blue sweater was hanging on the back of a kitchen chair. It was the sweater the bitch had worn at the bookstore. She grabbed it in her fist and pulled it to her face. It smelled like perfume, this sweater. No wonder the bitch was always getting pegged. Who wouldn't, wearing a sweater like this? She slid one arm deep into the sleeve, letting the other sleeve drape around her shoulders. Finders, keepers, dogface. Ooo, it felt good.

She moved around the table and sat down. There was a little leftover roast and a half-finished glass of wine, which she quickly swilled down, imagining Blondie sitting there next to her, talking to her, reading to her, asking her to go in the car with him. Just then Taffy let out his tiny growl.

Jesus H. Christ! If there was anything she didn't need now, it was some scrawny little mutt sniffing around her leg. Not when she was wearing the sweater and drinking this wine. The puppy was crawling around her nervously, low on its belly.

"Bye-bye, little doggie-poo."

Taffy looked up when he heard the voice. He could see the piece of leftover roast dangling enticingly from her fingers. Confusion clouded the puppy's eyes. He wanted the meat, but didn't trust her. Cautiously he craned his neck and took the meat in his mouth. Her hands flicked out in one practiced movement, seizing the dog by his neck and snout. "Let's see you swallow it now, poochface." Her fingers tightened around the dog's throat, his tiny whimpers lost in his mouth.

Then she heard the bed creak.

"Are you up?" It was the bitch's voice.

"Uh-huh."

"Did you hear something?"

"No. You're the one who hears things, not me."

"Listen, Tom . . . what do you hear?"

"You. I hear you, asking me if I hear anything."

"Tom, go take a look. I won't be able to sleep unless you look."

He sighed. "I'm going to get myself something to drink." He got up blearily and fumbled into his robe and slippers. Women. Jesus.

Tom padded into the kitchen and turned on the light. Now that he was wide awake he might as well enjoy it. Pouring himself a glass of milk, he added two ice cubes and opened a fresh box of Fig Newtons. His mouth full, he peered out the window into the garden. Nothing there. Reaching for another cookie, he spied a scrap of leftover roast on the floor. He picked it up and carried it to the disposal. "Damn dog, at it again." Then, as if to fulfill his masculine duty, he strolled into the living room to check the garden door. It was securely locked. He glanced around the room a final time and returned to the kitchen to fill his glass again.

Diana rolled over in her sleep. Her dream carried her

on an uneasy sea. Tumbling, lifting, falling, drowning. She wanted to scream, but she had no mouth, no voice. There was darkness around her, and fingers of light. And in the light a figure moved, looming over her, reaching for her. A figure grotesque and big and malformed, with a gaping hole of a mouth calling her name. The voice was getting clearer. Then she sensed it. This wasn't a dream. Someone was in the room! Diana bolted upright with a scream.

Two strong arms reached out to grab her. "It's me, honey," Tom said soothingly. "There's nothing out there. It's all right."

Diana clutched him tightly. "You scared me," she said, sounding like a little girl.

Tom squeezed her and let her down onto the pillow. "Everything's okay. Go back to sleep. I love you."

"Hold me," she whispered.

They spent the night in each other's arms.

7

Diana had known Dr. Allen all her life. Indeed, he had delivered her twenty-six years ago, when her parents still lived in Queens. In the years since then he had done very well for himself, so well, in fact, that he now had an office and apartment on Park Avenue.

But despite an acquired Manhattan indifference and an income approaching $120,000, Dr. Allen had a place in his heart for Diana that could have accommodated Madison Square Garden. Yes, he had brought her into the world, but his fondness for Diana was rooted in something deeper still. She was a continual reminder of why he had gone into medicine in the first place. She was the last link with his still-vivid memories of Dr. Walter Allen, his father, and Dr. Walter Allen, his grandfather, both of whom had spent their lives in the same New York neighborhood of Jackson Heights seeing the same families through the crises, joys, and sorrows of life.

Like a family homestead that is passed down through the generations, so the Allen family practice had been passed on to a young Walter Allen, III, when his father died right after World War II, a few short years before the old neighborhood disappeared under the onslaught of urban renewal.

Now only Diana Stewart remained to remind Dr. Allen of that once-cherished responsibility that his father had entrusted to him. Indeed, Dr. Walter Allen, Jr., had delivered Diana's father, as Dr. Allen, the son, had delivered Diana.

And so if sometimes Dr. Allen overplayed the part of the kindly old family physician, Diana thought she knew why and allowed him his role and was touched by the sincerity of his concern for her well-being.

Today was no different. Diana was sitting in Dr. Allen's office, watching him as he stood by his desk, perusing her medical file.

"Well," he said finally, "all the tests came out perfect. If good health and medical compatibility have anything to do with a successful marriage, you're off to a good start."

Diana smiled. If there was anything she was sure of, it was that she and Tom were compatible. "I'll work hard at the rest of it," she said.

Dr. Allen nodded. "I'm sure you will, Diana." He paused thoughtfully for a moment, then slipped into one of his frequent reminiscences. "Little girls sure grow up quickly. You know, it wasn't so long ago that I slapped that little pink fanny of yours. And a very pretty one it was."

"Tom says it still is," Diana replied, with a twinkle in her eye.

Dr. Allen gave an embarrassed shrug, then continued, "I don't mean to sound like a sentimental old fool, even if that's what I am. But I was very fond of your parents and I know how they loved you and I have a great affection for you, too. It would just make me very happy to know that if you ever have any kind of problem, Diana, even if you only need someone to talk to, you feel that you can come to me."

"I do feel that," Diana said simply. "And I know that you mean it."

"I just wanted to make sure."

"Dr. Allen, that's the nicest wedding present anyone could give me."

Dr. Allen had touched her in a most vulnerable spot. Since her parents' death, she *had* felt alone. There was

Tom, of course, and Sarah, but they were her age. In many ways she still thought of herself as a kid. It was nice to know there was an adult out there. Just in case.

Dr. Allen waved a finger at Diana in mock-anger. "And you can stop Dr. Allening me, too. When my patients get married, they call me Walter, Wally, or Walt. But no more Dr. Allen."

"But you'll always be Dr. Allen to me."

Impulsively she got up and kissed him on the cheek.

He chuckled, holding his head against hers. "You shouldn't upset an old man like that."

Diana smiled. "Flatterer. And liar. You're not an old man at all. You'll outdance everyone at the wedding."

"You know, I'd like nothing more," Dr. Allen assured her. "But I'm afraid that since my heart attack, I'm lucky to get away with a slow foxtrot."

"Wally," she joked, "if you can lead someone with my kind of stage fright down a wedding aisle with four hundred people looking on, I'm sure you'll be the life of the party."

Putting an arm around her shoulder, the old doctor started to walk Diana toward the door.

"Now, next time you come around, Diana, I want you to bring this Tom Johnson with you. It's about time I met the young man."

"Well, you'll just have to come to dinner then. I'll make you my specialty. Tom calls it Arabian Goulash, but it tastes better than it sounds."

He laughed and bade her good-bye. He had made her feel more confident, she thought, less alone. Perhaps that was as important as anything else he did.

◆◆◆

Another dull fucking day at home with dull fucking Joel. Sometimes she thought that was all she ever did. But that was before she had found that girl, and now life had started to have some gusto in it. She wanted to drag it out, make it last. The longer it took, the more fun it would be. In the meantime she was going to amuse herself any way she could.

She sprawled on her belly across the living room floor, in the middle of all the rundown, mismatched furniture. With a fistful of crayons she was playing with a coloring book, working on all those round-cheeked smiling children, making them people who would be her friends. She gave them twisted mouths, red eyes, and black, lifeless legs. They looked gaunt and haunted, as though they were in a concentration camp somewhere. But she didn't put bars in front of them. She knew that the bars were all in your soul.

She looked up at Joel, who was in the kitchen, feverishly peeling an onion, making another salad; he always made salad. She thought how he didn't even like eating salad. It was just another excuse to use his favorite old knife and twitch his nose. No one could peel a carrot, slice a tomato, core an apple, like Joel. His tool was so quick, precise, exact. Nobody liked cutting things up as much as Joel, watching the severed little bits of living tissues spring off from the larger whole.

She decided he was having too good a time over there. His nose was twitching like crazy. No way was she going to sit with the boring crayons when Joel was having all the fun. She'd get him good this time. She knew just how to do it, too. She always knew how.

She made her voice low and taunting. "Guess what I saw today, Joel?"

He didn't bother to answer her. He just kept on chopping away.

"Just guess." She made it sound very secret, very sly.

Joel didn't so much as lift his eyes.

She knew how to take care of that, too.

"I saw a man doing tricks on the sidewalk," she said. "He made a nickel come out of my ear."

84

Now she had him. She heard him stop chopping, then heard his feet, then she saw him come into the room, the knife still in his hand.

"Where was that?" He was trying to sound casual. "Was that in the neighborhood?"

He had taken the bait. Now she was going to reel him in slowly. "The man pulled a long scarf outta his pants and made four little strings into one big long one."

"Did little Laurie leave the neighborhood today?"

"My name's not little Laurie!"

"Well, you're little, aren't you?"

"Shut your face!" she squawked.

"Where – were – you – today – Laurie!" He was practically screaming.

"I went to Puerto Rico for a vacation. Ninety-nine fifty round trip. Three days, two nights."

"When is little Laurie going to learn there are a lot of sick people on the street with knives and guns. They're gonna get you, if you go walking alone. They're gonna make a pie out of you."

Joel was lashing out at her, but what he was really doing, as she knew, was pleading with her, pleading with her to stay home. But she had had it with that.

"Why don't you go on television, Joel, and win us some money, so we can go to Puerto Rico!" Laurie fired back.

Joel clutched the knife in his hand. The expression on his face indicated what he would like to do with it. "You little beast, come and give me a big kiss."

"No!" Laurie said. "No more kisses for you, Joel."

She smiled to herself when she said it. She knew he would start to whine now.

Sure enough, that wheedling note crept into his voice. "If I say I'm sorry?"

Her big fish was almost in the boat.

" 'Cause you know I am," he said.

85

The look of pain on his face made her grin. He was so much easier to handle when he got like that.

Tom waited at the fountain in front of the Plaza Hotel, immaculate in his blazer, looking like a model from the pages of *Gentleman's Quarterly*. Fresh and groomed and perfectly tailored. Seeing him there, framed against the elegance of the hotel and the lushness of the park, one wouldn't think there were such things in the city as ghettos or garbage strikes or looting.

Tom glanced at his watch. Diana wasn't late, it was just one of his quirks to know the time within five or six minutes.

"Tom, darling!"

He looked up. Through the crowd, across the fountain, he had a broken view of Diana in her favorite blue sweater. She was looking at him with an intensity at odds with the gaiety of her voice. Then, even more oddly, she saw him looking at her and ducked into the crowd, moving with a rapid, awkward gait. He opened his mouth to call out to her, but hadn't gotten a word out when her voice came again, and caused him further disorientation. It had come from a point far from where she had disappeared. He swung around just in time to catch Diana as she ran up and leaped exuberantly into his arms.

But Diana wasn't wearing her favorite blue sweater—she was looking very chic in a simple gray suit with a ruffled white silk blouse.

"It's official," Diana exclaimed, planting a warm, damp kiss on his cheek.

"What's official?" Tom asked in a dazed voice, looking back toward the fountain in puzzlement.

"We are! We're compatible, Doc just said."

"What did he say exactly?" Tom took her hand and they set off in the direction of Rumpelmayer's for lunch.

Diana went into her best imitation of Dr. Allen's

grandfatherly manner. "He said, 'Diana, go forth into the valley, be fruitful and multiply,' which means, for all you nonliterary types, that you and I are now free to fool around with the State of New York's blessing."

"Great," Tom grinned. "That's really great."

She tightened her grip on his hand. "And you know what else? We're going to have the biggest, poshest wedding New York's even seen. Okay?"

"No, Diana, we don't have to . . ."

"I know we don't, silly."

"Don't cave in to my parents," Tom said stubbornly.

"Then you have to tell me whether it's the caving in to your parents or the four hundred people that upsets you the most."

"It's the fact that our wedding isn't going to be what you wanted it to be. That's what upsets me."

"Yeah," Diana said wistfully, planting another big kiss smack on his cheek. "Well, you'll still be there, won't you?"

"If that's really the way you want it." There were a lot of times when he couldn't figure her out, but the times when she was puzzling in a way that charmed him were by far the best.

For a moment he wasn't going to say anything else. But there was something that had been on his mind for a long time, and now was as good a time as any to let her know. It wasn't easy. Self-revelation wasn't his strong suit.

"I just want you to know," he began hesitantly, "that if I hadn't met you, I'd probably be walking right now with some girl from Beekman Place who'd be talking to me about some society function or fashion show that I really didn't give a damn about. Instead, I'm . . . I'm very happy. You do know that, don't you?"

"It's chemistry," she announced. "The very first time I saw you, I could tell that beneath that Brooks Brothers uniform was a regular old T-shirt and a hairy chest."

Tom stopped abruptly and turned to face her.

"So your doctor really said we could have kids?"

Diana threw her arms around his neck. "Only if you follow my instructions."

8

It sounded as if the Modern Jazz Quartet was sitting right there in the living room playing "Pyramid." But they weren't. Tom's thirteen hundred and sixty-two dollars' worth of quadraphonic, concert-hall quality, high-fidelity equipment was just doing its job.

The Modern Jazz Quartet was about as far out as Tom Johnson allowed himself to go. They were quiet and intricate, and when you really listened, you could hear something going on. If you didn't want to listen, you could just use them for background music. Stan Getz, the same way. Genteel jazz was hard to come by, but Tom had managed quite a collection.

Rock had never made much of an impression on him. It was too loud, too raucous, too unbuttoned. This music was soothing, unobtrusive, like a double martini or a Nembutal.

So even if Tom couldn't play an eight-hundred-dollar sax like Stan Getz, he could damn well play his thirteen-hundred-and-sixty-two-dollar stereo.

The strange thing was that though the music was playing in Tom's apartment, Tom wasn't there. Neither was Diana. But the tape went round and round, and the Modern Jazz Quartet played "Pyramid."

There was one other sound in the apartment. A monotonous clicking. At first hearing, it might have been taken for an extra rhythm instrument, a castanet, maybe. But the beat was different and irregular. It hurried up, it slowed down, it went along furiously for a little while and then it stopped. And started again.

The sound came from the bedroom, where, spread out on the bed in casual disarray, were dozens of snapshots of Diana with her friends and family. Pictures taken at the beach, at school, at parties—a photographic history of special little moments of friendship and happiness. Except now those memories were desecrated. An odd, rectangular hole had been cut out of each picture. Where the hole was, Diana's left leg used to be.

The clicking sound was being made by a pair of scissors, which Laurie held in her hand. She sat on Diana's bed, wearing Diana's black leotard, with Diana's photograph album open next to her. She was cutting Diana's left leg out of all the pictures.

Laurie took another snapshot out of the album, went snick-snick with the scissors, and another left leg dropped neatly out.

She held the mutilated picture up in front of her face and looked through the hole. This was the most fun she could remember having in a very long time.

She rifled through the album until she found a picture of Diana alone; Diana was wearing a little two-piece bathing suit and standing in front of a beached sailboat. Carefully Laurie folded the photo in two, creasing it at the top of the thighs. She grabbed the crease between her teeth and ripped Diana's left leg out of the picture. It felt really good. God, did it feel good! Too bad it was just a game.

She scooped up the mutilated pictures, jammed them back into the photo album, and put the album back where she had found it.

But not the legs. She carefully picked the little scraps of paper off the bedspread and set them to one side. Maybe she'd take them home with her to look at later.

She got off the bed and opened the dresser drawers. They were filled with clothing. Secret clothing that nobody ever saw. Except that guy who lived with her. He probably saw it, all right. She grabbed a pair of panties and stuffed her fist down into the crotch. A lot of room in there. She brought the underwear up to her face. They smelled fresh and nice and clean, not like her own stuff. The bitch.

She slipped the panties on over her leotard. She stroked them. They felt terrific. Softer than anything she had ever owned. It just wasn't fair.

She went into the bathroom and looked at herself in the mirror. She pushed a clump of her hair to the right and held it there. It made her look more like the bitch, except when she let it go and it flopped back to the other side. If only she had some of that Lady Clairol spray to make it stay right.

What she did have was the goddamned dog jumping around, growling and yapping at her ankles, interrupting her, all excited like he had a wire stuck up his ass. He had been hiding in the bathroom like a smart little pooch, but now he was bothering her like a dumb one. Didn't he remember what happened the last time he messed with her? Did he? Did animals have a memory like that? They came back to the same place every day to get fed. The little sucker was definitely going to remember her this time.

She grabbed the puppy by the skin of its neck and dropped it into the toilet. She shut the lid and flushed. The dog swirled around, its hind legs pulled down into the hole. Desperately it clawed at the smooth porcelain bowl before it disappeared under a torrent of water. Then the suction eased, and the furry body floated to the surface, gasping for air and coughing up water.

Laurie turned her attention to the medicine chest. There it was, all that crap that made you pretty, all the stuff that made guys go after you and drive you to the beach in expensive cars and pour you drinks. All that stuff that made you look like *her*.

There sure was a lot of it. Rouge, cold cream, mascara, lipstick. Anybody could be pretty if they put enough of this stuff on. Jesus, was she going to look great!

Diana could hear the sound of the Modern Jazz Quartet coming through the door as she fumbled in her purse for her keys.

That was odd. Tom was supposed to be at the office till six, but there was his music playing.

Diana didn't like it. Normally she would have simply thought that her fiancé had changed his plans or come home early, but too many strange things had been happening recently, and even a comparatively minor occurrence, such as music coming through the door when music shouldn't have been coming through the door, was enough to alert all her warning systems.

So she was very careful when she opened the door and very careful when she closed it behind her. She turned to look into the apartment. And stopped.

And tried to suppress the scream that rose in her throat.

She could feel her eyes open wide in disbelief.

It seemed that the whole room was tilting. Every piece of furniture was missing a leg. The television stand, the chairs, the couch, the coffee tables, and the mahogany dining table had each been mutilated in the same way; one leg chopped off and missing.

And someone was still in the apartment . . . she could feel it.

"Tom . . ." she called out. But Diana knew he wasn't there. Images of Charles Manson and Sharon Tate flashed through her mind. "Tom, is that you?"

Hesitantly she moved a few steps into the apartment, her eyes covering the room, searching for the place from which someone could jump out at her. The light in the closet was on. She moved in a little closer. Then out of the corner of her eye she caught it. Her mouth contorted in horror. On the living room wall—the imprint of a human body!

It looked as if someone had covered himself in a thick red paste and pressed his body, both arms and legs spread-eagled, against the wall.

Stunned, Diana gawked at the awful thing in front of her. It was some kind of thick impasto the color of tomato soup. She was afraid to touch it. It looked like some kind of target.

And there was more. Above the head of the grotesque silhouette was a message. There, scrawled in red lipstick, written in the handwriting of a seven-year-old, were the words RE-MEMBER ME.

What did it mean? She recalled that Manson had written "Kill the Pigs" with the blood of his victims. Had something awful happened to Tom?

Her breath short, her throat constricted with fear, she rushed to the bedroom. The bed and night table and dresser were tilted, too; one leg from each was cleanly severed and missing.

Diana just stood there. She didn't understand it, but she didn't want to see any more. Her home had been desecrated. She didn't feel safe here any more. She didn't feel safe anywhere. She had no idea what this kind of random, wanton destruction could mean.

Except for one thing. She couldn't explain the feeling, but she was very sure that whatever was going on was not directed against Tom.

It was meant for her.

And then that thought was interrupted by the sound of the toilet flushing. There *was* somebody in the apartment!

She whirled around to face the sound and saw the bathroom door slightly ajar.

When she called out again, there wasn't much strength in her voice. "Tom . . . are you there?"

For a moment she waited, desperately hoping for an answer. But no answer came.

Rigid with fear, Diana crept toward the bathroom door. It took all her courage to traverse that small area of bedroom floor. She was sure her legs were going to buckle beneath her. Her hand reached out for the brass knob. In a sudden burst, the bathroom door flew open, almost knocking her over.

She had to force herself to look inside.

The bathroom was empty. The window was wide open.

Someone had been in there. But she didn't need a flushed toilet or an open window to tell her that. The bizarre butchery of their furniture was evidence enough.

She was too shaken now to deal with this alone. She rushed to the telephone and dialed Tom's office.

A voice came on the line, as impersonal as a computerized answering service. "Corporate Finance Group."

Diana was out of breath. "May I speak to Tom Johnson, please?"

"I'm sorry," said the voice. "He's in a meeting. If you'd care to leave your name and number . . ."

Diana simply didn't have time to listen to what the computerized voice would be willing to do if she'd leave her name and number. "This is his fiancée," she interrupted. "Tell him it's an emergency. Please."

The voice at the other end apparently wasn't programmed to call executives out of meetings if their fiancées were having emergencies. The voice didn't want to do it. The voice insisted that it wasn't really empowered to do it. Surely the young lady understood.

But Diana persisted, overriding the objections, finally making the voice understand that something of real urgency was taking place that had absolutely nothing to do with The Bank. The voice, apparently picking up

94

the vibration of panic, said that it would see what it could do. First, of course, it put Diana on hold.

Diana waited nervously. And then she heard a tiny sneeze. Taffy was standing in the doorway, soaking wet and shivering, practically crawling on his belly.

Even her own fear couldn't keep Diana from responding to the sight.

"Taffy!" she cried out, "What is it, baby?"

That was when Tom came on the phone.

Even before he spoke to her, he was angry. He had been in an extremely important meeting with some extremely important people, and as always in such circumstances he was concerned to show these men that he could hold his own, that he wasn't there simply because of who his father was. Such ambitions weren't helped along by being pulled out of a meeting because your fiancée was having some kind of a problem she thought was an emergency.

So when he picked up the phone, he didn't even say hello. "Diana, what's so important? Didn't they tell you I was in a meeting?"

He listened to the beginning of her wild story and then interrupted, "What do you mean? Was someone in the house?"

"Someone broke in."

"Did they take anything?"

The question hurt her, and she let it show in her voice. "I don't know. I haven't looked. Please, Tom, come home."

"Are you okay?" he finally asked.

"I guess so. I don't know. Can't you come home?"

"Don't panic. I'm leaving right now. Call the police, Diana. I'll be there in fifteen minutes, okay?"

"Okay," she said. "But hurry."

She hung up and immediately dialed the police. Taffy growled and bared his teeth at her.

◆◆◆

They didn't look like television cops. They didn't wear three-piece suits with fancy paisley silk linings or dirty old rumpled raincoats. They wore plain blue uniforms. As often happened in moments of stress, Diana allowed an irreverent thought to tumble around in her mind. Why was it that in all those years, nobody had ever figured out that Lieutenant Kojak was on the take? Nobody could finance a tailored wardrobe like his on a cop's salary. Look at what Columbo wore. The thought made her smile, and that in turn made Tom and the cops stare at her. Half-defiantly she returned their gaze, visibly sizing them up.

They were two of New York's finest. The older of the two was named Patchek, according to the nametag pinned just above his badge. Sgt. Harry Patchek. Not Harold; Harry, like your favorite uncle. Somewhere in his thirties, he had a flat, florid face and a bent nose that looked to have been hit more than once—from several directions. His hair was beginning to show flecks of gray at the temples, and there was a bit of a paunch pushing out over his shiny black leather belt. His blue coat seemed too small for his beefy shoulders, and his hands were scarred and broad-knuckled. He wore the expected world-weary scowl of stoic patience and suspicion, and gave such an impression of being the average big, dumb cop that you were tempted to believe it. Until you looked at his eyes, which were an odd shade of amber and as coldly intelligent as a barracuda's. It was as if they'd been sawn from sections of brass rod.

The second cop, William D. Timilty, according to his nameplate, looked like a college senior playing at policeman. He was younger than Patchek, and was only a corporal. His uniform was precisely pressed and his leatherwork and metal relentlessly polished. He had mild eyes and a mild presence, and had a habit of standing just to one side of Patchek and slightly to the rear, as if in deference to the older policeman's rank and age.

Notebook in hand, he appeared to be waiting for pearls of wisdom to drop from the senior partner's lips.

They looked to Diana like the original Odd Couple, two men linked together solely by the increasingly apparent fact that they both enjoyed their work. Diana did not know if that was a good thing or not. With cops you could never tell.

Patchek looked around the room again and then turned to Diana. "You're sure nothing was stolen?"

Diana shook her head. "I've looked, and nothing seems to be missing."

"And no sign of a break-in" Timilty said. It was a question, but he didn't phrase it like one. It sounded like a flat statement of fact, a reiteration of an earlier remark Diana had made.

"The bathroom window was open," she said again, wearying of the repetition. "I assume he just came in through there."

"He?" Patchek shot back. His tone said everything: How do you know it was a man? Did you see him? If you did, can you describe him? If not, why say "he"?

"I just assumed . . ." Diana began.

"You can't assume a thing in this town, lady," Patchek cut in. "That work of art you got on your wall there sure looks like a woman to me."

"I suppose so," Diana conceded. She wasn't about to argue with these men. They were wearing her down. They asked perfectly reasonable questions, they listened attentively, but they exhausted you. They made you afraid to sit down, lest that be taken as a sign of guilt. These policemen were obviously very good at what they did. She just wished that, as the injured party, she could feel that they were on her side.

Patchek stood in the middle of the room, looking at the thing on the wall. It impressed and puzzled him at the same time. Diana thought he looked like some out-of-towner at the Museum of Modern Art, staring at one of those wall-sized Jackson Pollock drip paintings, blaming himself that he couldn't figure out what in the world the artist meant.

Patchek dug his hand deep into his pocket as if he were going to pull a gun on the thing. "As near as I can figure out," he said, "this person smeared themselves all over with that stuff that was in the empty jars and tubes in the bathroom and then sort of attempted to, uh . . ." He struggled for the *mot juste*. ". . . affix themselves to the wall."

"Wallowed around in it, is what they did," Timilty added.

It looked that way to Diana, too, but it was making no sense. "Why would a person want to do a thing like that?" she asked.

Patchek exhaled a small breath of delight. This was more his turf. "Now that, ma'am," he said, "is something I don't know, any more than I know why people go walking around in overcoats with nothing on underneath or cut their initials into dead whores' bellies. I guess it gives them pleasure, is all."

Diana flinched. She'd been given a sudden, front-row look into the slime pit that constituted Patchek's everyday life and she didn't like it at all.

"A lot of pleasure," Patchek repeated, and watched her squirm. "Yes, ma'am," he went on, obviously relishing the moment, "some people in this town have got themselves some pretty original ways of getting off. This here could just be a cold-cream freak."

"Motivations is a tricky business," Timilty rejoined. "They're unique to the individual." He eyed the wall intently, as if hoping it would render up its arcane secrets to him. "Look here, Hank, I think I got something," he said.

Patchek walked over to the thing Diana was beginning to think had a right to be called, "Mural, School of New York."

"It's a hair," Timilty said.

"Sure is," Patchek agreed, peering at the place where his partner was pointing.

"Let's bag it," Timilty suggested.

Patcheck handed him what looked to Diana like a miniature plastic Baggie. Timilty took a tweezerlike implement from his shirt pocket and, with infinite care, plucked the hair out of the thick impasto of the mural, dropped it into the plastic Baggie, and sealed it.

The two men smiled smugly at each other, like they had just recovered the Hope Diamond. Diana didn't understand what the big deal was all about.

As if Patchek could read her mind, he set out to answer her question. "Well," he said, "now we got us a hair. Now we got a place to start."

"With just a hair?" Diana asked.

"Sure thing, ma'am," Timilty said, all quiet and reason. "It belongs to somebody. It's got a person that goes with it."

For an instant Diana was afraid he was going to continue, like the minister in *Our Town* who addressed his letter in ever-widening concentric circles, encompassing his town, his state, his nation, his hemisphere, and his planet, finally ending up with the Mind of God. But mercifully Timilty was willing to limit his conceptual horizons to an unknown person who had been attached to the hair.

Thank God, Diana thought.

Patchek immediately brought the issue down from such metaphysical speculation back into the dirt where he apparently spent all his time. "Miss Stewart, you wouldn't have had any falling out with, say, a friend or acquaintance lately, would you?"

"No, I haven't, Officer. And what does that have to do with anything?" Diana shot back, not bothering to hide the indignation in her voice.

Patchek turned back to the wall. Diana couldn't see

his face, but she would have sworn he was licking his lips. "I'm just looking at this message here, just exploring the possibilities, is all," he said, and waved his hand at the lipstick graffiti scrawled on the wall.

He underlined the message in the air. "Re-member me. Re-member me," he repeated, thinking aloud.

"Perhaps an affair that didn't work out?" Timilty asked, leaning forward eagerly.

"That's ridiculous," Tom protested feebly.

"Besides you said a woman did this!" Diana half-railed at the younger cop. "Your partner did."

"Sure," Timilty replied, with that same maddening blandness, "maybe he did. But there's more than just one kind of companionship, you know."

Diana could not have felt more violated if the cop had actually shoved his slimy hand up her dress. She was about to tell him what she thought of him, of his questions, of his demeanor, of his unspoken assumptions, of the whole stinking situation that had suddenly grown up around the fact that someone had penetrated *her* space, abused *her* property, when suddenly Patchek cut through her as yet unspoken tirade with the bluntness of three fingers of vodka cutting through a drunk's morning phlegm.

"Let's wrap this thing up," he said, speaking to the room at large.

Diana just stood there, livid, afraid to open her mouth for fear of what might come out. Patchek looked at Tom. "Could I speak to you alone, Mr. Johnson?"

"Sure," Tom said, too nonplussed to do otherwise, and in any case too accustomed to obeying authority to refuse. He turned to Diana and said in a voice full of concern, "Darling, why don't you lie down in the bedroom? I'll be there in a moment."

For once she was all too glad to accede to what sounded like a patronizing directive from her fiancé. At that moment she wanted nothing more than to get away from them, get away from what she was sure Patchek thought of as serious men's talk, get away and lie down and be by herself. And not think.

So Diana was no longer in the room when the ever-observant Officer Timilty discreetly opened her purse, pulled some hairs from her hairbrush, and carefully put them into another of his little plastic Baggies.

And she was no longer in the room when Patchek took the opportunity presented by Tom's walking him to the door to ask a few more questions. "Tell me, Mr. Johnson, have you and your girlfriend been shacked up a long time?"

It was the wrong way to say it. If anyone went along with authority, it was Tom, but there were still social distinctions one observed, and Patchek had just neglected one of them.

Tom stiffened, avoided the friendly arm that was just about to come to rest on his shoulder, and said, in a cold voice that would have been appropriate for a waiter who had just brought the wrong wine, and warm at that, "Miss Stewart's not my girlfriend, she's my fiancée."

"Yeah, that's right. She told me," Patchek said, trying to slide over whatever was eating at this rich WASP. "Have you known her long?"

"What are you after, Officer, a character reference?" Tom snapped back at him.

Patchek sighed. "Look, Mr. Johnson. I'll level with you. Sometimes people don't want to be in the situation they're in, and they pick some pretty strange ways of telling themselves that."

If there was one thing Tom didn't need, it was some philosopher cop, some Jimmy Breslin of the police force, drawing on all his observations of kinky young couples from Queens to tell him something was the matter with him and Diana.

"Just what does that mean?" Tom said, his gaze burrowing contemptuously down on Patchek.

Patchek waved a conciliatory hand. "Don't go getting your dander up, Mr. Johnson. Let me just give you the facts." And then he unreeled, in his flat monotone, the results of the logic and speculation that obviously made him what he was. "The upstairs neighbors are both on the Island for the summer—that's your testimony. There's no sign of a forced break-in—her testimony," he said, nodding toward the bedroom. "The hair off that wall is the same color as hers—fact. And that thing on the wall fits your girlfriend like a glove—my observation."

And having stunned Tom with his recitation, he allowed himself a last little insight. "You don't come across two bodies like that right in a row . . . if you know what I mean."

That tore it for Tom.

"Just stop it right there!" he demanded. "You're making a lot of assumptions, and they're full of crap."

Patchek looked as if someone had asked him what time it was. "Yeah, well, that's part of my job," he said, placing a placating hand on Tom's arm. "Look, we'll run that hair through the lab and tell you what our man says. We're down at the Nineteenth Precinct if you want to get in touch with us."

And he smiled again. And his younger partner smiled again. And both of them walked out.

Tom damned them as he watched them go, all the more upset because for a moment they had seemed so reassuring, so logical. Then he closed the door behind them and started toward the bedroom, where there was a young woman to whom he had committed himself but with whom he suddenly felt he had far less in common than he had with those two abrasive strangers, and about whom, he now thought, he might know very little indeed.

They shared the work. Tom held each piece of furniture on an even keel, while Diana stacked books to replace the missing legs. She tried to keep up a light banter by cracking little jokes about some of the titles and where they were ending up. But it didn't work. Nothing could make the job anything other than what is was: a grim reminder of a wanton and unexplained intrusion.

When all the furniture was finally standing upright again and Tom had cleaned the horrid smear off the wall, Diana made them sandwiches and milk. They sat in silence, eating mechanically, trying their best to avoid talking about the desecration but having nothing else on their minds.

"Want some cookies or something?" Diana finally chanced.

"No, thanks. I'm not that hungry."

"There's some ice cream in the freezer."

"Maybe later."

Then Diana couldn't stand it anymore and blurted out what had been on her mind all evening. "Do you think there could be a connection between the attack on the car and what happened today?"

"Yeah. New York City," Tom replied, and took a huge bite of his sandwich, as if to punctuate his statement.

"You don't think it's possible that maybe that person on the street came into the house."

"Honey," Tom explained, sensing her anxiety, "the

connection between all this is goddamned New York City. There are more loonies in twenty blocks of this town than in the entire Western hemisphere."

"I never heard of this stuff happening to anybody else," Diana continued, almost pleading.

Tom put his sandwich down, wiped his fingers, and slid across the couch to be next to her. "Now don't get yourself thinking that there are ghosts behind every door. We just drew the wrong card twice in a row." He sounded almost is if he were trying to convince himself. "We're not the only ones, you know. Some people get burglarized four times in the same year."

"I know how they must feel," Diana murmured sullenly.

"Now listen to me." Tom took both her hands and held them tightly. "You can't let the city get the better of you. I've lived here all my life. I know what I'm talking about. You let things like this spook you, and every time you hear the news you'll be too scared to leave the house." He stood up and gave her a pat on the cheek. "Come on, you'll see. We'll both feel better in the morning."

Tom took the plates into the kitchen and then went about laying his clothing out for the next day. It was typical of him that he did this every night. Not for him the casual grabbing of shirts and ties first thing in the morning before he'd even had his coffee. No, he did it the evening before and he thought about it carefully, and as a result his ensembles were always impeccable.

Diana sat in bed watching him, trying to guess which tie he would choose to go with the blue striped shirt he had set on the chair. Snuggling down beneath the covers, she made sure to keep his side of the bed unturned and neat, the way he preferred.

"Maybe something was stolen from the apartment, and we just haven't noticed it," Diana said, curiosity beginning to wash away her uneasiness. "Did you check your grandfather's coin collection?"

"No, I didn't check the coin collection, and it wasn't a robbery, and I really don't feel like talking about this for the rest of my life."

Diana snapped on the reading light, her signal that she didn't like the tone in which Tom had answered her. She picked up her book and glasses from the night table. She couldn't even remember what novel she had been reading and she didn't look now. She wasn't actually going to read, anyway; she couldn't concentrate. She was going to pretend to read, to shut herself off from Tom until he apologized. She opened the book and put on the glasses.

It took her a moment to realize that something was wrong and another to puzzle out what it was. The glasses. They were too bulky. She took them off and examined them. The frames were heavy black plastic, like the cheap ones you found in drugstores. Nothing like she had ever owned.

"Tom," she said, holding them out toward him, all thoughts of ignoring him now gone, "these aren't my glasses."

"They're certainly not mine," he said, hardly looking up at her.

"Oh, that's just terrific. The boogeyman strikes again."

Curious now, she wiped the lenses with the bedsheet and tried them on.

"That's weird! They seem like my prescription."

"Well, that's it, then," Tom said. "They're an old pair you bought sometime or other and forgot about."

"Come on, Tom," Diana said, exasperated. "I at least know whether a pair of eyeglasses belongs to me or not, don't I? And look how ugly they are. I'd never buy anything like this."

Tom slipped on his pajama bottoms and gave a deep, sarcastic bow. "All right, Diana, I apologize for thinking you might have bought ugly glasses."

That was the last straw. She turned off the light and

pulled the sheet up around her. Tom shut off his light and pulled back the covers on his side of the bed. Now the room was dark and quiet.

Oh, boy, Diana thought, this is going to be one of those nights. One of those nights when we lie awake beside each other, both pretending we're asleep, so we don't have to talk. Then she felt his body stiffen.

"What the . . ." He sat up, fumbling for his reading light, and switched it on.

Diana rolled over, aware that something was happening. Tom was hunched over, lifting the covers, peering down beneath them.

"Tom, what's—"

And then his howl shattered the night. It was a long, loud "Holy shit" of utter shock that bounced off the ceiling as he jumped out of bed. He stood frantically brushing at his pajamas, as if they were on fire.

Diana sat up by reflex and what she saw made her scream.

Tom's white pajamas were soaked with blood. Wet and red and covering him. Instinctively she reached across the bed. "Are you all right!"

He backed off, a look of fear and disgust on his face. "Don't touch me!" he bellowed, and made a dash for the bathroom, ripping desperately at the blood-drenched pajamas, trying to tear the cloth from his body.

"Tom!" Diana got out of bed after him. "Are you hurt? What is it!"

"That's what I want to know, goddamn it!" he yelled at her from the bathroom.

A moment later he stormed back into the room, wearing his bathrobe.

"What the hell's going on in this house?" His hostility seemed to be aimed at her.

"HOW—SHOULD—I—KNOW!" Diana said it as if she was talking to someone who was deaf.

Tom marched over to the bed and yanked off the covers.

He was expecting almost anything, perhaps the manifestation of some demented teenage prank—say, a dead rat, its blood smeared around—but he certainly didn't expect what he saw. He glared at it, half-hateful, half-nauseated. His entire side of the bed was completely soaked in thick, dark, half-coagulated blood. It looked like the top of a spoiled, gelatinous cherry cheesecake had been smashed into the sheets.

Tom had to keep himself from vomiting.

"Oh, God," he said, almost choking on the words.

Diana backed away, mute with disgust. She steadied herself against the wall. "Don't touch it," she implored.

"Those shithead punks!" He turned to Diana and shook his finger at her. "I just wish I had come in here while those bastards were doing this. I would have beaten their stupid brains in."

"I can clean it up, Tom. It'll only take me a couple of minutes," Diana said, with all the calm she could muster.

"Do it tomorrow."

"I can do it now, it's not too bad."

"I said do it tomorrow!"

"Don't talk to me that way." Her voice was confused and frightened, and it shook Tom out of his anger.

"I'm sleeping in the living room," he announced tersely, and started for the door.

"Okay," she mumbled, relieved that he had made the decision and assuming it included her.

Then he was gone.

If the bedding wasn't the mess it was, he probably would have dragged it off after him.

At least, that's what they did in those old movies Diana was always watching late at night on TV. Somebody square and middle-class, somebody who slept in pajamas— somebody like Robert Cummings—was always getting upset and self-righteous about some minor domestic matter. He would tear the covers off the bed and make a beeline for the couch. But since he was Robert Cummings, he usually tripped on the bedding and did a half gainer into an end table. His wife would call the family doctor and out of her genuine concern for her helpless husband, everything got patched up, including her husband's scalp.

Diana had the sick feeling that things weren't going to be that simple. Besides, they didn't make those kind of movies anymore.

By the time Diana got to the living room, Tom had already staked out the couch and had his back turned to her. She fetched a blanket from the closet and placed it over him.

"I'm sorry I yelled at you," he said, averting his eyes.

"That's okay. No harm done."

Diana returned to the bedroom, stripped the foul sheets and blankets, and put on a fresh mattress pad. When she went back to the living room, Tom was already asleep. She wanted to snuggle up next to him, but didn't want to wake him. So she lay down on the carpet and closed her eyes.

She didn't expect sleeping on the floor would be all that comfortable, but on the other hand she didn't expect it to be quite as hard as it was. It pressed into the back of her shoulder blades. When she rolled over, it squashed her breasts. She tried sleeping on her side, and the floor ground into her hipbone. There was no way she was going to get to sleep.

So she lay there thinking, her eyes wandering aimlessly to the walls and ceiling and bathroom, anywhere except in the direction of the bedroom. But what she was thinking only upset her more; her life was sliding away from her, and she didn't know how to stop it.

At dawn, when the sky was beginning to show the first signs of light, Diana gave up all thought of trying to get any rest and walked as quietly as she could across the foyer toward the kitchen. Maybe breakfast would calm her down. Moving quietly on her bare feet, she was hardly making any noise at all, but it was enough to awaken Tom, who had been having his own kind of bad night on the couch.

He stirred in his sleep and opened his eyes. "What time is it?" he mumbled groggily.

"Six thirty," Diana said, looking down at him.

"How come you're up?" he yawned.

"The floor down there's not too comfortable."

Tom looked at her in sleepy astonishment. "You slept on the floor?"

"You didn't really think I would sleep in that bed!"

They stared at each other for a long moment, and she couldn't be judgmental with him looking so sorrowful the way he did.

"I'm scared," she told him. "It's all so horrible."

Tom reached for her. "It's going to be all right, honey."

She hesitated at first, thinking how this wasn't going to be the answer to anything, but she gave in to his kiss and even kissed him back hard before pulling away. Tom reached for her, trying to get her back in his arms.

"Don't go," he protested affectionately. "I was having a nice time there."

"So was I," Diana whispered, but she didn't come back to him. Instead she walked over to her purse, which was still where she had left it on the table, what seemed like a hundred and twenty-seven years ago. Reaching inside, she pulled out a handful of brochures. She walked back to Tom and spread the folders over his reclining form.

"Here, take a look," she said. "With everything that was going on, I forgot to show you."

Tom picked up one of the colorful travel brochures and looked at it with some puzzlement. "Tahiti?" he asked.

"Glamorous Tahiti," Diana nodded. "For our honeymoon. Deserted beaches, a little hut under a big palm tree, no phones, a jug of wine, a loaf of bread, and you and me, brown and naked as berries. Waddaya say?" she asked him anxiously, almost trying to will herself out of the dreadful apartment into someplace where it was warm and safe.

He sat up straight, letting several of the brochures slide to the floor. "Let's go right now."

She smiled coyly, feeling a bit like a hooker, but not much caring, if it swept away the bitterness of the night before. "Can't you just see us there?"

He reached for her again, and this time she slid over easily, taking advantage of the narrow couch to be very close. Tom pulled open her bathrobe and slipped his hand inside her panties.

Diana couldn't help it, she knew it wasn't the right time, but the words practically tumbled out by themselves. "Tom, are we going to call the police?"

That was not what he wanted to talk about. He wanted to pretend they were lying naked on a beach in Tahiti.

"They've got plenty of evidence already. They know what they're doing. Let's not pester them, honey," he said stiffly, trying to drop the subject.

Diana broke loose from his embrace and sat up on the edge of the couch.

"But there's a whole bedful of blood in there. Don't you think they ought to know that?"

"I'll take care of it," Tom said. He sounded like someone promising to get the lawnmower fixed.

"You will?" Diana asked.

Tom sat up and put his arms around her again. He wanted to get back to Tahiti, but he couldn't get the weasel cop's words out of his mind. "That thing on the wall fits your girlfriend like a glove." He didn't believe it. It was too absurd. But Tom forced himself to peek over again to where the ghoulish outline of the washed-off body imprint glared back at him. It had needled him all night, until now all he wanted was to get it over with—to pull her off the couch and make her stand next to the damned thing, to once and for all get the doubts out of his head.

Instead he turned to Diana and murmured into her ear, "Just trust me, okay?"

"Okay," she said. And she did.

Tom sat in the waiting room of the doctor's office looking at old copies of *People* magazine. Cindy Garvey was leaving her husband. Cheryl Tiegs was returning to her husband. Suzanne Somers was telling the world how wonderful her husband was, and Farrah Fawcett was looking for a husband. Who were these women? Tom thought they might have been made up by drones in the editorial offices of *People* magazine. Did any of these women—what was the phrase?—freak out? Go bonkers? If so, how did their husbands handle it? Did they ever find blood in their beds, bizarre impressions on their walls? If they thought their wives were going ape, did these husbands come right out and confront them with it?

A uniformed nurse standing over him interrupted Tom's musings. "Mr. Johnson, the doctor will see you now."

"Thank you," he said, as he followed the direction of her outstretched arm to an opened door.

Dr. Allen walked across the carpeted floor of his office, took Tom's hand, and pumped it effusively.

"So you're the famous Tom Johnson," the elderly doctor smiled, still shaking his hand.

"That's me," Tom managed to say. "It was good of you to see me on such short notice, Doctor."

Tom was acutely embarrassed by most overt displays of emotion, especially when they came from people who didn't know him. And right now he felt as if he was in the conference room of a Holiday Inn in Iowa, being approached by the Regional Sales Chief for some new brand of vacuum cleaner.

"Well," Dr. Allen chortled, letting go of Tom's hand, "I just had to see what you looked like!" This was obviously true, because he just stood there staring at Tom, as if he were a life-size Rodin sculpture on loan from the Met. "That's a mighty fine girl you're getting there, young man," Dr. Allen finally said. "I hope you appreciate that."

"Yes, sir, I do."

The mood had changed. Tom thought he had wandered into an episode of *The Waltons*.

"Oh, I could tell you stories about that little one," Dr. Allen began. "You know, when she was born, she didn't have a hair on her head." The doctor chuckled softly, as if after all these years he still found bald babies warmly amusing. "But I gather this isn't a social call. Please sit down and tell me what's on your mind."

Tom sat down, and Dr. Allen slid back behind his massive teak desk. He clasped his hands together, attentively waiting for Tom to say whatever it was he had come to say.

Obviously the social amenities were over now, and Tom suddenly felt trapped. He didn't know how to begin. He was worried that the harmless old coot sitting across from him might think he was weird and unmannered. Not that he much cared what the old man thought of him one way or the other, but years of correct upbringing had ingrained in Tom the importance of making a good first impression, and this seemed to Tom an unlikely possibility, given what he was going to say.

"Well, sir," he stammered, "this might seem very odd . . ."

Tom was playing right to Dr. Allen's soft spot—helping the Decent, Confused Young Person.

"Son," the old doctor interrupted, chuckling benignly,

"I've sort of guessed what was on your mind when you called, and, Tom, I applaud your coming to me."

"Sir?" Tom asked, genuinely bewildered. Somehow the setting had changed again, and the Walton farm had given way to the varsity locker room, and Tom was talking to the Coach.

"Son," Coach Allen said, "you're afraid you might have caught something and you don't want our Diana to know about it or contract it herself, am I right?"

The phrase "our Diana" held undertones Tom didn't even want to think about.

"No, sir," Tom laughed nervously, "it's nothing like that. I almost wish it was." Then he paused and said aloud what he had been telling himself ever since he had first decided to call Dr. Allen. "Well, there's no easy way to do this."

He reached inside the pocket of his elegantly tailored poplin jacket and withdrew a small brown envelope. He felt like a CIA operative.

"Sir," he continued, "there's a piece of cloth in here, a piece of bedsheet, actually. It has blood on it. I have to know if the blood is Diana's."

Dr. Allen took the envelope from him. He handled it gingerly, as though he were afraid it might explode.

"You're certainly full of surprises, aren't you, young man?" Then his voice got more professional and less friendly. "Of course, you understand I couldn't think of doing what you're asking unless you tell me what this is all about."

"Please, sir," Tom implored, as sincerely as he could, "I know you don't know me, but you must know that I wouldn't do anything to hurt Diana. If the blood isn't hers, then it's best I don't say anything at all."

"You can tell me something, can't you?"

"I can't. I promised Diana I wouldn't," Tom lied.

He would have given anything to know what was going through the old man's mind.

"Well, you've certainly put me in an awkward position, haven't you?"

Tom didn't answer. He just looked at Dr. Allen, letting the honesty pour out of his eyes. He watched the old man convince himself that it was all right to do this thing.

"I'm extremely fond of Diana," the doctor said, after a while. "I hope you know what you're doing, young man."

Tom smiled reassuringly. He didn't permit himself a sigh of relief until he had left the doctor's office.

◆◆◆

Diana and Sarah stopped at a hot-dog vendor near the Eighty-sixth Street entrance to Central Park. At twelve o'clock they were one of his first customers, and the wieners were slightly undercooked. Central Park was bustling with activity, but not with weekend strollers, fun-loving teenagers, or overage jocks. This was the weekday morning shift: scores of preschool tots and their mothers pushing every conceivable kind of two-, three-, and four-wheel baby carriage invented by man.

"Have you ever noticed that young mothers always cut their hair short?" Diana observed, gobbling down the last piece of hot dog.

"It's part of the job requirement," Sarah replied. "Short hair, short nails, and long days."

"Too bad for Tom. He's crazy about long hair."

"Well, he won't be when it's full of baby food and hasn't seen a curler in two weeks."

Diana laughed aloud and dodged a reckless tricyclist, who sped on his way between the two friends.

"I really want another hot dog," Sarah ventured wishfully.

"Those things are at least two hundred calories, Sarah. You know you shouldn't."

"I shouldn't have had the first one, either."

They sat down on a bench in the shade of a leafy tree

and for several minutes neither of them said a thing as they soaked up the sun's rays.

Then Sarah had a sudden burst of insight. "Do you remember that pact we made freshman year that we'd never marry before we were forty? We were convinced it would take at least that long to get all the experience to make the right decision. So what's our punishment for breaking a pact?"

Diana shrugged. "I plead innocent on the grounds we were both crazed virgins."

"It was fun being virgins," Sarah protested.

"Yeah. You remember all those nights we stayed up talking about how we wanted it to be the first time?"

Sarah giggled and smiled widely. "We could always talk to each other, couldn't we, Dee?"

"Since always," Diana answered, "husbands or no husbands." And even as she said it, she knew she couldn't hold it in anymore. So despite her promises to Tom that she wouldn't tell anyone, she told her best friend, haltingly at first, then with a rush. All the not-quite-connected strangenesses. The horrible mutilation of the apartment. The blood in the bed, the stain on the wall. And most of all, Tom's distance, his not-quite-concealed annoyance with her.

And when Diana had finished, good old Sarah had some plain and simple, garden-variety, chicken-soup things to say and one very sensible suggestion to make.

"Why don't you come stay with me for a few days?"

Diana shook her head. "I just can't walk out on Tom and leave him alone in the apartment. I'm getting married in six weeks; what kind of wife would do that?"

"The kind whose future husband refuses to do anything when the woman he's supposed to love is scared out of her mind. That's what kind."

That was Sarah again. Diana could always count on her best friend to take her side.

"I know Tom," Diana said. "He doesn't want me

to get upset. Cool under pressure. I think his whole family pride themselves on it."

"Well, you're not a Johnson yet," Sarah said flatly, "and you're sleeping at my house, whether you like it or not."

"I can't, Sarah. I want to, but I can't. I have to do it his way. Besides, the police said that in most of these cases the weirdos who do these things hardly ever come back to the same place twice."

Sarah looked neither impressed nor convinced.

"Oh, yeah," she said. "Well, remember Becky Rivers, that girl from our Freshman English class?"

Diana nodded absently, wondering what in the world Becky Rivers from Freshman English had to do with anything.

"Well," Sarah went on, "I ran into her at Bloomingdale's last Wednesday, and she said that her apartment's been broken into three times in less than a year, and once when she was sleeping right in the next room." Sarah couldn't resist another zinger. "You won't believe this, but she finally did marry that nurd from Williams who was always coming up for weekends. Remember him?" She shook her head, conveying eloquently that she could conceive of few worse things in life than marrying the nurd from Williams.

Diana didn't answer. She had been watching a friendly Irish setter come bounding across the grass, wagging its tail. It nuzzled up to her leg, and she patted it with something more than affection—almost with gratitude. Dogs were smart. Dogs didn't come bounding up to crazy people with their tails wagging. Anybody knew that.

"Look," Sarah said, shifting gears again. "I'll make up the guest room when I get home, so if you change your mind, just give me a call. This may be Tom's way of handling things, but I know if it was me, I'd be going out of my mind."

With a suddenness that surprised both of them, Diana started to cry, as if Sarah's words had pressed a button releasing a rigidly contained impulse. She began to shake with the tears.

"I am going out of my mind," she managed to say. "I keep having this feeling that somebody's watching me."

Sarah glanced across the path to where a man was sitting on a park bench not too far away from them. He wasn't doing a thing. He wasn't watching them. He wasn't reading. He didn't even appear to be thinking. Sarah wondered why he was sitting so near to them, so obviously doing nothing. Maybe he was Diana's mysterious enemy, amusing himself by being so close, exulting in a feeling of power at seeing his prey so obviously distraught.

Sarah decided she had seen too many Hitchcock movies. She handed Diana a handkerchief.

"It's really spooky, you know?" Diana sniffled, wiping her eyes. She felt awful, breaking down this way. "I'm sorry, Sarah, I'll be okay."

Sarah put an arm around her. "Don't worry, Dee, maybe it's over already. This other stuff's probably just in your mind."

"God, I hope so." Diana had started to regain her composure. "You're still coming to dinner tomorrow, aren't you?"

"Of course we are," Sarah said. "I'm bringing the wine, remember?"

"I keep thinking that if I just stay busy, like having people over to dinner and stuff, then things will straighten themselves out."

But as soon as she said it, she bit down on her lip. She knew she didn't believe it. Not for a second.

Usually Greg enjoyed his relaxed twice-weekly games of squash with his old buddy Tom. The perfect opportunity to talk about cooze, work off the booze, and have a little fun—except that today there were no laughs. Tom was taking it seriously, for Chrissake, and coming on like some vicious Canadian hockey player who had been hit in the head with a puck one too many times.

He was murdering the ball, smashing it into the wall, picking it out of the corners, stretching to the limit for daring saves, skidding all over the floor. He moved like a jai lai player on speed, and Greg simply wasn't ready for it. If he had learned anything at all in his life, it was that you had to keep things in perspective, and a fellow who went around looking like he was perfectly willing to assassinate a squash ball simply wasn't keeping things in perspective.

It was after one particularly vicious point, which Tom had played as if the squash ball was eighteen communists who had raped his sister, that Greg threw his hands in the air in a gesture of surrender and said, "Okay, I give." He leaned against the wall, exhausted, and let his expensive squash racquet fall to the expensive floor of the expensive squash court in his father's expensive club.

Tom bounced around nervously, obviously eager for more action.

"Come on," he said, "let's play another."

"Not me, old buddy. You're a mean mother today. Aren't you getting laid these days?"

Tom smiled. "How come last time I won, you told me it was because *you* weren't getting laid?"

Greg knew what was turning Tom into a wild banshee, even if Tom didn't know himself. And it wasn't the fact that Diana might be behaving like a frigging psycho. Tom's real problem was that he was hooked on a pair of sensational legs.

Hell, Greg could understand that. Matter of fact, he wouldn't have minded hiding his salami between those legs himself. But that didn't mean you had to marry the fucking legs, for Chrissake. It didn't even mean you had to like the person they belonged to.

Take Lisa, for instance, which was something he always liked to do. With her little tiny voice and that empty barn between her ears, she gave "dumb" new interpretations.

But it was equally clear that Lisa had just about the finest set of tits that had ever been discovered on a woman since the dawn of recorded history. So all a sensible man had to do was to put his mind on other things whenever Lisa said something and then gorge on her tits when he got home.

How to say all this to Tom? That was what Greg was thinking about as he ambled into the locker room. He couldn't do much for Tom, but Greg decided that at least he could tell his friend how to cut his losses.

"Let me tell you," Greg said, getting out of his sweaty squash clothes. "You've got to look on the positive side of this thing with Diana. You're lucky it's happening while you're still engaged. Otherwise you'd be stuck with the hospital bills on top of the furniture bills."

Greg was describing his own personal vision of hell. Imagine marrying a broad because you were crazy to fuck her, and then she went off her gourd and got carted away to the hospital, which meant that not only was she in a place where you couldn't fuck her but you were paying to keep her there. Jesus!

Tom shot him a nasty look. "I just can't believe it's Diana doing all that," he snapped.

Greg thought that perhaps he could drive his point home with an old-fashioned maxim. "You ought to follow my golden rule of romance, ol' buddy. Never get involved with a broad that's smart enough to flip out."

The next thing Greg knew, he was pinned up against a row of cold metal lockers with the heel of Tom's hands digging hard into his shoulders.

"That's not funny, old buddy," Tom snarled in his face. He said it the way Greg imagined Italian gangsters told people it would be a good idea if they were not seen around town anymore.

"Hey, asshole, cool off," Greg warned, pushing Tom away. "It's not my fault. Anyway, things could be a lot worse."

Tom obviously didn't think so. "Oh, yeah? Like what?"

Greg thought of the absolutely worst thing he could imagine.

"Like my father going crazy and giving all his money away to charity."

Tom didn't even bother to answer him.

10

Had Leonardo da Vinci ever sliced open the belly of a dog? Had he ever peeled away the skin of a man's arm? Hell, no! It was so obvious to Joel. Da Vinci, the little faggot, had someone else do the dirty work for him, while he just lay back and did the drawings.

And that was why Joel thought that his own anatomical drawings were every bit as good, maybe even a little better, than da Vinci's. Joel wasn't the kind of person who went in for false pride or inflated what he did all out of proportion, but he just had to say it, if only to himself. He knew he'd never invent the submarine or paint the Mona Lisa, but if you put da Vinci's anatomical drawings next to his own, who would say da Vinci's were better?

The "cutaway" drawing of a dog that he was meticulously sketching at the moment was an excellent case in point. Da Vinci's dog was just your basic side-shot of the animal's exposed flank. It was useless as a practical teaching tool. It made it difficult to focus one's attention, to really study what the canine anatomy was all about. A drawing like that was too unwieldy, too emotional, too caught up in the notion of a dog's body as a thing of beauty.

Joel stepped back from his easel, kicking aside the medical books that had spilled off the table and now lay strewn across the concrete floor. For six hours he had immersed himself in the animal sketches that hung before him. One was a cutaway drawing of a dog, the animal's hide peeled back to expose its raw musculature and bone structure. For his purposes he had not drawn the dog entire, but had carefully disarticulated its body so that the animal's legs, trunk, neck, and head were separated from each other—as if it were a cardboard cutout with metal fasteners on the end of the limbs.

Alongside the dog was a drawing of a rabbit, disarticulated in the same way. It excited Joel to think how he would spend the remainder of the evening detailing the differences in the vascular topography of the two animals.

That's when he felt a pressure on his back, a hand on his arm, and the hot stinking breath of a face peering over his shoulder.

Damn! She was like a jealous cat in that respect. If you showed interest in anything else in the room besides her, she'd be over in a second, snooping around, poking her face where it didn't belong.

"That's real good, Joel," Laurie murmured into his ear. "That's a real good idea."

Joel ignored her. All she wanted was to distract him from his work.

Ignoring her just made her press harder. "Is that a dog or something?"

Sometimes she could be such a dumb shit. When you were the equal of da Vinci and you drew a dog, it was goddamned well a dog.

"I'm working now, go away," he mumbled.

"I can see what you're doing. You're gonna fuck up another dog, aren't you?" Then she whispered into his ear, making it sweet and secret and evil. "I know you are."

She waited a minute for him to answer, and when he didn't, she whispered again into his ear, like a plaintive little girl this time. "Can I help?"

Joel spun around and swatted her on the rear. "Get out of here. Go watch the TV."

Grabbing a pencil, she scratched a line from the dog's

neck to its torso. "The first thing you got to do is connect all the parts," she advised.

He caught her hand and twisted it back until she gasped in pain and dropped the pencil.

Laurie wasn't allowed to touch his drawings. She knew that.

"You ever do that again," he warned, "and I know one little girl who's gonna wake up one morning without her plastic leg."

The corners of her mouth curled up in a smile. "No one would do that, Joel. Not even you."

"I might. Or I might replace it with something better while you're sleeping."

"Yeah, like what?"

"Like a monkey's leg." As soon as he said it, he could tell she was scared. Her fear was useful to him, and he decided to impress the situation on her but good.

"Don't think it hasn't been tried," he continued, " 'cause it has. In Germany, during the war. A Dr. von Kreeger tried to graft the appendage of a fully matured ape onto a Jew. And I'll tell you right now," he went on, bringing his face closer to hers and lowering his voice, because he knew that would frighten her more, "if he had had more time, another year maybe, we would have seen some amazing breakthroughs."

The information didn't frighten Laurie, it only excited her. She tugged at his sleeve. "Those Germans, they could've helped me, huh, Joel?"

He looked into those wide, pleading eyes, but by now he was lost in his own peculiar vision. "They were the first ones to make a mechanical hand with fully articulated fingers. What they knew about prosthetics . . ."

Laurie moaned like a child in pain. "No!" she screamed. "Not prosthetics! What did they know about making me a normal person who can go dancing and driving in a car?"

Not that again, Joel thought. They always got back

to that. No matter where they started out, she always got back to that, and it always affected him the same way.

"Laurie," he said, his voice imploring her, "don't you start in again."

But she could sense her advantage and she wasn't going to stop now. "Make me normal, Joel. You know how to do it. You do it for the animals. Do it for me."

He had told her before and now he'd have to tell her again. "It's not possible. The animals all die after ten days."

"Rinkus is still alive."

"That was an exception."

"Make me an exception," she begged.

And now he really wanted to cry, because wasn't that what everyone had asked throughout time, throughout history? Make me an exception? Make me special? Make me different?

Except, God help him, she wasn't saying, "Make me different." She was saying, "Make me the same." And he knew that was impossible.

"I can't," he said, his voice trembling with emotion. "I don't know how, Laurie. I'd give you my own leg if I could."

She smiled slyly. "Then let's try that, Joel."

It wasn't so bad when she got manipulative. It was only when she was genuinely needful and vulnerable that he didn't know what to do, that he was reminded of his guilt, that he was helpless before her. How could he ever make her understand that the problem was Science?

"It's not just another operation," he said, struggling with the words. "I can do the operation. It's a question of genetic structure. The animals, they all die of massive tissue rejection."

"You funny kunkus! Kiss you tissue, kiss you tissue!"

She was retreating again into her private language, hurling invective, hating him for what had happened so long ago.

He grabbed her by the shoulders and shook her, harder than he intended. "Stop it, Laurie! Stop it!" It hurt her and it made her afraid of him again.

He shouted in her face, begging her with his screams. "Can't you ever understand? There's nothing I can do!"

But he knew that she would demand again. And that still he would have no answer for her. That there would probably never be an answer for her.

11 _____

Somehow Diana had managed to turn her attention to getting the apartment ready for dinner with Tom's parents. Even in the best of circumstances she would have dreaded having to confront that genteel inquisition all over again, but given the way she felt now, she wondered if she would live through it. Still, she had replaced the furniture—Tom's willingness to spend money on new furniture was immensely reassuring to her—and she had covered the place where the awful body had pressed itself to the wall with a delicate oriental silk print that reached from floor to ceiling.

Now she was having something else done to the apartment; she was making it safe.

Martin Horton, a middle-aged man in bib overalls, was just finishing with the last of an amazing assortment of locks, which made the inside of the front door look like something Houdini in his prime would have been afraid to tackle. There was a slide bolt and a dead bolt, there were two different key locks, and there was a police lock, with its long metal pole extending into a floor socket. By the time someone worked his way through that door, Diana could be in Chicago.

The locksmith slammed the dead bolt home and made the appropriate adjustments to the others.

"There," he said, with a workman's pride. "Unless them cat burglars and jewel thieves are packing howitzers these days, you got nothing to worry about."

"Are you sure?" Diana asked.

Wouldn't that be the ticket? she thought. To have nothing to worry about.

The locksmith walked over to the living room window and latched shut the brand-new locks he'd just put on the sill. Then he did the same at the door leading out to the garden.

"Sure, I'm sure," he said. "I've been in this business twenty-seven years. Last time I did a job like this was for some scumbag up in Forest Hills. Six hundred and twenty-seven dollars' worth of locks in a two-room apartment. Now there was one scared man. He was some pimp or low life like that, a man with enemies. A nice girl like you—you just want to keep the general riffraff out, am I right?"

"I suppose so." Diana had no intention of telling Martin Horton why she wanted the locks. First of all, it was none of his business, and second, he would think she was nuts. She could see him attempting to amuse his next clients by telling them about the crazy girl who had bought all the locks because she thought somebody was trying to get her. Probably that poor man in Forest Hills had the same terror, too. A man who lived in a good neighborhood like that wouldn't spend that kind of money on locks, not unless he was terrified to the depths of his soul. And what did Martin Horton know about that?

Diana and the locksmith were facing each other, so neither of them saw the dirty red ball that came sailing over the garden wall and landed near the barbecue.

The locksmith sat down at the table, glanced at his watch, and started figuring out the charges on a greasy pad of paper.

"Are you sure the alarm will go off if a window's broken?" Diana asked. "How do you know if you don't test it?"

A thin, sharp, street-wise face appeared at the top of

the garden wall. Caucasian, male. The kid couldn't have been more than eleven or twelve.

"When Martin Horton spends an entire morning in a four-room apartment," he said, looking up at Diana, "that's one apartment that's safe. I'm telling you, this is one secure apartment."

"I know," Diana said. "I appreciate that."

The kid hoisted himself to the top of the wall, perched there silently for a moment, and lithely jumped down into the garden. He went to where his ball had landed and retrieved it.

Through the garden doors he saw the two people talking. Intrigued, he walked up to the doors with quiet, nonchalant confidence and peered inside. His curiosity momentarily satisfied, he tossed his ball back over the wall and clambered up after it, disappearing to the other side.

"Like I always say," Martin Horton told Diana, "I'm supposed to be selling locks, but what you're really buying here is peace of mind, am I right?"

Diana nodded. But only because she hadn't seen the intruder.

✦✦✦

Taffy was growling again, and Diana thought it was about time that she took him to a vet. If it hadn't been a Sunday morning, she would have done it right there and then.

Instead she put Taffy's bowl of Purina Puppy Chow down on the living room floor and waited for him to jump in and wolf it down. But the little dog snarled and backed off, distrust and confusion all over his face.

Now Diana was confused, too. "Taffy, baby," she said, following after him, "what's the matter?"

Cornered now, the puppy growled again, more ferociously this time, baring his teeth.

Diana was getting worried. She took the bowl over to

Tom, who sat on the new living room couch listening to a tape of Gato Barbieri while staring unhappily at a piece of paper in his hand. It was Martin Horton's bill for materials and services.

"Tom," Diana said, "I think Taffy's sick. You try and feed him. He won't take any food from me."

She handed the bowl to Tom, who took it from her and set it down on the floor beside him.

Taffy inched his way over to the bowl, took one sniff, and began to eat.

"Well, I'll be damned," Diana said.

Tom shook his head and tapped the bill with his finger. "Diana, do you realize you spent four hundred and fourteen dollars on locks? Don't you think that maybe you're going a bit overboard?"

"Not if it keeps us alive."

Tom looked as though he wasn't too willing to remain alive in a world where people spent four hundred and fourteen dollars on locks.

"Maybe I can write it off," he said.

Diana sat down beside him. It was time to change the subject. When Tom started talking about money, he sounded like his father.

"Honey, is there anything special that you want me to fix for your parents tonight?" she asked. Diana knew she should have been planning this meal for days and days, the way good wives-to-be were supposed to, but she just hadn't had the heart.

"Dad loves roast beef," Tom answered.

"We had roast beef at your house. Besides, mine would pale next to your mother's."

"Then why don't you make steak? It's tough to ruin a good piece of meat."

Lord, Diana thought, he can really be a charmer when he wants to. But she was determined to keep this light and happy, if it were at all possible. She put her arms around him and curled up close.

"Tom, I thought that because this was the first time your parents were coming to dinner at our apartment, we'd make them something special. You know, something that would make it a specially memorable evening."

"Why is it," he said, his eyes brightening with amusement, "that I get the distinct impression you know exactly what we're having for dinner tonight?"

"Curry and kebab," Diana said, getting the words out quickly.

Tom's expression would probably have been much the same if Diana had told him she planned to serve whale meat.

"Indian?" he exclaimed.

"Indian," she answered.

"You know that's not my parents' style," Tom said.

Diana went over to the tape recorder and turned it off.

"I've made it before. It's delicious. It's different. It won't be too spicy, if that's what you're worried about." She took his hand. "Come on, keep me company. You can help me shop."

Tom got up and started out the door with her, but he was clearly not pleased. "I really don't think my parents are going to like even the idea of Indian food," he said. "I mean, you wouldn't serve them a taco or Puerto Rican food, would you, because that's how they're going to see it."

"Darling," Diana said, getting him out the door before he could change his mind. "What's missing from your parents' life is adventure. Believe me, they'll be thrilled with this."

"What's missing from my parents' life is Indian food. So let's keep it that way, okay?"

The night breeze made the garden a cool and pleasant place to eat dinner. Sarah, Diana, and Mrs. Johnson were all wearing shawls, and the men had kept their jackets on, except for Tom, who had loosened his tie, rolled up his sleeves, and was sweating under his collar.

He was watching his mother's fork pick its way through a plate of hot Indian food as cautiously as a hunter creeping through a jungle full of poisonous snakes. The fork skirted the dangerous curry, passed over the unfamiliar kebab, and pounced delicately upon some reasonably safe-looking vegetables.

Mrs. Johnson raised the forkful of vegetables to her disapproving lips, but couldn't manage to put them in her mouth.

"What a filthy country India is," she said. "Years ago Henry and I flew into Bombay on our way to Bangkok. We couldn't get off the plane, the stench was so terrible."

She looked at her fork as if it contained a tribe of filthy Untouchables.

Tom knew his parents and he knew that right now they were being as polite as they had ever been in their entire lives. He could tell that what his father wanted to do more than anything else was spit the food he had in his mouth onto the ground. His mother looked as though she thought she was being poisoned. Perhaps deliberately.

"This is marvelous, Diana," Mrs. Johnson lied. It was a tone she would have used to address a maid. "It's . . . original, very different."

"Thank you, Mrs. Johnson," Diana answered.

Sarah was having trouble keeping a straight face. She decided to stir things up a little. "Oh, this is nothing for Diana," she said nonchalantly. "Her kabuli palau in pomegranate sauce nearly wiped out our entire Freshman English class."

From the expression on Mrs. Johnson's face it was obvious that she was thinking about kabuli palau in pomegranate sauce and wondering what unspeakable things it might contain.

"Now you know why I'm marrying Tom," Diana beamed. "He appreciates my more exotic culinary efforts."

She looked at her fiancé, hoping for a nod of encouragement.

"Tom is just like his father, dear," Mr. Johnson told Diana. "He's a meat and potatoes man, aren't you, Son?"

If Tom had been on trial for his life he would not have weighed his answer more carefully.

"Sometimes," he said quietly.

With this evasion the food-related conversation that had kept the evening alive sputtered and died, and for what seemed like a very long time everyone just sat there.

A dinner party with people sitting around not saying anything was an unsuccessful dinner party, and Mrs. Johnson felt called upon to exercise her social skills, even though she was growing increasingly less fond of the hostess.

"Tell me, Sarah," she said, "do you work, too?"

Sarah smiled. "Well, I've been threatening for the last year and a half to join Diana's ballet class. In the meantime I do some volunteer work at the Whitney." Sarah put emphasis on the impeccable name, which Mrs. Johnson could not possibly disapprove of. "But nothing full-time," she added.

"Of course not," Mrs. Johnson said, looking straight at Diana.

"Sarah has a six-year-old daughter," Diana quickly explained. "Besides, if any of you want to join my ballet class, you're going to have to wait. It's been closed all week. Some gang broke in and vandalized the place."

"I think I read something about that," Jack volunteered. "Wasn't that the one where someone was killed?"

"I knew the man," Diana said softly. "He was the night guard on Wednesdays and Thursdays."

There was a momentary silence until Mrs. Johnson picked up where she had left off.

"You sound like quite a busy lady, Sarah. I've always felt that raising a child properly is a full-time job. I know that I always made a point of being there when Tom got home from school."

"You were always there, Mother," Tom agreed. "And I'm sure Diana has no intention of working once we have children, either."

Diana swallowed hard. No intention of working? What was he saying? How many times had she and Tom discussed it; once their children were in kindergarten, she would continue her career. Thanks a bunch, Tom!

Somehow—none of them could ever have explained how—dinner was finally over, and everyone moved inside for coffee and dessert. Sarah helped Diana carry the dirty dishes into the kitchen. Two of the plates were still heaped with curry and kebab.

"It's trench warfare out there," Sarah said, under her breath. She handed Diana a carving knife. "If you're going back out there, you'd better arm yourself."

Diana opened the oven and reached inside. "I don't need it," she said. "I have this!"

She stood there triumphantly, holding a simmering pan of swirling, viscous orange goo.

Sarah looked at the pan and wrinkled her nose.

"What is it?"

Diana smiled with sly satisfaction. "Tangerine cream pie. His mother's gonna hate it."

The two girls giggled and headed into the living room, where Diana set down the steaming orange concoction.

Tom watched his mother cast a suspicious eye on the dessert and then shoot her husband a wary look. Goddamn it, Tom thought, why couldn't Diana have at least served a normal dessert? Like sherbet. Or vanilla cake. Or eclairs. Anything except for this orange crud—and the awkward silence that accompanied it.

Worse, Tom could see his mother would be of no help

with the social amenities this time. The burden of salvaging the evening had fallen to him.

As Diana began spooning out portions for her guests, Tom got up from his chair and walked over to his tape deck. "How about a little Stanley Turrentine?" he asked no one in particular. "He's a terrific saxophone player."

If there was one thing Tom knew, it was that his parents wanted to hear Stanley Turrentine about as much as they wanted to see Taffy do tricks. But at least the music would be something to talk about. He pressed a button, and in a moment there was Turrentine, lush funk over strings, making some kind of try for the disco market.

"Another cup of coffee, Mrs. Johnson?" It was all Diana could think of to say.

"Please," Mrs. Johnson said, staring at the orange stuff in front of her. "But I don't think I'll be having any dessert, dear. It looks a little heavy for my taste."

And that was the last calm thing any of them said.

Suddenly Stanley Turrentine stopped playing, and in his place came the hiss of the tape recorder and then some kind of low, guttural whine, like a sick animal's death call. Diana shot to her feet to see where the hideous sound was coming from. Then the ghastly whine turned to words, and it was obvious that the sound was coming from the stereo speakers. No one in the room even knew what half the words meant, but their intent was unmistakable.

"TOMMY, WHERE'S MY BLUE NIGHTIE" demanded the voice. "GIVE IT TO ME, TOMMY! THE NIGHTIE'S MINE. I NEED IT FOR THE WEDDING. GIVE IT TO ME GOOD, YOU FAT KUNKUS."

The voice was alternately pleading, cajoling, insistent—then violent.

SAVE ME ... SAVE ME ...
SAVE ME A PIECE OF CHICKEN!
GET THAT PINK THING OUT OF MY FACE.
YOU'VE MADE A MESS ON ME.
WHY DIDN'T YOU FEED THE DOG, JERKUS.

Everyone stared at the speakers, as if expecting some half-human beast to jump out and devour them all. Then they recognized the voice, and one by one they turned their eyes from the speakers and settled them on Diana. It was unmistakably her voice saying things that no one there had ever heard anyone say. The voice continued in its vile, inexorable way, getting deeper, rasping, chanting out some evil, rhythmic litany.

TIGHT AND JUICY, LOOKIE SEE.
STICK YOUR WORM RIGHT INTO ME.
IN THE HAIRY SACK, STUPID.
DO IT FROM THE BACK, STUPID.
THE AIR CONDITIONER'S BROKEN, YOU BITCH.
IT'S TOO HOT IN HERE.
HONEY. THE PUNKUS IS FUNKUS,
LOOK UNDER THE BED.

Tom stared at Diana, then buried his face in his fist as if trying to crush out the sounds he was hearing. Diana stood there in shock, mouth slack, eyes glazed.

"Stop it!" Tom screamed finally, as if the sounds were choking him to death. "I'm going to stop it!" He rushed over to the tape recorder and ripped the plug out of the wall.

"God Almighty," he shouted, and stood shaking.

Diana was rooted to the floor in stunned silence. Finally she spoke in a fragile whisper. "I never said any of those things."

"Disgusting," Mrs. Johnson blurted out.

"Evelyn," Mr. Johnson cut in with icy calm. "I think we'd all better be going. It's getting late."

Sarah and Jack got up, as if that was the best idea they had ever heard.

"I know that sounded like my voice," Diana managed to say, "but it wasn't me."

Sarah put an arm around her friend and hurried her off toward the kitchen.

"It's going to be all right, Diana."

"It wasn't me, Sarah. God, please someone believe me."

When they were alone in the kitchen, Diana leaned against the counter for support and practically begged Sarah for an explanation. "What were those words? You heard it! What was it saying?"

"I don't know."

Diana shuddered at the thought. "It was so sick."

Sarah hugged her friend. "You said it wasn't you, Diana, and I believe you. I do."

"But . . . it was my voice, wasn't it, Sarah?"

From the foyer Jack shouted for his wife. "Come on, Sarah. I'm waiting for you."

"Hold your horses!" Sarah snapped back. "Now listen, Diana, tell Tom once and for all it wasn't you and then go on as if nothing happened. The best thing you can do now is try and act normally."

"Do I have to go out and say good-bye?" Diana asked, in a pitiful voice.

"No, they'll understand." Sarah gave her another hug and turned to leave. But Diana couldn't let her friend go. She said the first thing that came to mind. "Do you want to take some dessert home for Nina?"

Sarah shook her head. "I'd better be going. Promise you'll call me tonight if you want to talk?"

Diana squeezed her friend's hand gratefully. "I will, I promise. Thanks, Sarah."

Diana waited and listened as the good nights were exchanged in the foyer. When everybody else had left,

Mr. Johnson spoke sternly to his son. "I'll see you first thing tomorrow morning in my office."

The young man nodded disconsolately.

When Tom had finally closed the door behind his parents, Diana came out of the kitchen like some trapped, beaten animal and glanced around to make sure that everyone was gone.

"Tom, please . . ." she began, but that was as far as she got.

"That was the most disgusting, perverted thing I have ever heard. Why, Diana?" Tom's words snapped at her like a whip. "Why would you ever do a dumb thing like that? I know you dislike my parents, but—"

"Tom, that wasn't me. I didn't record that."

But Tom remembered what the cops had told him and pressed on angrily. "Christ, Diana, if you're having second thoughts about our relationship, why don't you just say it to my face?"

"Stop it, Tom! You can't really believe that was me!"

"I believe I can recognize the voice of a woman I've known for over two years." He strode to the hi-fi, grabbed the plug, and waved it at her. "Shall we run it again? What's the name of the tune, Diana? Last waltz with parents? How to end a marriage before it's begun? Or just your idea of a little after-dinner humor?"

"Sarah knows it wasn't me," Diana faltered, a sob escaping her throat.

"Then maybe you'd better marry Sarah. You certainly see her enough." He dropped the hi-fi cord and turned to face her. "As they say, some people have funny ways of telling you they want out of a relationship." Then he was gone, slamming the bedroom door angrily behind him.

Diana spent the night on the couch. Not sleeping, not getting undressed, not even lying down. She just sat there, staring into space, while Tom slept in the next room.

She wondered how he was able to sleep. She thought about what he had said. He just assumed it was her. He was sure it was her. It was something she had done deliberately to humiliate him in front of his parents. That was what he was thinking about; that was all he was thinking about.

And for the first time a horrible notion crossed her mind. What if it was me?

She got up and walked over to the tape recorder. But she couldn't bring herself to turn it on. Finally she found the courage, and the strange, obscene flood of words filled the room again. She stood there listening, hot tears pouring down her cheeks.

♦♦♦

Tom walked briskly along Wall Street past the people scurrying to get to work on time, some of them eating breakfast rolls on the run. He had a very good idea of what his father was going to say and he had no idea at all what he was going to say in reply. But not even for a small moment did Tom consider not showing up at his father's office as instructed.

At exactly nine o'clock he entered the imposing granite building and saw the brass plate by the side of the entrance, elegantly understated in a way that only very old money knew how to do: JOHNSON AND BEYNES, INVESTMENT COUNSELLORS.

Tom knew his father believed he was attacking that brass plate with a sledgehammer—indeed, attacking the building's very foundation—by his continual refusal to work there. The first Johnson was Tom's great-grandfather, Alfred Johnson, who had founded the firm in 1873. He had bought out old Mr. Beynes in 1879, but the brass plaque had already been put up, and Tom's great-grandfather had never been one for unnecessary expense. So the firm was still Johnson and Beynes, and had been that for so long that there was never any thought of changing it.

On the eighth floor Tom got out of the elevator and walked down a rosewood-paneled hall decorated with pictures of gentlemen in red coats on their way to hunt foxes. He stopped at the desk of an elderly receptionist, who had been there for as long as he could remember.

"Hello, Mrs. Mitchell. Could you buzz my father, please? I think he's expecting me."

The old lady's eyes lit up.

"Tom, it's so nice to see you. You never come by any more."

"Things have been a little hectic," Tom said, hoping to avoid a conversation about how it used to be when he did come around.

Mrs. Mitchell just smiled, as though she understood exactly what he meant by things being hectic. "Just a moment," she said, "I'll check to see if your father's in."

She knows damned well he's in, Tom thought. There was no way he could get in or out of his office except past her, but she said it because she said it to people thirty times a day, perpetuating the system that permitted people to be polite to one another.

She pressed the button on her console and spoke into the phone. "Carolyn, Mr. Johnson's son is here to see him."

She hung up the receiver and turned back to Tom with another bright smile. "You can go right in. Your father's expecting you."

I bet he is, Tom thought. He took a deep breath and went inside.

Mr. Johnson's office reflected its occupant perfectly; correct and imposing. Several citizenship and humanitarian awards were displayed prominently on the walls. Mr. Johnson spent about twenty seconds in perusal of some papers Tom knew he wasn't really reading at all and then got up from his desk to shake hands with his son.

"Hello, Tom, I'm glad you found time to stop by."

"I bet you are," Tom shot back.

Mr. Johnson breathed in sharply. This was not going to be as easy as he had hoped. For a moment he wished he had done this another way, such as taking his son to lunch at one of his clubs. He looked Tom squarely in the eye. "Please sit down, Son."

But Tom didn't sit down. He remained standing. "Let's cut through the crap, Father. Why don't you just say what you've been wanting to say for the past year?"

Mr. Johnson had a momentary impulse to discuss the unnecessary use of the word "crap," but decided that he had far more important things to talk about this morning.

"Your mother went home extremely distressed yesterday evening," he began.

Tom wasn't going to buy that, either. "Mother certainly was in fine form last night, wasn't she? I'm surprised she didn't bring along her own silverware."

Mr. Johnson rose from his chair. "For the past twelve months you've been throwing this petty little relationship of yours in our faces, and I think we've had just about enough of it."

"And just what do you intend to do about it, Father?"

"The girl's not my problem. She's yours. What are you going to do about it, Tom?"

Tom wished to hell he knew. Against his will he heard himself apologizing. "Diana's been going through some rough times. She's been under considerable strain recently."

"Stop making excuses for the girl," Mr. Johnson scolded. "Last night was a lot more than just considerable strain. Let me be very frank," he continued, with no such intention. "You know your mother and I have always found Diana to be an extremely intelligent young lady—"

"I never asked for either your approval or Mother's," Tom cut in, "and I don't need it now."

"I'm afraid you do," Mr. Johnson said, in a voice far sharper than he usually permitted himself. "Now, I can understand your attraction to a girl like that and why you choose to live with her. Hell, I had a few flings myself in my day before I met your mother . . ." Mr. Johnson hesitated a brief instant and then continued. "But a lifelong commitment is something else again."

"I'm aware of that, Father."

"I don't have to tell you," Mr. Johnson went on, "you're one of the most eligible bachelors in town. There are any number of suitable, attractive women available to you."

The daughters of your friends, Tom thought bitterly. He had a vision of his father and his friends taking over the Waldorf Astoria for the night and presenting all those women to him on a ramp, smiling and holding their teacups just so.

"You're a good businessman, Son, and a good businessman doesn't throw good money after bad."

For a moment Tom wondered what in the world his father was talking about. Then it was made all too clear.

"Your mother and I haven't sent out the wedding invitations yet and have no intention of doing so."

Suddenly Tom was no longer concerned with whether or not he behaved like a gentleman in this office, where one always did. He was enraged. He saw his father standing there, smug, self-assured, positive that just about the best thing on earth was to be Henry Johnson, II, and advise old chums about which tax-free municipal bonds to buy while taking in a very nice percentage for himself.

"Diana's not one of your goddamned investments, Father," Tom said, in a tone harsher than he had ever before used with Henry Johnson, II. "I happen to be in love with her."

"I knew you'd rise to her defense, Tom. I wouldn't expect any less of you."

God, he was good. He could defuse any argument, co-opt anybody.

"But the time to make absolutely sure is now, Son, before you've made an irrevocable commitment. In any case, Diana is not an emotionally well girl."

With that, Tom began to pay attention again.

"I've taken the liberty of contacting Dr. Edward Graham. He's one of the best psychiatrists in the city and a good friend. He'll be waiting to hear from you. You owe that much to the girl."

My God, Tom thought. No wonder he's so rich. He's so slick, an eel couldn't catch him. First he's presumptuous enough to arrange a head doctor for Diana. Then he gets me to make the call. Then he convinces me I owe it to her to betray her. Jesus, he must be something to see when dollars and cents are actually at stake.

"So that's the bottom line as far as you're concerned?" Tom sneered at his father. "I pay a shrink, and it becomes his problem, not mine."

"Son, I know it's not easy admitting one's mistakes."

"Well," Tom scoffed, "that's not your problem either, is it, Father?—seeing how you never seem to make any."

But Tom knew that a puny little salvo like that wasn't going to upset the equilibrium of a man so self-satisfied, so unshakable, and so obviously sure of the fact that there was nothing in the world that he couldn't straighten out, couldn't fix, with one well-placed phone call.

The old patriarch stared back at his son. He didn't enjoy the victory. It was just something that had to be done.

Tom turned and walked out the door. He felt like slamming it and would have done so if he hadn't been convinced that his father was at least partially right.

12

Tom had breezed by Diana and walked out of the apartment on his way to Wall Street without so much as a "good morning," and yet somehow, from somewhere, Diana had managed to find the inner strength to drag herself to work at the bookstore.

She would never understand how she was able to do such seemingly difficult things as shower and dress and get on the bus, unless it was out of that same need to latch onto the mundane and commonplace that made her talk about dinner to Sarah that day out in the park.

Not since the afternoon four months ago, following Tom's marriage proposal over lunch at Orsini's, had Diana been as preoccupied as she was today. She thought it an accomplishment just to be able to go through the motions of her job adequately enough to avoid embarrassment or reprimand. Only four short months ago, her preoccupation had been the result of a marvelous euphoria.

As Diana struggled to unpack the three cartons of new books that had just arrived from Doubleday, everything she had been holding back came rushing in on her again, and it became overwhelmingly imperative to talk to Tom.

Leaving the books still in their cartons, she walked over to her desk and dialed Toms' office number. A well-dressed, fiftyish lady, who made shopping a profession and lunch a Caesar Salad at La Grenouille, suddenly appeared at Diana's side, hovering like a hummingbird, waiting for the "shop girl" to be finished with her phone call so she could get an answer to her urgent question.

"Excuse me," Diana told the lady, "I'll be with you in a moment."

"Do you have a *McGuffey's Reader?*" the woman said abruptly.

"If you'll excuse me just a minute, I'm on the phone," Diana answered a bit too curtly, and the woman returned her a frosty smile.

Finally Diana had Tom's secretary on the line. "Hello, Judy, this is Diana. Has Tom come into the office yet?" Judy's answer reminded her, more clearly than she would have liked, that this was not the first time this morning that she had felt an uncontrollable urge to talk to Tom "right now."

"I know you've put all the messages on his desk," Diana said, embarrassment flushing her face. "I just thought he might have come in and gone right to a meeting." It was bad enough to have to plead with Tom. To have to plead with his secretary was unconscionable.

Diana listened to more of Judy's bland excuses and then added, "You're sure you don't know where I might reach him? There's nothing on his calendar?" She waited until she got the answer she knew she would get and then apologized for the second time. "I'm sorry to be calling all the time like this, but I really need to talk to him. Please be sure to tell Tom I called again."

Diana hung up the phone only to find herself staring into the face of a now very irate customer. "Miss, could you tell me where I might find a copy of *McGuffey's Reader?*" the lady demanded.

"If we have one," Diana said, pointing, "it would be over there in the children's section."

That wasn't good enough. "Could you show me, please?" the lady ordered.

"Of course," Diana said wearily. She walked over to

the children's section, located a paperback copy of *Mc-Guffey*, and handed it to her.

The woman looked at the book, but wouldn't accept it. "I would like this in hard cover, please," she said.

"I don't think they print the book in hardback anymore."

"That's most unfortunate, because I do need an original edition. For a gift. Children need all the encouragement they can get to read the proper things, don't you think?"

"Yes, ma'am," Diana said. At that moment she would have agreed to almost anything to get the woman out of her hair.

But the woman ran on insistently. "Well, then, what should I do?"

"If you're looking for an original *McGuffey*, you'll have to go to a used bookstore. Maybe even a rare bookstore."

"Could you recommend one?"

Diana drew in a deep breath. She knew this speech by heart. "The best and biggest is probably the Strand, at Twelfth and Broadway, and if they don't have it, there are several other used bookstores around the corner, on Fourth Avenue."

"It's awfully warm out today," the woman said. "Isn't there someplace closer?"

"Not for what you want," Diana answered, exasperation starting to creep into her voice.

"Well, then, write down the address of this Strand Bookstore, will you, please?"

Diana wrote the name and address of the bookstore on a piece of paper and handed it to her.

"What's the best way to get down there, would you say?"

On your broomstick, Diana thought. But she answered, "There's an express bus going downtown, right across the street."

"On which corner?"

"One block down, on Forty-seventh Street."

"And would you happen to know how often they stop?"

Damn you, Diana thought. What do you want from me? To her own amazement, and certainly to the amazement of the lady standing in front of her, she suddenly found herself shouting, "I don't know how often they stop! I don't work for the bus company, I work for Scribner's! If you want to know the bus schedule, call the goddamned bus company! Why do you people always act like you own the store?"

"Pardon me!" the lady snapped, "There's certainly no need to be nasty about it."

Diana tried hard to pull herself together. "I'm sorry," she mumbled, "really, I'm terribly sorry. I didn't mean to shout at you like that."

But then it got worse. Before Diana realized it, she was crying, and she rushed off the floor, her face in her hands.

She stumbled blindly to the phone in the stockroom and called Tom for the fourth time in three hours.

Tom had never been in a police station before, and the experience wasn't proving reassuring. He didn't know what he had expected, but it wasn't this. The room he was in—Central Receiving, according to a badly lettered sign on the wall—was long and narrow, painted that bilious green that seemed to have been invented solely for government institutions. The floor was of faded linoleum, chipped and scuffed, and the fluorescent lights overhead gave everything a pale and alien pallor.

This much didn't surprise Tom. It somehow fitted in with the image one got from novels and movies. So did the heavy-mesh cage surrounding the overweight sergeant seated at the high desk. But nothing Tom had seen or read had prepared him for the low, pervasive din of misery that echoed through the room, rushing in from the doorways and corridors that led into it. A sound made up of questions and answers, lies and promises, weary shuffling, the creaking of leather, clanking of metal, occasional muffled yells, screams, threats from the depths of the building. It all blended into a low moan, more felt than heard, which bored into Tom's bones as he stood there, chilling him with the reality of the place.

Worse, perhaps, was the smell. The pervasive odor of detergents, pungent cleaning products, of endless rounds of scrubbing and mopping. But behind that odor, woven into and through it, were others. The stale smell of sweat, of blood and vomit and uncontrolled bowels.

It was a piece of the real New York, and Tom wasn't sure he could handle it. For a full twenty minutes he had been waiting on his feet, watching the traffic flow through the room, unable to make himself sit down on one of the empty wooden benches, too worried about what slimy pimp, prostitute, or lowlife might sit down next to him. By the time Sergeant Patchek came walking out of the back room looking rumpled and harassed, Tom had seen so much riffraff pass by that he was ready to recommend the electric chair for misdemeanors.

Tom recognized the cop immediately and stepped forward. "Sergeant Patchek, Tom Johnson here. You were at my apartment last week."

Patchek stared blankly at him before making the connection. "Yeah, sure, I remember now. You're the guy whose girlfriend was having all those, uh"—he groped for the proper word—"the problems, right?"

"Look," Tom replied, "all I want to know is whether you've gotten any of the lab reports back."

Patchek thought about it for a couple of seconds, then something clicked into place. "Didn't we get back to you on that? It must have gotten lost in the shuffle. Yeah,

I remember that one. You know that hair on the wall? Well, bad news, buddy, it matched your girlfriend's. It was her own hair up there in that red crap."

The next moment slowed into a hundred parts as the words burrowed their way into the gray cortex of Tom's mind, hammering their message down his shivering spine, releasing the condemnation and panic he had been fighting all day. It was only his instinctive need for logic that permitted him to plow forward through the paralyzing fog of emotion. When he finally spoke, his voice was shaking.

"What about the fingerprints?" he asked urgently.

"All the fingerprints in that house were either yours or your girlfriend's."

"Are you sure?" Tom was pleading now. "It's important."

Patchek sighed wearily. People never wanted the answers he had to give them. "It's always important," he said, "and we're always sure. The lab doesn't lie. And if you ask me, that girl ought to have her head examined."

"When I want a medical opinion," Tom shot back, "I'll ask for it."

And he did. A little more than an hour later he was sitting across the desk from Dr. Allen, who was regarding him with a mixture of distaste and distrust that not even his professionalism could keep off his face. On the desk between them lay the piece of bloodstained sheet Tom had brought in nearly a week before.

Tom cleared his throat nervously. "Well, Doctor?"

Dr. Allen continued to look at him awhile. Then, he spoke, slowly and deliberately. "Before I answer your question, Mr. Johnson, I have a few of my own. First, I want to know what the purpose of all this is—I am assuming for the moment that this isn't some kind of sick joke."

Tom shook his head, already certain of the answer Dr. Allen was going to give. "No, it's not a joke."

"Then what is it? What's going on here?"

"I can't tell you, Doctor. I really can't."

Dr. Allen leaned across his desk. "Young man, if you feel some sort of embarrassment, either for your sake or Diana's, remember that I brought her into this world and that in my many years of practice I have heard things even you would not believe."

Tom shook his head again miserably. "It isn't that, Doctor. It's just that I'm not sure myself what's going on. All I can tell you is that I'm doing this for Diana's sake. I came to you because I know you care for her as much as I do."

Dr. Allen rose and paced to the window, looking out on the Park Avenue traffic. "You are asking me to violate a professional ethic, young man. Worse, you are asking me to violate a friendship. You bring me this . . . this thing, ask me to analyze it for you, and then refuse to tell me where you got it, why you want it, or what use the information will be put to."

Tom gripped the edge of the desk, steadying his emotions. "You know where it came from. It was in our apartment."

"Brought here without Diana's knowledge."

"Yes," Tom admitted. "But I swear to you that it was necessary. I also swear to you that as soon as this thing is resolved enough to permit me telling you what's happening, I will do so, sir."

Dr. Allen shook his head. "It's been my experience that secrets between friends always bring grief." He came back to the desk, shaking his head. "I don't like this, Mr. Johnson. Not a bit."

"But you'll do it, sir," Tom stated, willing it to be so. "Because Diana and I both need your help."

Dr. Allen looked from Tom to the bloodstained piece

of bedsheet, then back to Tom. "Don't cause me to regret this."

"I won't," he answered in a voice more forceful than necessary. "You have my word."

The physician picked up a folder and studied it. Then his face hardened, and he gazed back evenly at Tom. "Yes, Mr. Johnson, Diana's blood is on that sheet. It's her . . . menstrual blood."

Tom was almost sick from the thought of what Diana had done. "You're certain?" he insisted. "I mean, there's no chance you could be wrong?"

Dr. Allen shook his head. "In this case, no. Diana has a peculiar white corpuscle count. We've known about it since her birth. It's most definitely her blood, Mr. Johnson." He tapped the torn linen with a bony finger and fixed Tom with an accusing stare. "Do you know what else is on this sheet?"

"No."

"Animal blood, Mr. Johnson. The blood of a dog." He drilled a finger in Tom's direction. "Now I ask you again, young man, what is going on here? I am Diana's doctor. I think I'm entitled to some explanation."

Tom rose unsteadily to his feet. "I'm not even sure there is an explanation."

Tom chose to walk the twenty-six blocks home to his apartment. It was ninety-five degrees, and the sun pounded relentlessly down on the Manhattan streets. Sweat poured over his chest and under his arms, but he didn't even think to carry his jacket. He had too much on his mind.

The hair was hers. The blood was hers. The voice on the tape was hers. There was but one inescapable conclusion; that Diana herself had been doing those awful crazy things and God knows what else. So what was he supposed to do now? Tom thought to himself. He would have to move out of the apartment—no, he'd ask Diana to move. After all, it was his apartment. But what if she refused? Then he'd go to Greg's, have a lawyer call her. No, he couldn't do that, he wasn't that kind of guy. Wasn't it obvious someone had to talk to Diana? She needed help. Professional help . . .

By the time Tom got home, nothing was any better or made any more sense. When he opened the door, Taffy came bouncing up, inordinately happy to see him. Tom called out, as he always did.

"Anybody home? Diana?"

No answer. That was okay. He wasn't sure he could face her right now, wasn't sure he could sit in the same room with her and look at her and not tell her what he had been doing. And if he told her what he had been doing, he would have to tell her why, and what it meant, and what he thought. He just wasn't up to that.

The only thing he felt like at the moment was a cold beer and a nice cool shower. He went into the kitchen, took a Löwenbräu from the refrigerator, and walked back to the bedroom, stripping off his sweat-soaked clothes as he went. The apartment had never seemed quite so hot, and the air conditioner was broken as usual.

He finished his beer and, clad only in his underwear, shuffled into the bathroom and turned on the shower. When the water was just the way he wanted it, he slipped off his shorts and got under the blast, sliding the heavy opaque glass door shut behind him. He felt better almost instantly. If nothing else, at least he would be comfortable.

Tom closed his eyes as the soap poured down his face. He didn't see the figure that stepped abruptly into the bathroom to stare at his body through the opaque glass.

But then, reaching for his washcloth on the bathtub floor, he caught a glimpse of the blurred silhouette. He wondered how long Diana had been standing there without so much as a hello.

"Hi!" he called out. "How you doing? I'll be out in a

minute." And then, feeling better with the water coursing down on him, he decided he might as well say it. He'd have to, sooner or later. "We have a lot to talk about, Diana."

She didn't answer him. Well, that was understandable. She had been telephoning him all day, and he hadn't taken one of her calls.

"Could you get me a clean towel, honey?" he asked, his voice placating.

And the silhouette disappeared out of the bathroom.

The thought of the dog's blood on the bedroom sheets flashed through Tom's mind, and he shuddered involuntarily. He wondered how the hell Diana had gotten it.

A moment later a white bath-towel flopped over the top of the shower-stall door. Through the opaque glass it was impossible for Tom to make out the pair of scissors clutched tightly in the silhouette's knotted fist.

"Thanks," Tom called out. He searched for something more to say. Might as well at least start this on a friendly basis. "Boy, am I beat."

No response.

"Are you okay, Diana?"

The silhouette just stared at Tom's nude body.

"I tried reaching you at work, but the line was busy."

A lie, but still there was no response.

The silhouette disappeared out the bathroom door again.

Tom shook his head. This was going to be even tougher than he thought. Well, the sooner he started, the sooner it would be over. He stood exhausted under the water, taking as much energy from it as he possibly could.

A dull, metallic thumping noise interrupted his reverie. He looked around. It had sounded distant.

Then he heard it again, louder this time. Two quick

thumps and then a sharper one. Finally, he placed it. It was in the pipes. The plumbing system. It was probably on the frig again.

Then the water stopped completely. His body still dripping with suds, Tom looked up at the shower head. The pipes thumped again, one last time, and a blast of water hit him full in the face. Hot, scalding water, and he was directly beneath it!

With a howl Tom tried to jump back, but there was nowhere to go. Instantly the stall was clouded with steam. He slipped and fell, thrashing under the punishing blast. It was the hottest thing he had ever felt. It was killing him, turning him a bright-red. He screamed in agony.

Using the corners of the tub to brace himself, Tom struggled to his feet, the water still boring down on him. He pulled at the shower doors to slide them open. Something was blocking them. He tried again. Still they wouldn't budge. He pressed his body tightly against the back wall, grabbed for the towel hanging over the shower door, and tried to shield his groin with it.

But the water kept pouring down on him. It felt like a thousand burning matches were being held to his body at the same time. It was tearing his skin off.

Half-mad now, he screamed for help.

"Diana!!"

No answer.

He called out again, "Diana!"

He couldn't see the figure standing there smiling, watching his thigh pressed against the glass, seeing the shower doors shake and rattle against the pair of scissors that had been wedged in against them as securely as a lock.

Tortured by pain, out of his mind, Tom grabbed for the back brush and began to pound away at the opaque door. A crack went racing down the glass. He slammed it again. That was good enough. A huge gaping hole exploded in the shower door.

Tom could see the scissors now, wedged in tightly, blocking his exit. Enraged, he yanked the scissors away, rifled the door back, and stumbled out onto the bathroom floor. Shards of broken glass bit into his feet and he howled again. The steam followed him out, enveloping him like a cocoon.

He slumped against the wall, gasping for breath. The tile was torture against his back. Then abruptly the water stopped, and there was quiet.

Crouched and bloodied on the bathroom floor with his head throbbing from the awful hurt, Tom neither saw nor heard Diana enter the apartment.

He did see her a moment later as she passed through the foyer carrying two large packages into the living room. She seemed relaxed and calm. He wondered how she could be so carefree after what she had done to him. Maybe she thought he was dead.

Again he caught a glimpse of her. She was heading for the kitchen now. He struggled to his feet, the scissors clutched tightly in his hand. He was probably going to need them.

His robe was hanging at the far end of the bathroom. He threw it on and stood breathlessly, watching and waiting for her, trying to figure what she would do when she discovered he was still alive.

Then he saw her walking back toward the living room. Something metal glinted in her hand. Diana was carrying a large steel butcher knife. Tom craned his neck, his eyes following her every move.

Maybe she only intended the shower to soften him up, to make him helpless. But he wasn't helpless. He had the scissors. It was stupid of her to leave the scissors where he could get at them.

He slipped his weapon under the robe and stalked

out of the bathroom to confront the woman he had wanted to marry. When he hit the living room, Diana was busy cutting the string off her Bloomingdale's packages. The sudden sound made her whirl around. Tom stumbled toward her, bloody and disheveled.

"My God, Tom! What happened?"

Diana rushed toward him, still clutching the butcher knife.

Tom backed away and raised a hand in warning.

"Stay away from me!" he ordered.

The intensity in his voice stopped Diana in her tracks. "What did you do to yourself?" she gasped.

"Put the knife down, Diana."

"What?" She was hardly aware that she still held a knife.

"Drop it, Diana," he barked as he pulled the scissors from under his robe.

Suddenly all Diana's self-protective instincts were at play. She was as wary and cautious as she had ever been in her life.

She spoke to Tom in a soft, placating manner, exactly as she might talk to a very small, very dangerous child. "We're playing a game, right? Like in the movies. Drop the gun, Louie and all that, right?"

Tom advanced on her slowly, the scissors held tightly, like a dagger.

"It's no game," he shouted. "Put it down."

Diana backed off, not certain anymore whom she was dealing with. "I tried calling you all day," she pleaded, "Didn't they tell you?"

"Put the knife down, Diana. I won't ask you again." And he raised the scissors to show that he meant business.

"We've got to talk about this," she managed to say, despite the panic rising in her stomach. "Whatever's happened, we can sit down and talk about it."

Tom smiled reassuringly and extended a hand in her direction. "Sure, Diana, right. Just give me the knife."

There was no way Diana was going to give up her butcher knife. Not while Tom was coming at her with those scissors in his hand. And why was he so bloody? Had he already killed someone with the scissors? Was she going to be next?

"You first," she said. "Put down the scissors."

Tom stared back at her defiantly. "Of course, darling, just as soon as you do."

She was wearing that extra-special white dress and having one stinkin' good time. She couldn't hear what they were saying, but she could see them through the window, and that was good enough. At least for now. The way they were circling around in there, it looked like they were going to kill each other, which opened up all kinds of possibilities. Like wrapping up Diana's body in a garbage bag and dragging it over to Joel's place. He'd know what to do with it.

Or else if Tom didn't end up with a knife in his gut, then she'd just march right up and show that blond prick that she could make him just as happy as the bitch had.

Either way she couldn't lose. And she had done it *all by herself*. Just like the grown-up that Joel was always saying she should be. Now if something would only happen, if those two in the house would just get on with it.

Then they moved closer to each other, she could see it through the window, and her breathing got faster and shallower, the way it did sometimes when Joel really knew what he was doing.

A yellow stain of urine spread itself across the beautiful white wedding gown.

The screams from the house were so loud and she was so excited that she didn't even notice.

Tom was shouting at Diana. "I suppose you didn't give me the towel, either, right?"

"No, I didn't give you any towel," Diana insisted bitterly. "How could I give you a towel when I wasn't even here?"

"You're lying to me," Tom screamed, his eyes blazing. "You were the only one who was ever in this apartment and you know it."

"Tom," Diana pleaded, trying for whatever thin shred of trust might still exist between them. "What is happening to us?"

"You're going crazy, that's what's happening to us!"

Diana looked at him as though he had just slapped her across the mouth. There it was, it was out and he had said it.

"You can't believe that," she said very quietly.

"Oh, no? I'll show you how much I don't believe it. I'm getting the hell out of here. I'm not staying here another damn minute and I'll be goddamned if I am going to go to sleep in the same house as a crazy woman who likes to play games with scissors and butcher knives!"

"Please, Tom, don't leave me here alone," Diana begged, setting her knife down on the table. "You can't just leave me here."

"I'll be at Greg's tonight," he answered.

Tom dressed in silence, trying his best not to look at her, even though she stood staring at him all the while.

Then he was out the door and gone. Leaving her alone . . . except for whoever it was who had actually done that horrible thing.

Like a windup doll whose spring had broken, Diana began dashing frantically around the apartment. Locking windows. Shutting blinds. Closing curtains. She bolted all five locks on the front door. But it still wasn't any good. She still didn't feel safe.

She sat on the couch panting heavily, sweating profusely, and not just from exertion. Two minutes passed.

She had to talk to someone, anyone, so she got up and dialed Sarah's number.

Jack answered the phone. She wished it had been Sarah, but Jack would understand.

"Jack," she said, "this is Diana."

"Hello, Diana." Jack didn't sound talkative. In fact, he didn't sound pleased to hear from her at all.

"Jack, can I stay with you and Sarah tonight? Tom and I had an argument, and he went to stay at Greg's house."

"Gee, Diana, you caught us at a bad time," Jack replied sheepishly.

Sarah called out to her husband from the next room, "Who is it, honey?"

Before Sarah had finished speaking and before Diana could hear the familiar voice, Jack had clamped his hand over the receiver. He yelled back to his wife, "It's for me. One of my students." Then he took his hand off the receiver and spoke into the phone. "Listen, Diana, Sarah flew to Cincinnati to see her mother. It was sort of unexpected."

That wasn't at all like Sarah, Diana thought, to leave town without telling her. "Well, can't I come over anyway?"

"I really don't think it would look right," Jack said.

Don't pull this shit on me now, Jack, not now, Diana felt like saying. But instead she pleaded with him.

"Come on, Jack. Tom's not here, and I don't want to be alone in the apartment."

"Not tonight, Diana. It would just look funny, with Sarah not being here and all. I suggest you go to a hotel. Good night now."

And before Diana realized what had happened, he had hung up on her.

"Thanks a lot, Jack," she said into the dead phone, and slammed the receiver down.

Somehow Diana got through the night. She might have dozed off once or twice, but she couldn't be sure. In the morning she dragged herself off to Scribner's, still tense and exhausted. She was standing on the main floor giving another of her standard speeches to another standard customer when a man came barging in like Patton at the head of his tank corps.

For a moment all Diana could see was a figure practically goosestepping across the floor at top speed, and it was only when the person was right on top of her that she realized it was Tom. He barged into the conversation, grabbing her arm and propelling her toward the door. For all he cared, she could have been talking to Mr. Scribner himself.

"Come on," he said, "I have a cab waiting for us outside."

Diana shook herself loose from his grip. "Where are we going?"

"I'll tell you on the way," he said, and grabbed hold of her arm again. "Where were you last night?"

Maybe those phone calls had been his. She hadn't wanted to answer them. "I stayed at a hotel," she said, wondering why she was even bothering to lie to him. "You're hurting my arm."

"I'm sorry," he said, "but we're late." And he started dragging her toward the door again.

And again she shook herself loose, wondering if she had been right the night before; maybe it was he who had gone mad.

"Whatever this is," she said, "can't it wait a second? I'm in the middle of work, you know."

"Diana. I've made an appointment. There's a cab waiting outside with the meter running, and I want you to come with me right this minute."

Then Diana became aware that Mr. Russell, the priggish, gray-haired store manager, was standing next to them. "Is there some trouble, Miss Stewart?" he asked.

"No, sir. None at all."

"We can't expect customers to wait for us while we conduct our personal business, Miss Stewart."

"Yes, sir," she answered.

Tom was furious. "Diana, if you don't come with me right now, that's it. It's all over."

The memory of Tom walking into the bookstore the day they had met flashed through her mind. Today she was wearing the same blue dress. It had become one of her favorites. In a second she had made up her mind. If Tom was willing to give it one more shot, whatever it was he had up his sleeve, assuming it wasn't an eight-inch icepick, she would try to go along with it, if only to show him she still cared.

She turned to the manager. "I   rry, Mr. Russell, but I'm afraid I'm going to have to take the afternoon off."

Mr. Russell's voice had worlds of quiet menace in it. "If it's that urgent."

For the third time Tom took her arm, but this time Diana let him. "This had better be awfully important," she told him. "I might not have a job tomorrow."

"We're going to see a psychiatrist," Tom said.

Diana stopped dead in her tracks. A bolt of lightning could not have rooted her any more firmly to the floor.

"A what?" she exclaimed.

She said it loud enough and incredulously enough for half the store to turn and stare at her. Maybe she had a job thirty seconds ago. She certainly didn't have one now.

But that didn't bother her. She felt too tired and confused to fight back, even if she could have figured out who or what to fight. She allowed herself to be led, unresisting, to the waiting taxicab.

Dr. Edward Graham was a surprise to both of them. He was a surprise to Tom, because he was under sixty-five. In fact, he was far closer to forty, and he seemed as though he might be a nice fellow. This second part was what surprised Diana. She thought she liked him. He was the kind of guy who seemed genuinely interested in finding out what was on your mind, and without any subliminal thoughts about groping you after he had become your pal, either. But as soon as she acknowledged that feeling, Diana was on guard against it. Part of his professional baggage, she thought. They're taught how to be concerned and trustworthy, and as soon as some sucker buys the act, they pounce on you.

Yet even as she was ready for betrayal, Diana still found she liked him.

"The most positive sign of all, Diana, is that you wanted to come here," Dr. Graham began. That was all he had to say. The honeymoon was over.

"I didn't want to come here, Doctor," Diana objected. "I'm doing it for Tom."

Dr. Graham smiled while Diana watched the light from a desk lamp bounce off his horn-rimmed glasses. Nothing seemed to ruffle this man's professional composure.

"Tom has told me about the unusual events of the last several days," he said, "and we both thought it might be helpful if you were to talk about them in your own words."

Well, Diana thought, if he was going to be that honest with her, she would be that honest right back. As far as she was concerned, they could just sit there all afternoon being honest with each other.

"What I say doesn't seem to mean very much to anyone these days," she replied.

"It'll mean something to me, if you feel like sharing it. But of course I don't like anyone to feel coerced in this office."

So this was his pleasant way of saying, put up or shut up.

"Well, I do feel coerced," Diana said loudly, letting her anger show. "Coerced into coming here, coerced into putting locks on the doors because some sick person is trying to ruin my life, and coerced into looking over my shoulder at every street corner because I think someone might be following me. So don't worry, Doctor, if I feel coerced in this office, it's just icing on the cake." And she gave him her own version of his dazzling smile.

"Diana," Tom said, as if talking to a child, "Dr. Graham is only trying to help you. I think you're over-reacting."

Dr. Graham waved a placating hand in Tom's direction. "No, that's all right, I can understand why Diana's upset."

Then you're a better man than I, Gunga Din, Diana thought.

Dr. Graham went on, "Tell me, Diana, have you actually seen this person who follows you around?"

A seemingly innocent, concerned question, but Diana recognized a trap when she saw one. "No, I haven't," she answered. "But I have seen the furniture in my home mutilated, my dog scared half to death, and the imprint of a human body smeared on my wall."

"But have you actually seen this person doing these things, Diana?"

A good maneuver. Very crafty. Her inquisitor obviously knew the answer, but she had to play along. "Of course I haven't," she replied. "I just told you I've never seen the person."

Dr. Graham nodded again. "What if I told you that the person who's following you around is the same person who's vandalizing your apartment."

That seemed like a straightforward, sensible remark to make, so Diana answered it in a sensible, straightforward way. "I'd believe you. I've thought about that myself."

Dr. Graham's smile seemed to applaud her for her honest common sense. "Can you think of any reason why someone would want to do these things to you in particular?"

To Diana the reason was all too apparent. "Because someone obviously has a very disturbed mind."

Tom gave Dr. Graham a quick sidelong glance, but not so quick that Diana didn't catch it.

"Diana," the doctor continued, "I'm going to ask you two more questions, and I want you to answer me very frankly, because it's extremely important for both you and Tom that you do. First, I want you to tell me, as irrational as it might seem, whether you've ever felt any guilt about your parents' death."

Dr. Graham glanced down at the police reports sitting on his desk and then looked his patient straight in the eye. For the first time since they had started talking, Diana felt Dr. Graham might be treating her like something other than just a meal ticket.

"It's not really guilt," she began, and then she paused for a moment, trying to formulate what it was. "Well, maybe it is a kind of guilt. I guess with my job and Tom and moving to New York, I didn't spend as much time with my parents as I should have. I was really the only family they had and I didn't even manage to make it to my father's sixtieth birthday. I just hope they knew how much I loved them."

Dr. Graham nodded understandingly. It occurred to Diana that psychiatrists really had a pretty easy job. They could sit there and nod understandingly for twenty years, just waiting for their patients to go broke.

But not this doctor. He was going to give you your money's worth.

"Tom has told me that your parents were on their way down from Rhode Island to meet him when the tragedy occurred." He paused thoughtfully and went on, "Do you think, Diana, there is any possibility at all that what's been happening in Tom's apartment is your unconscious way of punishing Tom and yourself for your parents' death?"

Diana felt like kicking herself. She had stupidly stepped into a pool of quicksand, and the only two people who could throw her a rope were busy finding nails for her coffin.

"I want to get one thing straight once and for all," she said, her throat tightening. "I am not doing crazy things in my own apartment and I am not going to sit here any longer listening to either of you make these absurd accusations."

Dr. Graham ignored her and plowed ahead. "As your doctor now, Diana, I'm going to have to insist that you face up to the truth. The police have been doing lab tests, and I want you to know what they've found. The hair from the body print on your wall, the blood on your bed sheets, and the voice on the tape recorder in your living room were all undeniably yours. As hard as it might be for all of us to face up to, Diana, that is what has been happening to you. And that is the reality that we're all going to have to deal with together."

The guilty verdict hit Diana so swiftly and unexpectedly that for a long moment all she could fix on was the doctor's license to practice hanging among the diplomas on the wall. When she spoke, she was deadly calm, in a way that Tom knew meant trouble.

"I don't want to put you in a position where you might have to violate your professional ethics, Dr. Graham, but I'd like to know how you came by this information."

"It's nothing to be ashamed of, Diana," Tom spoke up reassuringly. "It's an illness like any other illness. That's why we're here."

Diana ignored him. "Dr. Graham," she demanded, "where did you get your information?"

"From Tom, of course," Graham answered. "He cares about you, Diana, and he wants to see you well again."

Diana stood up, shaking with rage, towering over her fiancé. "You mean," she said slowly, "you knew all that stuff, and you didn't tell me?"

Tom had the kind of grin found on the face of eleven-year-old boys who are caught playing with themselves. "I thought it was information the doctor needed to have," he said, squirming in his seat.

"Well, bully for you," Diana said, her voice cracking with anger. "Now what do you two propose to do? Put me in a mental ward?"

"Come off it, Diana," Tom said, "you're only making matters worse for yourself."

She looked at him with a contempt she would have thought herself incapable of feeling.

"Please sit down, Diana," Dr. Graham advised. "I know how painful this must be for you. I've handled many cases similar to your own. People have all kinds of different reactions to the loss of their parents. Tom told me how close you were to yours."

"Oh, he did, did he?" Diana said, her outrage increasing with every word. "What other private little goodies did he tell you behind my back? Did he tell you how often we make it? Did he tell you what turns me on?"

"Diana, please," Dr. Graham implored. He didn't like the way this first session was evolving. He preferred people with mild, malleable problems. "We can work all this out together, Diana, but we'll need your cooperation. Believe me, I do understand how upsetting this must be for you."

"No, you don't!" she burst out. "You understand I'm crazy because he told you I'm crazy." The inflection she used for the word "he" left no doubt about whom she meant or how she felt about him. "Why don't you both go screw yourselves!"

And before either man quite realized what was happening, Diana had turned and stormed out of the office.

For a long moment Tom just sat there, feeling embarrassed and confused. Then, as if seeking a medical opinion, he asked, "Should I go after her, Doctor?"

"Well, somebody certainly should," said Dr. Graham, who wouldn't have gone after her himself if they'd offered him the Nobel Peace Prize for it.

Irving J. Cohen had never heard anything like it in his life. Irving J. Cohen had been driving a cab in Manhattan for upwards of thirty years and had every reason to believe that he had heard and seen it all, and until a few minutes ago he thought he had.

That was before a very pretty girl had flagged him down in front of one of those fat-cat Park Avenue apartment buildings. No sooner had he pulled over to the curb than some overage prep-school type came barrelassing out of the building like the cops were after him and grabbed the girl by the arm. They immediately got into one cockamamie fight about whether or not they were going to get into the same cab, and Preppy must have won that, because he did get in with her, and as soon as they had given their destination, they were back at it, clearly oblivious to the fact that Irving J. Cohen was right up front, where he could hear everything, and some of it was pretty raw. Now they seemed to have reached some kind of important impasse.

"Is that final, Diana?" the Preppy said. "You won't go back to see him?"

"You're goddamned right it's final," Diana said, and she sounded like she meant it, too. "You've given him so much loaded information he thinks I'm a homicidal maniac. If I ever walk in there again, that pompous quack will have a straitjacket ready for me."

Preppy tried to appease her. "Listen, Diana, we don't have to use Graham. We can find another man."

Just then Diana apparently realized something. "*You* think I'm a homicidal maniac! Don't you!"

Preppy did his best to be calm and reasonable. "Let's say I think it's highly possible that you're emotionally disturbed, and we ought to find out. And furthermore, I don't think it's such a good idea for me to stay in a house where my fiancée is brandishing butcher knives and trying to burn me to death."

Irving J. Cohen thought he'd have to go along with Preppy on that, even if this Diana didn't look to him like the kind of girl who'd go around doing things like that. And after upwards of thirty years driving a cab, Irving J. Cohen prided himself on being a pretty good judge of character.

Diana obviously didn't think she was the kind of person who went around doing things like that, either. "Are you sure it's safe for you to be sitting here in the cab with me?" she said, her voice bitter with sarcasm. "I might stab you to death with a hairpin or something."

"This isn't easy for me, either, Diana. I'm trying to do what's best for you."

"Then trust me, goddamn it!" Diana screamed, loud enough to break Irving J. Cohen's eardrums and with enough anguish to break his heart. He punctuated her grief with an abrupt stop at a red light.

"Unless you agree to see another doctor," the Preppy threatened, "I'm not even coming home with you."

Diana started to retort, paused, and looked hard at Tom, a curious, detached look as if she were seeing him for the very first time. "You mean that, don't you?"

"I damn sure do," Tom answered. "I'll have someone pick up my clothes in the morning."

Diana replied without a moment's hesitation. "You won't need to pick up your clothes or my psychiatry bills. I'll be packed and out of that apartment tonight."

The finality of her tone silenced Tom's comeback. Before he realized what was going on, Diana had opened the car door and was halfway out.

167

"Listen to me, Diana. . . . " He tried to take her hand, but she pulled away. "Good-bye, Tom." Then she was out on the street and lost in the traffic.

Even though he had the light, Irving J. Cohen felt sorry enough for the so-called homicidal maniac to watch in the rearview mirror and make sure she had another cab before he put his foot on the gas and propelled Preppy on his way to what was undoubtedly going to be a very lonely night.

13

The thumbtack punctured the kneecap and drove through to the plaster. The leg drooped forward awkwardly, as if broken at the thigh.

Laurie stepped back and thought how really lousy her room would be if she didn't have those three hundred and fifty-seven pairs of gorgeous paper legs thumbtacked onto the four walls. Everywhere. Floor to ceiling. You could hardly see the plaster. Her favorites were over the bed, where she could play with them. Cher's, Cheryl's, Farrah's, and three pair of Chrissie Evert's. They weren't just for decoration, either, they got you thinking.

If God came in all of a sudden and said she could have any pair of those legs for her very own, which pair would she choose? Strong and athletic or slim and elegant? Long and supple or short and powerful? What would be really terrific would be to have several pair, to mix and match for different occasions.

As usual when she was having a nice time thinking of things like that, Joel came in and bothered her.

"How come you haven't fed the animals?"

"I fed Rinkus," she told him, hoping he would go away.

Fat chance. She could tell right away from that hangdog look on his face that he was going to stick around and try to "communicate" with her.

He walked over, sat beside her on the bed, and brushed the hair back from her eyes. That was one of the ways he showed affection for her. Like she was one of the dogs.

"Are you okay, Laur?"

"I been thinking."

"About what?"

That was another way he showed affection for her. He made her think he wanted to know what was on her mind. He probably got it off the television.

"That no one around here gives a fat funkus about me." Then she decided to stick him one. "You ever had a girlfriend, Joel?"

He got up from the bed, his face red. He was so easy to get flustered that way. He turned his back to her and stood looking at all the limbs.

"You're sort of my girlfriend," he muttered. Then his attention was caught by a newspaper clipping, the edge of which stuck out from behind a pair of shapely calves. That was strange. Laurie could hardly read.

"If I'm your girlfriend, how come you never give me any rings and shit? How come?" Laurie needled him.

"I can get you a ring, if that's what you want," he said, but that's not what he was thinking about. His hand went to the leg mosaic and pulled off the limbs covering the clipping.

The resemblance made him gasp. He snatched the yellowed newsprint off the wall to get a closer look at it.

Laurie sat upright on the bed. She knew trouble when she saw it. Joel shoved the clipping of Diana Stewart's smiling face in front of her nose. "So that's where you've been going! You've been lying to me."

"Let's go and kill her, Joel. We'll kill her and bring her back home with us."

"You've seen her, haven't you?" Joel asked angrily.

"We're in the same ballet class, fish face."

Joel sighed in exasperation, then spoke with fierce intensity. "Has she seen you, Laurie? If she's seen you, you have to tell me."

"Go fuck yourself, Joel."

"Answer me, Laurie. Has she seen you?"

"It's none of your bee's wax."

"Don't you understand? If they catch you, they're gonna take you away from me." He was pleading with her now. "Can't you see? I'm doing it for you."

"Then how come you never give me any of these?" Laurie lifted her dress and wiggled around in a pair of pink lace panties that fitted her perfectly.

Joel looked as though someone was playing on the soles of his feet with a lit cigarette. "Where did you get those?" he asked.

"I took them from her house."

"Have you lost all your senses going over there?" Joel was shouting at her now.

"Where else was I going to get them, maggot mouth? I asked you for a blue sweater. Did you get me one? No. I wanted a pair of new glasses. Where are they, Joel? I asked you for a white dress for the wedding. Okay, where is it? I don't see it, Mr. Stinkum. You think I look good like this? You like my hair this way?"

"It's nice enough like that." The guilt was creeping into his voice.

"I can't sell books looking like this," she roared viciously. "Admit it, Joel, you never wanted me to look like a pretty girl."

She sneered at him in expectation of the answer.

Joel spoke to the floor, his voice barely audible. "I didn't want you to leave me. You would have left me."

His whining, the easy way he knuckled under, enraged her more. She picked up a magazine and hurled it at him.

"I hate you!" she screamed. "I really hate you."

He tried to look away, but the intensity of her gaze held his eyes.

"You know I'd do anything for you," he said. He was in total misery now. "Just swear you'll never leave me."

171

Her eyes widened with excitement and promise. "I'll swear it, Joel. But you got to swear something, too. You can make me look like her."

He stared back into her hungry eyes, a glimmer of understanding flickering across his face, and suddenly she knew that everything was going to be all right. Sooner or later he would do what he had to do. And then sooner or later she'd be dancing up a storm.

✦✦✦

Diana had been sitting on the couch in the darkened living room for hours. A small framed photograph of Tom lay in her lap. The room was so dark she could no longer see the features clearly, but that made no difference. She had them memorized. She closed her eyes and could see him in a thousand different poses. Maybe she would just sit there forever, remembering how he looked. Like that old lady in *Great Expectations* who had stopped time by keeping her room the way it was when her lover decided not to marry her. Just sitting there in her wedding gown, waiting for the end.

Her eyes searched the room, gorging themselves on memories of Tom: his squash racket leaning against the television, his warmup jacket draped loosely over a dining room chair, the plastic magazine rack crammed full of his investment reports. Her gaze wandered to the collection of porcelain ballerinas on the mantel. Frozen in their lovely poses forever, time had stopped for them, too. How many had been gifts from Tom? His way of letting her know what he found so difficult to say.

Her eyes darted around the mantel, recapturing those lost moments. Even in the darkened room Diana could make out that her collection wasn't as she had left it. Why was the little ballerina with the blue tutu and white crown propped up awkwardly against the back of the mantel? A panicked moan escaped from her throat.

She got up to take a closer look and put a hand to her mouth to muffle the scream.

Her little figurines were still standing, but all had been horribly mutilated. The left leg of each one had been broken off like a toothpick. Missing and gone.

The small but senseless destruction sickened her. But beyond that was the sudden, mindless, crawling fear of whoever it was that had dismembered her little dancers.

"Tom?" Before Diana realized what she was doing, she had called out.

She knew that was foolish. Tom wasn't here. He'd never be here. She could die in this apartment, and no one would know.

Rushing into the bedroom, she found her suitcase and tossed it on the bed. Scooping up armfuls of clothes, she stuffed them into the bag. She rifled through the closet, tearing her dresses off their hangers.

Until she came to her wedding gown.

Moments ago, she had thought of sitting alone in a gown like that until she died, but now the sight of the dress in which she had planned to be married moved her nearly to tears. Gently she took it out of the closet and held it in front of her. She felt as if she were looking at a pair of tickets to a play she wasn't going to see because the person who was supposed to take her had died. Pressing the gown to her body, she moved in front of the full-length mirror for one last look.

The ugly yellow stain that had spread across the lower part of the dress was unmistakable. Still, she couldn't bring herself to believe it. She held the dress up to her nose and inhaled the stench of urine.

She gagged both from the awful smell and from the fear that rose in her throat like nausea. She ran into the bathroom and stayed there for a long time, racked with heaves, until it seemed that not only everything in her stomach but her stomach itself had come up.

When she entered the living room again, she was shaking with rage as much as sickness. Some sort of hazy, indefinable line had just been reached, beyond which she could not be pushed, no matter what further indecencies were heaped on her person.

She was through with simply waiting for the house to cave in. Enraged, Diana marched to the garden doors and threw them open. A scream burst out of her lungs; part fury, part fear, it echoed into the night air.

"I'M STILL HERE, YOU BASTARD, SO COME AND GET ME! COME ON! I'M WAITING FOR YOU!"

The force of her own voice startled her, and for a moment there was deathly silence, as though she had been wrong and she really was alone.

A rush of elation swept through her body. She had hit rock bottom, but at least the ground there was firm, and she was standing up again. Then a thing so mind-boggling happened that even in the midst of the horrifying next few seconds, Diana was sure her mind had snapped.

A face sprang suddenly out of the darkness inches away from her own; a face that, even though it was grimy, surrounded with stringy hair, and distorted with rage, Diana instantly recognized as her own.

"Give it back, you cunting maggot!" the face croaked, in a harsh, mad whisper. "Give it back! It's my turn now."

"Please, no!" Diana cried out to herself.

She retreated into the living room, bewildered, panic-stricken, her heart pounding uncontrollably, unable to get her mind around the amazing thing that she was seeing.

The girl with the face like hers advanced into the room with a strange, halting gait, and Diana kept backing away, until she felt something behind her and realized she couldn't back away any further. Diana pressed herself against the wall. She felt her muscles going limp with terror.

"I'm gonna make a pie out of you," the intruder hissed. Her mouth cracked in a smile of intense satisfaction. She reached out and ripped Diana's blouse open.

"I know what you're hiding in there," the girl squawked, pinching Diana's breast.

Diana slid along the wall, shamelessly inching her way toward the front door. "Please don't hurt me," she pleaded.

The girl's open hand drove Diana's head sideways against the brick wall, leaving a red, stinging pattern on her cheek.

Pain and hysteria fought in Diana's face. "Take anything you want," she begged, when she was able to speak. "Go ahead. You can have anything."

"You've got to give it to me, cocksucker," screeched the girl with the face like hers.

Terror crawled along Diana's nerves. Her face was drained of color. She had no idea what the apparition was talking about.

"I'll give you whatever you want," Diana babbled. "Just leave me alone."

The girl reached out and placed her fingers gingerly on Diana's left leg. With maddening slowness she moved her hand under Diana's skirt and up the exposed thigh. It was a caress both reverent and lustful.

"Your turn," the ugly face whispered. "Feel mine."

Rigid with fear, Diana tried to press herself still further into the wall. She felt a pressure between her legs. The girl had jammed her knee up between Diana's thighs. But it didn't feel like a knee. It didn't feel like flesh. It was harder than that. It had no life.

"I said, feel my trunkus," the girl shouted, her hot, putrid breath showering Diana's face.

Diana turned her head away, but did as she was told. She reached beneath the girl's dangling skirt. She felt something firm and cold, and in a moment of disbelief realized that her hand was touching metal and plastic.

"How about that, cunto? Feels good, doesn't it? Smooth as a baby's ass."

Diana's nerves snapped. She screamed aloud. A swift glint of white light swept through the darkness, and before she could articulate the thought, Diana's motor reflexes reacted to the weapon in the air. She lurched awkwardly to the side an instant before the knife came crashing down into the wall where her left leg had been.

Diana broke away and bolted for the kitchen. The electric carving knife lay on the counter. She picked it up, flicked it on, and stood in the dark, brandishing the carving knife before her like a sword, waiting for her assailant to strike again. She stood there for a long time, the hum of the battery-powered knife the only sound in an otherwise silent house.

Twenty, maybe thirty, minutes passed, and Diana found enough courage to venture into the living room. Cautiously she moved from room to room, checking into closets, behind doors, under the bed. There was nobody there.

Diana was alone again.

The girl had left and taken the tortured face with her.

Usually Dr. Allen slept peacefully and without dreams. He was satisfied with his life as it neared its close; he had done what he had set out to do, and perhaps even more important, he had harmed no one. He had never become famous, he had made no startling medical breakthroughs. He wasn't even a celebrity within his profession, like, say, the head of neurosurgery at one of the fashionable Manhattan hospitals, whom the interns followed around as though they were movie stars. But he was satisfied with what he had done. A lot of men had accomplished less. So he slept peacefully and without dreams.

Except for tonight. Tonight he dreamed he was hiding

in a dark closet somewhere in the hospital and someone had found out where the closet was and was pounding on the door, trying to chase him out of his hiding place.

The dream was so inexorably real that it jolted him into wakefulness. He turned on his bed light. To his amazement, the pounding continued.

It took Dr. Allen a moment to realize that he hadn't been dreaming after all, that someone was actually out there, pounding on his door in the middle of the night. What did they think he was, some kind of country doctor?

He pushed his feet into a pair of slippers, threw on the silk robe by his bed, and made his way through his apartment, turning on lights as he went and mumbling, "I'm coming, I'm coming," under his breath.

For a moment he did not recognize the distraught, disheveled creature standing on the other side of the doorway. She was wild-eyed, confused, and disjointed.

Diana's words came tumbling out, stumbling over each other in frightened haste. "I have to talk to you. I'm sorry I woke you. I know it's late, but I have to talk to you."

Dr. Allen blinked away his disbelief and led the girl gently by the hand into his apartment. But Diana did not calm down. If anything, she became more incoherent.

"She hit me and I couldn't stop her. She was in the house. She was after my leg. She tried to cut it off."

There are certain rare occasions when a physician's primary function consists of pretending he knows what it is his patient is talking about. Tonight, though, Dr. Allen felt that role far too difficult to play.

"*Who* came after you, Diana?" he asked.

"She's going to come back. I know she will." There was a terrible urgency in her voice.

"You just sit down right here, child. I'll make you some coffee."

"No! You have to listen." Diana was clutching at his

arm. "I saw her with my own eyes. . . . She came to get me."

"I'll listen to you, Diana, but you have to calm down. Let me get you something hot to drink."

When Diana had been coaxed into a chair, the doctor went to the kitchen, put on some coffee, and returned with a glass of water for her. Not for the briefest moment did he feel unreasonably put upon. This was a child he had brought into the world. He had a responsibility for her.

No sooner had Diana gulped the water down than she was going again a mile a minute. "There's a cab downstairs. I told him to wait. I didn't know if you were home. The girl had a butcher knife and she looked like me."

The last sentence pushed Dr. Allen into dark waters in which he was not prepared to swim.

"I'll take care of the cab," he said. "You just sit here and calm yourself."

He got his wallet and left the apartment.

Diana inhaled deeply and tried to put her thoughts back in order. She could count on Dr. Allen to help her, but sitting alone in an apartment again gave her the creeps. She didn't feel safe anywhere. Not even here.

And then suddenly it wasn't a silent apartment anymore. At first it was barely audible, a gurgling kind of sound. Diana sat perfectly still, trying to figure out what it was she had heard and where it had come from. Dr. Allen lived alone and had for many years. But she was certain she had heard something.

A loud breathy sigh whistled through the apartment. Diana recognized that sound. She cursed herself for not having been more cautious. Why hadn't she thought of it? She had been followed here. Sheer terror rooted her to the floor. The breathing got louder, heavier, more tortured. It was coming from one of the rooms right off from where Diana was sitting and it seemed to be getting closer.

Diana whirled around toward the sound, expecting the thing to come bursting into the living room, for one final struggle. She grabbed a thick metal ashtray from the coffee table and clutched it tightly in her cocked fist.

Dr. Allen was back inside the lobby, having paid off the cabbie and seen the man's knowing smirk at a person of his age, dressed in bathrobe and pajamas, paying the cab fare for a pretty young woman who had come to see him in the middle of the night. Well, let the man think what he liked. If people were going to make mistakes about him, they might as well be flattering.

He pressed the elevator button and looked up at the dial. It was on five. His floor. Was Diana leaving the apartment? He wanted to take the stairs, but he was already agitated and afraid for his heart. Then the elevator began its descent and opened. There was no one inside. When Dr. Allen got out at the fifth floor, he was surprised to find his door slightly ajar. He pushed it open and stepped inside.

The apartment was empty. There was a slight indentation on the couch where Diana had been sitting. Dr. Allen felt the cushion; it was still warm. The sound of heavy breathing filled the room, breathing he knew wasn't hers.

"Diana?" he called out.

There was no answer.

"Diana, where are you?"

He heard a tiny rustling sound from behind a chair in a corner of the room. He walked over and looked in back of it. Diana was there, curled up on the floor.

He spoke to her as he would to a frightened child. "What are you doing there, Diana?"

"The kitchen," she managed. "There's someone in the kitchen."

"There's no one in the kitchen, Diana."

She looked up at him, doubt crowding in her eyes. He smiled confidently at her. "You wait here, I'll show you."

He walked into the kitchen, where the coffee percolator was bubbling away as he had left it, sending its hot vapor into the air with the loud sound of labored breathing. Dr. Allen unplugged the percolator, and the breathing stopped.

A moment later the doctor reentered the living room, the percolator in one hand, a coffee cup in the other.

"See?" he said, smiling. "It's just a coffee pot. Nothing to be afraid of. Here, why don't I pour you a cup."

Diana blushed at her foolishness. She got up from the floor, took the cup of coffee from him, and sat down on the couch.

"Thank you," she said. "I guess I must seem paranoid to you."

Remarks like that were always a sign of hope to Dr. Allen, a sign that the patient was willing to discuss his problems. So he tried to open the door to such a conversation.

"What are you afraid of, Diana?"

Whatever answer Dr. Allen might have been expecting, he was not expecting the reply he got.

"I have a twin sister, don't I?"

It was a question so surprising to Dr. Allen that for a moment he could only stare at Diana, the way a pathologist might study a cadaver.

"I do, don't I?" she persisted. "You know I do."

The events surrounding her birth had been buried and forgotten as far as the old doctor was concerned. He wasn't going to lie, but he didn't want to tell her anything that would upset her more than she already was. Avoiding her gaze, he took her hand in a way he hoped was both reassuring and fatherly.

"It's the past, child, leave it alone," he said uneasily.

"Please, what are you hiding from me?" Diana implored in a tiny voice of utter desperation.

Could he tell her? Tension knotted the muscles on the back of Allen's neck. This wasn't the time or the place to reveal to the girl what had been kept hidden for all these years. Yet even as he convinced himself of that, his eyes opened to a vision of hot white operating lamps, breath-soaked surgical masks, and sterilized rubber gloves snapping tightly over freshly scrubbed hands.

Dr. Allen gulped a breath of resolve. "I guess maybe we should have told you, Diana, but there was never any reason to. Your father, God bless his soul, didn't want anyone to know, not even your mother."

"Didn't want anyone to know what?" her voice demanded.

"I've never lied to you, Diana, and I won't now. It is true, you were born a twin . . ."

"Then it was her," she whispered suddenly. He could feel her grip tighten, her body stiffen.

"No," the doctor insisted, "only you survived the birth. Your sister died painlessly the day you were born."

"But she didn't die," Diana objected sharply.

"I was there, Diana." His voice was calm.

"But I saw her! I saw her a half-hour ago."

"That's not possible, Diana," the doctor continued firmly. "Your father could have told you. He was with me that day. I guess it was just one of those things he tried to put out of his mind. I don't know if he finally did. . . . I never could."

Especially not now, not while he was looking at her. Every time he saw her, he remembered the terrifyingly strange events of twenty-six years ago. He sat down on the couch next to her, cradling her hand in his lap, and began to tell the story that rushed back at him from the past.

14

January 26, 1955. It would be the most amazing day that Dr. Allen ever spent in the practice of medicine, and yet it had begun quite normally with another baby to deliver—one aspect of his work that Dr. Allen didn't even particularly enjoy. But baby doctoring was the key to establishing a solid family practice, and judging from his growing referral work, Dr. Allen could deliver babies as well as anyone.

On top of that, today's delivery was special. The expectant mother was practically family. Dr. Allen's father and grandfather had been doctors to the Stewarts of Jackson Heights for what seemed like forever, which was why it was going to be a particular pleasure to bring another Stewart child into the world.

But not an unalloyed pleasure. Dr. Allen was afraid the birth was going to be a difficult one. Mrs. Stewart was a delicate, small-boned woman, and he had always suspected he might have trouble with her.

Now, huddled over the operating table with Dr. Allen was his brilliant but somewhat temperamental twenty-seven-year-old assistant Dr. Raymond Brock. Three nurses were in attendance beside them.

The contractions were coming quicker and stronger. Mrs. Stewart began to scream. There *was* going to be trouble. More trouble than even Dr. Allen had thought. It wasn't going to be a nice, pleasant day, after all.

The pregnant woman heaved and gasped and moaned,

bucking against the operating table as if it were a torture rack.

"It's coming faster now," Dr. Allen assured her. "It's all right, keep pushing . . . push . . . come on now, Barbara, bear down, help me."

The baby was in the birth canal now. It was moving, but the contractions weren't pushing it forward.

"Help her with the contractions," Dr. Allen instructed a nurse.

He pressed a stethoscope to the lower part of her abdomen, but couldn't make out the baby's heartbeat through all the commotion and noise in the room.

With each contraction of the uterus the nurse pushed down hard on Mrs. Stewart's stomach, trying to force the baby downward. It wasn't any good. Something was holding it back. Dr. Allen couldn't understand it. The cervix was dilated to a full 10 centimeters.

"Breathe out, Barbara. Keep breathing like I showed you," Dr. Allen coaxed her. "I think it's gonna be a big fella," he added, as if an explanation would resolve what was quickly becoming a serious problem.

The baby was kicking now against the vaginal walls, which were fully extended and ready to burst. Mrs. Stewart grunted and heaved with the pain of the effort. Her screams were almost incoherent, except for the repeated plea, "I want my baby, I want my baby."

Sweat streamed down her face, she pursed her lips, the veins stood out on her wet forehead.

"We're almost there, Barbara," Dr. Allen assured her.

Then Mrs. Stewart screamed as if her insides had been ripped out.

"Anesthesia!" Dr. Allen snapped.

Brock tried clamping a black rubber mask over the patient's nose and mouth, but Mrs. Stewart turned her face away. "No, don't . . . I want to see my baby."

Brock cupped her chin in his hand and yanked her

face back under the mask. For a moment Mrs. Stewart refused to breathe, but then the pain was too great, and she sucked in the sweet-smelling gas that would bring on sleep. Her legs went limp, and her feet were placed into leather stirrups.

Brock turned to Allen, his eyes filled with accusation. "It's too late for a cesarean. The baby's no longer intrauterine."

"Prepare for an episiotomy," Dr. Allen answered. There was urgency in his voice.

He looked at the woman spread-eagled before him, her pubic hair shaved. "Sponge," he said, holding out his gloved hand.

He dipped the sponge into brown antiseptic and scrubbed the perineum from the outer genitalia to the rectum. A nurse took the sponge from his hand and replaced it with a small pair of scissors. Dr. Allen glanced up at the anesthesiologist for a final okay.

"All right by me," the man answered.

Inserting the sharp point of the scissors two inches into the vagina, Dr. Allen cut a straight line through the thick musculature down toward the rectum. As the muscles freed themselves from their pelvic moorings, the vagina and birth canal expanded instantly. Gently Dr. Allen inserted the large tweezerlike forceps between the labia, moving the instrument along the vaginal walls. Feeling the baby's head between the metal tongs, he pressed down delicately and began pulling the infant out of its mother.

It was harder work than Dr. Allen had thought it would be. The top of a tiny head was finally visible. "Here it comes," Allen said, his hands trembling with the tension. Then he got his first surprise. "Holy Jesus, there's two of them—twins—she's having twins!" He was almost shouting.

One head, emerged, then another, purple and wet.

Brock hovered over the mother, fascinated. "I think they might be conjoined, Doctor."

"I can't tell," Allen said. "One of them's having trouble. That's it, now. Ease them out."

"Oh, my God!" Dr. Brock said, and one of the nurses had to turn away.

Dr. Allen cut the single umbilical cord and lifted the two babies upside down high over his head.

Suspended in the air, framed by two surgically gloved hands practically as big as they, were two little girls, joined at the waist and perfect in every respect except that they shared one middle leg. Three legs for the two babies. Siamese twins. That's what they were.

Dr. Allen slapped them on the fanny, and they cried in unison.

Out in the waiting room Dr. Allen found the nervous young father, Norman Stewart, sitting in an armchair beside a mountain of cigarette butts.

How to begin? Dr. Allen swallowed hard. They didn't teach you this in Med School.

"Norman, could I speak with you?"

Norman Stewart's face showed he feared the worst. He jumped out of his seat. "Is anything the matter?"

Dr. Allen's eyes darted around the busy room. It was a bad place to talk. The men's room was nearby. Not exactly the most intimate surroundings, but it would have to do.

"Why don't we go in there?" he said, motioning toward the door. "We'll have some privacy."

Norman Stewart walked along beside him as if he were on his way to the electric chair.

"Dr. Allen, please, is my wife all right?" he asked.

"She's perfectly okay."

Norman Stewart felt relieved. But not for long.

When Dr. Allen had finished explaining the situation,

the young man looked as though someone had clubbed him in the stomach with a baseball bat. He leaned against the tiled bathroom wall, tears streaming down his face.

"It can't be," he mumbled. "We took all the tests. We're normal people!"

Dr. Allen put his hand on the young man's shoulder. "I'm sorry, Norman, but it wasn't anybody's fault. Now, I need your help. The twins are joined at the waist . . ." he hadn't told this part yet and stumbled over it quickly— "and there's only one leg at that juncture. One middle leg that they share."

Stewart pulled Dr. Allen's hand off his shoulder and looked for a moment as if he wanted to crush it. He stared into the doctor's face with agonized intensity.

"What did you do wrong?" he asked

Wearily Dr. Allen extricated himself from the young man's grasp. "It's nobody's fault," he said. "Surely you must know that. Now, please, I'm going to have to ask you to control yourself."

The young man made a great show of calming down.

Dr. Allen kept his language simple and direct. "Your twins are in critical condition. There's a circulatory problem that must be corrected. As conjoined twins, they have an extremely slim chance of surviving. If we separate them now, one of them will die, but the other has a damned good chance of making it."

Stewart looked as though he himself had only a slim chance of surviving the turn of events that had been dumped in his lap. Finally he spoke. "And what are the chances for the other one?"

Dr. Allen shook his head. "We'll do our best, believe me, but I can't operate without your legal consent."

"How can I decide to let one of my children die?"

At least Dr. Allen could make that part easier. "I'm not asking you to let one of your children die, I'm asking you to let one of them live."

For a long moment Stewart just stood there thinking.

"All right," he said finally, "you can operate, on one condition. I don't want anyone to know we gave birth to"—he found it difficult to use the term—"Siamese twins. No one must know. Not even my wife."

Good heavens, Dr. Allen thought, the man's worried about what his friends are going to think. "The hospital can't do things that way, Norman," he said.

The young man answered with fierce intensity. "I don't want my wife spending the rest of her life wondering if both her babies couldn't have been saved."

"Your wife will understand. These things happen," Dr. Allen said, and thought to himself, Once in how many cases? At least the young man had a better reason than he had given him credit for.

"I can't do it, damn it," Stewart burst out. "Unless you give me your personal guarantee, I will not do it."

Dr. Allen looked nervously at his watch. There wasn't much time. He took some papers out of his vest pocket. "All right," he said, "you have my word. Now, I'll need your signature on these."

He handed the papers to Stewart, who flattened them against the tiles of the men's room wall and signed his name with a trembling hand. He looked at them for a moment before handing them back.

Only then did Norman Stewart ask what otherwise would have been his first question. "Are they boys or girls?"

"Girls."

The now-weary father gave him a long, hard look. "Don't make me regret this, Doctor."

Dr. Allen nodded, but all he was thinking was that if this went wrong, he'd have to live with it as long as Norman Stewart.

+++

Sitting on the couch beside Diana, the old man finished his story. "You were the lucky one. Your sister died on the operating table. The doctor assisting me took her body down to Autopsy."

Diana shuddered at the chilling throught and slumped back, weakened. Her mind was roiling, racing forward with the possibilities, trying to fit these new pieces into what she already knew to be true. There were still so many unanswered questions.

"And no one ever told my mother what happened?" she asked incredulously.

Dr. Allen shook his head. "She never knew."

Instinctively Diana's hand went to her side.

"That's how I got my scar, isn't it?"

"That's what it's from, Diana."

"I hated that scar when I was a little girl."

"We always told your mother that the operation had been for a circulatory problem," the old man added.

Diana had sat attentively while he was telling his story, but now she started to unravel again as the present came rushing back. Her voice was harsh and sharp. "You lied to my mother, and now you tell me that my sister died on the operating table. How do I know that's true?"

"We sent the body to Autopsy," Dr. Allen repeated. "I, for one, know she was dead."

"Who pronounced her dead? Did you? Did you see her die?"

"Get hold of yourself, Diana. You're getting hysterical."

"Someone's out there with my face, my voice, and she's trying to kill me!"

Dr. Allen was starting to lose patience. "That's ridiculous, Diana. Maybe you saw someone who resembles you, but . . ."

"The girl I saw was missing a leg!" she shouted.

Dr. Allen had had enough.

"Diana," he said firmly, "I spoke to Dr. Graham today.

I know you've been under great emotional stress. Otherwise I wouldn't allow you to talk to me like this."

Diana wasn't going to be deflected by protocol. "I want you to show me my medical records," she said.

"For what purpose?" Dr. Allen was suddenly stiff and guarded.

"I want to see in writing that my sister was declared dead."

"Diana," Dr. Allen said, with the air of someone who had repeated the same thing fifty times, "You'll just have to trust me. I told you, I signed the death certificate myself."

"But were you the last one to actually see my sister?"

Dr. Allen thought for a moment. "My assistant was, I suppose. He took the corpse down to Autopsy."

"What was his name?"

"For God's sake, stop it, Diana!"

"Why won't you tell me? I want to talk to him." She was shouting again.

"Because," Dr. Allen said, choosing his words carefully, "I think this has gone much too far already and I refuse to indulge this strange obsession of yours. Finding this man's name won't make you any better."

"Doctor, I am getting sick and tired of everybody lying to me and telling me what I see and don't see and knowing what's best for me." Diana stood up. "Now, if you won't tell me who your assistant was, I'll find out for myself."

Diana turned and ran out of the room. She knew exactly where she was going and what she was doing. She had been here many times before. Dr. Allen's office formed part of his apartment, and just off the room where he saw patients was a small private study where he kept his files. Diana went straight for the study, located the file cabinet containing the S's, and had it open by the time Dr. Allen walked in behind her.

"Diana," he said sharply. "I am not going to allow you to go through my files."

"Then tell me the name of the man who last saw my sister," she told him, and went on looking.

"You won't get it from me," he said, slamming the file drawer shut so quickly that Diana had to jump back to keep her hand from being caught. He angled his body up against the cabinet.

Suddenly the last of Diana's control cracked. She scooped up the phone from the doctor's desk and hurled it against the wall.

"Can't you see," she wailed, "you're the only one who can help me! I have to find her before she finds me."

The doctor grabbed her by the arms and tried to restrain her.

"That's enough, Diana," he said, as firmly as he could.

"No, it's not," she raged. "I have to know that man's name!" Infuriated, she broke loose from his grasp, snatched up a long, thin letter-opener lying on the doctor's desk, and in a quick motion pressed it against the old man's throat.

"Now, tell me his name," she demanded. Diana would have been aghast if she could have seen at that moment how much she looked like the girl who had held her pressed against the wall earlier that night.

Dr. Allen had never been more terrified in his life, but he knew that to show it would be a mistake. He spoke with as much calm as he could muster. "I've known you all my life, Diana. I know you wouldn't deliberately hurt me."

Diana increased the pressure against his throat. "I will if you make me, damn it. Just tell me his name."

Dr. Allen saw the maniacal intensity in her eyes, and it scared him. "Brock," he said. "Dr. Raymond Brock."

"Thank you," she answered, her tone strangely subdued. "Now please move away from that cabinet."

She kept the blade at his throat until he obeyed her.

Then she opened the file drawer and started rifling through it again.

"What are you doing?" Dr. Allen asked.

"I want to see my medical file," she told him. "I guess I'm not as trusting as I used to be."

She took out her file and slammed the drawer shut. Then, as the doctor watched her, she walked out of the apartment without so much as another glance his way.

15

On the way downtown in a cab, Diana kept thinking about it. The idea was so extraordinary that she couldn't retain it in her mind for more than a few minutes at a time. She would ponder it, consider it, accept it, and then, just as if someone were forcing her to look at a particularly ugly sight, her mind would veer away and come to rest on more mundane matters: Tom, her friends, her dog, her job.

And then she would be forced to think about it again. She was a freak. Something exhibited in sideshows. Something people paid to see. A Siamese twin. The realization of what she and her sister would have looked like together gave her goose bumps, and she shuddered.

But each time she shuddered, the thought kept returning that they had both been conceived in the same act of love. They had shared a mother, a father, and the first nine months of life, as well as a bond of flesh larger and sturdier than any umbilical cord. If her parents had been still alive, would they have reached out and loved her sister like a daughter? Maybe this was what her father had wanted to tell her about before she had children of her own. What other secret could be so awful and personal that he had asked that it be hidden from her own mother? In frightened, lonely despair, Diana could not help feeling used, cheated, driven blind into this life-or-death situation which would not have happened, *could* not have happened, if only she'd known the truth.

Then in a moment of cold sobriety, she realized that this really was "life or death" survival. Not the way her friends used the term, of getting through an unpleasant day, or bouncing back from an affair gone sour. But an honest-to-God fight for physical existence.

The cab pulled up in front of her apartment, and Diana bounded out onto the street. She could not avoid thinking that she had just done something her sister was unable to do. No doubt she would be having a lot of thoughts like that in the days to come.

Standing on the curb, she spoke to the cab driver. "Could you wait for a moment? I just have to get my dog. I'll be back in a minute."

"The meter's running," the cabbie answered. "I got all day."

That wasn't good enough for Diana. "You won't leave, will you?" she asked.

"Lady, you haven't paid me yet. I'm not going anywhere."

Diana ran up the steps and into the brownstone.

She didn't look back, so she didn't notice the dirt-encrusted black van parked halfway down the block.

Laurie was just so excited that she couldn't sit still. She had gotten Joel to help her, like she knew she would, and he had gotten the van out and waited with her for two hours, and now the bitch had finally arrived and would never be able to get away again.

"It's her," Laurie said, exulting. "I'm gonna get her this time."

"I don't like this at all," Joel said, looking at the Checker cab down the block.

God damn him! If he tried to chicken out, she'd kill him. Or worse.

"You swore!" she reminded him.

"It's not the right time."

Jesus, what a whiner he was. Couldn't he see this was going to be a piece of cake? It was so easy now. "I can get in from the garden and shove a rag down her throat," Laurie announced.

"The cabbie's waiting for her, can't you see that?"

"I'll get him, too!" she moaned. Here we go again. With Joel, it was always something. The cabbie was there or it was raining out or the animals weren't fed or he had to take a dump. But not today, Joel. He had agreed to do it, and they were going to do it, even if there were fifteen cabs waiting outside.

"Just shut up," Joel told her. "You're totally self-centered."

Here comes Mr. Bad Mood, Laurie thought. Spoiling the fun like always. "Joel," she asked, "did you bring those chocolates along? I feel like eating some chocolates."

"Would you stop talking to me about what Laurie wants all the time?" Joel sighed.

"You know what I want!" she said viciously.

And nobody was going to stop her. Not him, not anybody.

Diana sat on the edge of the bed, pulling a pair of pantyhose over her foot and up her calf, straightening the nylon smoothly along her thigh. Ever since she was old enough to be conscious of physical matters in a sexual sense, people had thought she had exceptional legs. In high school, boys had sat where they could look at them. Once, her biology teacher had told Danny Doyle that if he would pay half as much attention to the lectures as he did to Diana Stewart's legs, he would probably get an A. She had been so embarrassed that it was all she could do not to jump up and run out of the classroom.

Diana's fingers slid up and down the thin scar that extended five inches down the side of her hip. Since as long as she could remember, her concern with the scar seemed to wax and wane with the summer months. The bathing-suit months. And yet even in the winter Diana rarely undressed without some peek, however quick and furtive, in its direction. She was overly self-conscious about her little defect. She knew that. It was so small and fine that Tom hadn't even noticed it for an entire month until one bright Sunday morning in bed.

But now, Diana knew that scar was proof that another living human being had once been attached to her.

Her sister.

Her twin.

Her Siamese twin.

Her co-freak.

She reached down for her shoes and saw the electric kitchen knife, still lying on the floor near the bed, its batteries having run out.

"Taffy!" she called out.

She slipped on her shoes, tossed a few more things into her bag, and snapped it shut. She was ready to leave now and she wasn't going to hang around and play games with the dog.

She called out, sharper this time, "Come on, Taffy, damn it, this is no time to fool around. Come here!"

On that, she got a response. A low growl from the living room.

She walked into the foyer and was able to identify the sound as coming from behind the large, red leather armchair. She cut a wide arc around the chair and now she could see her dog curled up into a tight little ball, shaking with fear, still emitting his wary growl.

"Come on, Taffy, the taxi's outside."

But the dog backed away from her, with a show of teeth.

Diana followed him. "Taffy. It's okay. Come on, baby. Come here right now."

But the dog refused to obey and backed deeper into

the corner until he had nowhere else to go. Crouched on its haunches, snarling softly, baring his tiny teeth, the little puppy waited, his eyes riveted on Diana's beckoning hand.

That was when Diana understood not only what was the matter with Taffy now but also what had been the matter all along. Her sister. The girl who looked like her, who had undoubtedly been alone in the apartment with her dog. Who had undoubtedly done God knows what to the animal. No wonder the dog was confused. No wonder Taffy was afraid of her.

Diana bent down slowly, opening her arms, speaking as gently as she could: "Come on, Taffy. It's me, Diana. Here. Smell my hand."

The animal's rear arched in the air and his head fell onto his front paws. Diana's hand reached out to stroke him, and with that, the crazed dog lunged with sudden, shocking force straight at her throat. Diana heard a small clicking noise and realized that the puppy's tiny teeth had imbedded themselves firmly in the flesh of her neck.

"Taffy!" she screamed. The dog was hanging from her throat. She slapped at him with an open hand, knocking him to the floor, and clutched at the toothmarks planted in her neck.

The puppy crouched on the carpet, staring back at her, dazed and muddled. Then, gathering his legs together, summoning all his strength, the animal whirled around and rushed head-on directly for the garden doors.

Diana never knew exactly what the dog wanted to do. She didn't think that animals committed suicide. Probably he just wanted to get away, wanted to get outside, and was so confused that he didn't even realize the glass doors were shut.

The little puppy hit the door at full speed, shattering the glass, while letting out a horrendous, woeful dying yelp that Diana would never be able to forget.

He hung as if in midair, half in and half out of the

room, caught in midflight, impaled, skewered on jagged shards of glass.

Diana didn't move. She couldn't. She stared in stunned silence. Her mouth hung open a little, but otherwise her face was without expression.

She knew she should have buried the animal, but she couldn't bear to do it. In fact, she couldn't bear to stay in the apartment another minute, with her blood-soaked pet stuck there, like a tiny model airplane on a desk pedestal. It was as much as she could do to walk into the bedroom, pick up her purse, and leave the apartment.

She didn't even hear the cab driver when he asked her if she hadn't forgotten the dog she had come to get. And she didn't see the dirt-encrusted black van pull out of its parking space as the taxi made its way toward First Avenue.

Diana had only one thing on her mind. She was going to the hospital where she had been born and she was going to find Dr. Raymond Brock, who had taken her sister down to Autopsy and who, God willing, held the answer to the mystery of how her sister was still alive.

In the early morning hours New York's venerable Gotham Hospital was fairly quiet. A few people slouched on benches against the walls, waiting their turn to be treated, each, in one way or another, casualties of the New York night.

A bored middle-aged nurse sat behind the reception desk, a small guarantee that no one would die alone in the waiting room.

Diana walked up and stood before her desk. "Hello, ma'am. My name is Diana Stewart. I'm trying to locate a Dr. Raymond Brock."

"I've never heard of him," the nurse said confidently, hardly bothering to look up at her inquisitor. She flipped quickly through the Rolodex on her desk and shook her head. "Nope, like I said, he doesn't work in this hospital. You can look him up in the Yellow Pages under P for Physician."

"He's not listed in the phone book, I've already checked." Diana explained. "I know he used to work in this hospital. He used to be an intern here. He helped deliver me."

The nurse was not interested in Diana's autobiography. "I'm trying to tell you, this doctor of yours doesn't work here anymore." Then she added, "They might have his record in the inactive files up on Eight."

"How do I get there?" Diana asked.

"Dearie, do you know what time it is?" the nurse said, finally looking Diana in the eye.

Diana glanced at the large wall-clock, which the nurse could see just as easily as she could. "Six forty-five."

"This whole place isn't open twenty-four hours a day, you know," the nurse snapped. "Those offices upstairs don't open till eight thirty."

Diana had come too far to be stopped by petty bureaucracy. "But it's urgent. Please, isn't there someone who can get those files for me?"

"There's no one now, dearie," the nurse said, "but you're welcome to sit here and wait until eight thirty."

Diana was trying to think of another approach when the phone on the reception desk rang. The nurse picked it up, happy to be rid of Diana even temporarily. "Main floor reception," she answered. "Just a minute, I'll have him paged."

She looked up and saw that the girl she had been talking to was gone. Impatient people, she thought. If no one had time to wait anymore, it was no problem of hers.

There were a lot of gray metal steps on the way up to the eighth floor, and Diana was exhausted by the time she had climbed all of them. She prided herself on being in excellent shape, but she had been through a lot that night both mentally and physically.

She leaned against a wall, drawing breath into her lungs. The muscles in her legs ached, and they reminded her of why she was here. Cautiously she pushed open the door that led to the eighth floor.

As soon as she stepped into the hall, she realized what was meant when they say "quiet as a morgue." For all she knew, it was a morgue.

Trying to be as silent as possible, she walked down the hall, looking at the painted signs on the glass windows of the office doors. None of them was what she wanted. Some of them didn't even make sense to her. Chemo Compounding, Urinalysis Lab, Brain Scan Testing Unit, Electromyography Research. She kept on walking.

Then she saw it: Personnel Inactive Files.

She tried the doorknob. It was locked. Of course. She didn't think that anything was going to be made easy for her ever again.

Looking up and down the corridor to make sure no one was there, she slipped off her shoe. Lifting her skirt, she wrapped it tightly around the heel, hoping that the cloth would serve to muffle the blow. With a short, sharp punch, Diana smashed the glass.

She was a criminal now. This had to qualify as Breaking and Entering, and yet she didn't hesitate for even a moment as she snaked her hand through the hole she had made. She found the knob and turned it and with a step was inside. Out there in the hall the place had only felt like a morgue. In here it looked like one. Nothing but row upon row of dust-covered, gray metal file cabinets. She had the feeling that if she opened one of the drawers, she would find that it contained a tiny corpse.

Choking back her nervousness, she set out to find the file cabinet she wanted, the one that contained the records of Dr. Raymond Brock. For a full minute she groped in her purse for a book of matches, not daring to turn on the overhead lights.

Even with the help of the matches she made a few false

starts. These people had no idea of how to organize anything. A librarian would go crazy in here. The files within the cabinets were alphabetized well enough, but whoever had arranged the cabinets seemed to have placed them entirely according to whim. C was next to F, and D and E were off in a corner by themselves. But finally she found the B's—they were next to the T's—and after blowing off some dust, she read the identification card on the drawer, BLUMENTHAL–BUDNER, which confirmed her finding.

Diana was shaking as she opened it.

Frantically she flipped through the tan file folders until she found the one labeled BROCK, R. She felt as though she had climbed Mount Everest. A moment later she had the folder out and opened it with quivering hands.

It was empty except for an official-looking document stapled to the inside, which bore the letterhead of the New York State Supreme Court and was dated November 18, 1958. Signed by an assistant district attorney, it was a subpoena for all the hospital's records pertaining to Dr. Raymond Brock.

Diana could hardly keep from crying.

Numbly she put the folder back in its proper place and closed the file drawer. All of this had been for nothing.

And then she was hit with another thought. She had suspected—no, she knew—that this Brock hadn't taken her sister to the autopsy room as he was supposed to have done. Now she had found a subpoena for Brock's records. Obviously the man was a criminal. They didn't subpoena a doctor's records for no reason at all. Who knew what horrible things such a person could be capable of?

No one saw her as she walked back down the hall and waited for the elevator. Still, she felt a surge of relief when the elevator came and she began the ride down.

On the seventh floor she noticed the elevator operator. More particularly, she noticed his hands. They were old and wrinkled, the blue veins sticking up under the skin.

It was worth a try.

"How are you today?" Diana asked, as cheery as possible.

"Fine. Just fine," the operator answered, and turned to face her.

Bingo! Just as she thought. He was an old man. His face was wrinkled, his teeth were not his own, his pants were held up by suspenders. He'd probably been working here forever. Surely since before she was born. At least since before Brock had left the hospital.

She waited until the elevator started down again and then said, "Have you been working here a long time?"

"Sure have," he told her. "If you call thirty-seven years a long time."

"You must know a lot of the doctors, then."

"'Course I know 'em." His tone made it clear that he was offended that she should think otherwise. "All the doctors know old Izzy."

Diana sucked in her breath, and delivered the big one, "Did you ever know a Dr. Raymond Brock?"

The old man thought for a moment. "Dr. Raymond Brock?" Then comprehension crossed his face. "Oh, I sure do remember Dr. Raymond Brock. He had an office on the fourth floor. Used to stink up my elevator with his cigars. Not a relation of yours, I hope," he chuckled.

"Do you ever see him around here anymore?"

"Not since 1958. I remember, 'cause I hurt my knee and had to go on nights. That happened the week before he left."

As casually as she could, Diana asked, "You wouldn't happen to know where he went then, would you?"

The old man shrugged. "Went to jail, is where he went. It was a real big case. Had all kinds of news reporters down here talking to everybody, interviewing everyone. They even talked to old Izzy, but I didn't know anything."

With that, the elevator stopped at the main floor, and the old man opened the door.

"Thank you very much," Diana said, as she left the elevator. "You've been very helpful."

But the old man was still thinking about how he had hurt his knee and had to be put on nights. "You know," he said, "in all my thirty-seven years, I've only been sick twice."

Diana gave his hand a reassuring squeeze. "You're looking good, Izzy," she said, and headed for the street.

Diana smiled to herself. She felt an excitement well up within her that, a moment ago, she would not have believed possible. Her adrenalin was pumping, and her fear was gone.

She wasn't crazy, she was right.

They had told her she was imagining things and they were wrong. Because even Dr. Allen hadn't seen the baby die. He had given it to this Brock. And this Brock was some kind of criminal. The kind who had a big trial. The kind they came to write articles about. Even that tired old elevator man remembered the doctor more than twenty years later.

This Raymond Brock obviously had quite a past—and Diana thought she knew just where to find it.

They watched Diana leave the hospital and they followed her in the van. The traffic was light, and it was easy to keep up. In the back seat Laurie could scarcely contain her excitement at the sight of her quarry walking right in front of her. Walking on those legs.

"Closer!" she hissed at Joel.

"Not yet," he said. "We'll get her at the corner of Sixth."

Laurie pounded her fists against the seat in frustration. The van pulled to within a few feet of Diana. "Where's the Mace?" Joel demanded. "I'm going to need the Mace."

Laurie looked around for the can and couldn't find it. "It's not here," she groaned. Jesus! What if they'd gone through all this, and it was working out perfectly, and then they didn't have the goddamned Mace?

"It was on the back seat, genius," Joel said.

Laurie searched frantically under the seat.

"We can't do it without the Mace," Joel threatened.

"Don't you think I know that?" Her hand scuttled around crablike under the seat for a while longer, and then her fingers touched metal. But she couldn't get a grip on it.

"I can't get it, Joel! It's under the seat."

But then she caught hold of it, spun it around, brought it out, and tossed it triumphantly onto the front seat beside Joel.

"Here it is," Laurie announced proudly.

Joel must have been as pleased as she was, because he speeded up the van, moving parallel to his prey.

"Okay," he said. "Have you got it straight?" He went through it once more for her, to make sure. "I'll stop the car five feet in front of her. I'll get out and spray the can in her face. You open the rear door, and I'll push her in. The Mace'll knock her out. You just put the blanket over her."

"Just be careful of her leg," Laurie said.

"I'll worry about the leg. You just put the blanket over her."

At that moment the light at the corner turned red, and the Dodge Omni in front of them came to an abrupt halt. Joel jerked to a stop behind it.

Laurie leaned forward, reached around Joel, and slammed her palm down on the horn.

"We're gonna lose her!" she wailed.

Joel pushed her hand away angrily.

"You do that again," he shouted, "and we're going home."

Laurie sat back abruptly and folded her hands in her lap, a caricature of the good little girl. But her eyes were moving all the time, and she was worried.

"Where is she?" Laurie whined. "I can't see her!" Why did Joel screw everything up all the time? "You lost her, Joel!"

"Get ready," Joel barked. "She's two blocks down."

Then the light turned green, and the van surged forward. They were lucky. There wasn't too much traffic at this hour of the morning, and before long they were cruising right beside her again.

Through the dirty van window Laurie watched her favorite left leg moving along near the curb. She loved it. She hated it. She wanted it for herself.

"Any second now," Joel said, and even his voice was tight with the excitement of it.

Laurie couldn't take it any more. The frustration was too much for her. To be so close to what she wanted and not make a move for it was unbearable.

"I'm gonna get her," she cried, and threw open the van door.

It bounced off a parked car and slammed shut.

Joel cursed Laurie, and his eyes shot to Diana. She hadn't noticed anything. Well, that's what you call luck.

"You're going too slow," Laurie protested.

He gave her another of his long-suffering sighs. "I knew I couldn't work with you."

And then the sexy legs screwed up everything by turning the corner and starting toward Fifth Avenue.

"Where's she going?" Laurie howled. She rolled down the window.

"Damn," Joel cursed. "We'll never get her on Fifth."

In fact, they were lucky they ever found her at all. She had gone down a one-way street where the van couldn't follow, so they had to go up a block and double back, Laurie wailing all the way because they had lost her, and Joel trying to calm her down. Joel, too, thought maybe they had lost her, until they got onto Fifth Avenue and raced back to Forty-second Street, and there she was, going up the long row of steps to the main branch of the New York Public Library.

When Laurie saw her, she nearly jumped through the window.

"Stop the car," she screamed. "Let me out."

"She's going into the library," Joel said, but that didn't make any difference to Laurie. She'd go in there and drag the girl out by the hair if she had to.

Joel started to slow down, but a policeman waved him on.

Laurie couldn't stand it any more. There she was, going into the library, and if they didn't get her now, they might never have another chance half as good as this one.

"Stop the car!" she screamed again. It was an order this time, and the threat behind it was far worse than anything the policeman could have come up with.

Joel drove the van halfway up onto the sidewalk and stopped. They scrambled out of the vehicle and bolted up the stairs, not noticing the people who were staring after them and not even hearing the dumbfounded obscenity of the policeman on Fifth.

Diana had found the newspaper room, but discovered it wasn't just a matter of walking up and asking for the newspaper you wanted. First of all you had to fill out a request slip, and then someone had to go and get the newspapers, which were not newspapers at all but rolls of microfilm. Then an attendant took you down a hall to a special room, where there was a machine that enabled you to look at the microfilm. It seemed wonderful to Diana that they were able to compress such a vast amount of information into such a tiny space. Just holding the small box of microfilm in her hand made her feel good. This was something she knew how to do. This was Research.

"Is this the entire *New York Times* for 1958?" she asked the acne-faced attendant as they walked down a gloomy corridor in the bowels of the building.

"Just the last four months," the young man answered. He walked slowly, trying to make the conversation last. "If you don't find what you're looking for, I'll get you the rest. You know how to work the machines?" he asked, hoping that she didn't.

"Yes, I've used them before, thank you."

They came to a door, which the attendant opened. He switched on a light, revealing a small, windowless room containing nothing but three microfilm-viewing machines with a chair in front of each. It was early in the day, but the room was already stuffy.

"Better try to get your work done in the morning," the attendant said. "Gets broiling in these rooms by noon."

Diana smiled. "Thanks, I'll try."

"Just bring the film to the desk after you're done," he said, smiling back at her. He knew he had to be there when she returned. He'd skip lunch, if necessary. All the good-looking chicks were up in the magazine room. Down here you could go a month without seeing one. And this girl was one terrific looker.

He left, closing the door behind him, anxious for her to finish as soon as possible.

Between Smith College and Scribner's, Diana wondered how many weeks of her life had been spent in front of a microfilm machine. Probably far more time than she had ever spent with Tom. In just a few minutes she had the film threaded and the machine working.

The front page of *The New York Times* for September 1, 1958, filled the screen. She focused the lens, then got up and turned off the overhead light, making the small print easier to read.

Alone in the dark, her face illuminated by the bluish light from the viewing screen, she began turning the handle of the spool, anxious to get the date she was looking for. Headlines passed in front of her like a blur . . . Stock Market Hits Record High . . . Tyrone Power Dies in Spain . . . U.S. Puts Four-Ton Missile into Orbit . . . Cardinal Roncalli Elected Pope . . . Pasternak Wins Nobel Prize for *Zhivago*. That was news to Diana. She had always thought *Doctor Zhivago* was terribly overrated. But in any case, it sure was becoming clear that 1958 was an eventful year for the medical profession.

Joel hadn't been inside the New York Public Library for years, not since his student days. Laurie had never been inside the library, any library, in her life. The place bewildered and frightened her. There were people all over the place, reading, not making a peep. Just like Joel was always doing. What was their problem? How did they make money? And what the fuck was the bitch doing here?

"So if you're so smart, where is she?" Laurie practically screamed at Joel.

"Shut up, goddamn it," he whispered to her. "You have to be quiet in here. If you're not, they'll kick us out."

"I'll stuff a rag down their throat."

"Would you be quiet? Please, Laur."

"Maybe," she replied.

"Look," he instructed, "you just stay right here by this desk." They were standing in the periodicals room. "Don't move, you understand? I'll find her."

Sure, Joel thought to himself, and maybe find a cure for cancer while I'm at it. This was going to be impossible. The library had eighty-eight miles of corridors, reading alcoves, book stacks, and offices.

Joel had as little idea of where to start his hunt as he had about why the girl had come here from the hospital in the first place. He scurried past the main circulation desk and entered the cavernous reading room. Weaving between the long, wooden tables, his eyes searched for the familiar face. He knew that face like he knew his own. Any small piece of it would be enough to trigger his recognition. An eye, an ear, even a chin would do.

Then it hit him. Of course she wouldn't be in the reading room, she'd be in the medical reference section! He smiled. That's why she had come to the library. That's what she was looking for. Right this minute little Miss Stewart was probably searching through the T's, hunting down the books and articles on Twins. She was looking for herself.

Joel returned to the information desk. "Could you tell me where you keep your reference material on medicine?"

The librarian had it memorized. "Medicals on 7, A103 to K532. Periodicals are on microfilm in the basement, sub-level 3, rooms 340 through 353."

Joel hurried down a long corridor. It was all so logical. He heard his keys rattling against the can of Mace in his pants pocket.

Laurie would be so proud of him.

Diana reeled the microfilm forward to November 18. She searched the paper cover to cover, but there was no mention of Brock's subpoena. She raced the film ahead past Thanksgiving and Pope John's investiture. Finally, on December 8, she found what she'd been looking for.

It was right on the front page, a picture of a man in custody, deliberately covering his face with a hat. From the left-hand corner the headline loomed out at her.

GUINEA PIG SURGEON CONVICTED
OF CRIMINAL MALPRACTICE

Dr. Raymond Brock of New York City was convicted today in State Supreme Court of six counts of criminal malpractice stemming from surgery performed on the person of Mr. Franklin Fleming, also of New York City. The surgeon faces a maximum sentence of thirty years in jail. Mr. Fleming remains today in critical condition at Mount Sinai Hospital in Manhattan. Both the defendant and his counsel, Mr. Lewis Nelson, refused comment on the court's decision. . . .

Diana sat staring at the screen, riveted by its testimony. Two new names. Two new leads. Franklin Fleming and Lewis Nelson. A patient and an attorney. They would know something about Brock. They might even know where he could be found. She was so absorbed in this information and its implications that she didn't notice the door to her windowless room open briefly, admitting a funnel of light from the corridor. A man stepped inside and silently closed the door behind him.

Quietly he moved up behind Diana, his impeccably shined shoes reflecting the light from the screen. Standing directly in back of her, he waited for a moment, considering his next move. Then his arm reached out beside her, inches away from her face.

Diana saw the hand out of the corner of her eye and reached out to grab it, stifling the scream that filled her lungs. She whirled around to face her antagonist.

A diminutive Chinese man smiled down at her and nodded profusely.

"So sorry. Just cleaning," he said, pointing to the ashtray next to her machine. "No problem now."

"Oh, my God," Diana sighed, trying to compose herself.

The Chinaman emptied two wastebaskets, offered a few more "So sorrys," and left the room.

Quickly Diana looked through the *Times* for the few days following, checking to see if there was any further mention of Brock's trial. But there wasn't. It was as if the city had convicted the man and then forgotten about him.

But she bet that Franklin Fleming hadn't forgotten. She wanted to find Fleming, to find out what Brock had done to him. To ask what had become of the Guinea Pig Surgeon.

Whatever he had done, Brock had to be out of jail by now, the way the court system was these days. Even if he'd blown up half of Manhattan Island, he'd be out by now.

Diana rewound her spool of microfilm, shut off the machine, and hurried out into the hallway. She smiled at the young man at the desk in the newspaper room, gave him back his box of film, and left so quickly that he didn't even have time to begin the speech he'd been carefully working on ever since he'd seen her.

For all that the stacks looked like in the near-windowless gloom, Joel might just as well have been in the catacombs beneath Rome. Except that he was seven floors above the streets of Manhattan and surrounded not by tombs but by tomes, thousands of them, in every language and size. Joel scurried past the shelves of books, the titles flying by like the credits to an old movie.

The medical reference section was as big as a hockey rink, but in twenty-five minutes he had covered it all. He dropped his bulk into an old wooden chair and cursed Diana repeatedly. He had been wrong. The girl wasn't here. Laurie would never forgive him.

Then Joel was up and out of the chair like a shot, sprinting madly through rows of dimly lit books. Why hadn't he remembered it before? The library had only two exits. If Diana was still in the building, he had another chance. He crashed into a medical student, sending an armful of notebooks tumbling to the floor. Joel excused himself perfunctorily, but kept on running. The girl would probably leave the library the way she had come in. If he waited at that exit, he'd have better than a fifty-fifty chance of getting her.

The library basement had lots of phones but not a single phone book. Diana had to return to the main floor for that. Opening the city phone directories, she was lucky right away. There was a Franklin Fleming in the Bronx, the only Franklin Fleming in the book. For a moment she debated calling him, but decided against it. If he was gone or moved or dead or out of town or not the right Franklin Fleming, she wouldn't have been able to stand it. He had to be the right Franklin Fleming.

She copied down the address and phone number, left the building through the Bryant Park exit in the rear of the building, and crossed Forty-first Street to get a cab going uptown.

It was only when she reached the other side of the street and was standing at the curb waiting for a taxi that she noticed a crowd on the sidewalk in front of the library. Some kind of demonstration, Diana thought, and looked closer to see what it was.

But it wasn't a demonstration. Several people, including four policemen, were gathered around a large, dirty, black van that was parked all the way up on the sidewalk, practically on the steps of the library. What kind of kook would park a van there?

She flagged down a cab and gave the driver Fleming's address. Bodily fear had left her and had been replaced by a gnawing anxiety, an obsession for piecing together the puzzle of Raymond Brock's whereabouts. You couldn't put baby-stealing past a man like Brock.

16

After Diana left his apartment, Dr. Allen had been unable to get back to sleep. He had never been so shaken in his life. To have a sweet young girl like Diana suddenly appear in his office in the middle of the night pressing a letter-opener against his throat threatened the foundations on which he had built his life.

For what seemed like hours he had lain in bed, tossing and thinking about what had happened, reconstructing in his mind the events of the last few days: the early-evening phone call from Dr. Graham, the odd visits and requests from Tom Johnson, Diana's half-mad but consistent ravings, and the bizarre circumstances of a birth that still gave him the shivers. And as he pondered all this, his thoughts kept returning to a man whom he had not seen for twenty or was it twenty-five years, a man whose face he could no longer even picture in his mind, but a man whom he clearly remembered never having liked or trusted or enjoyed working with—Dr. Raymond Brock.

Brock had been only one of a number of interns who had been assigned to him by the hospital for a three-month exposure to the work of the general practitioner. It was a matter of pride for Dr. Allen that he had steered more than one of these young doctors into the unglamorous but necessary field of general medicine. In fact, many of these now well-established G.P.s came by his office even today to thank Dr. Allen for being the inspiration in their professional lives.

But Dr. Allen recalled never having made much of an impression on Brock, who had always seemed quiet and efficient, but not in a manner that gave you confidence in him. Instead the man made you uneasy and wary. You could never tell what he was thinking. Brock had always been one of those frontiers-of-science boys, always talking about new technology, concerned only with making great medical breakthroughs, the kind of healer to whom Dr. Allen referred as being more interested in "patents than patients." The kind of doctor who did the profession a favor by going into the lab rather than the wards. Judging by the jokes that used to circulate in the doctors' lounge concerning Brock's blood-relationship to Burke and Hare, the famous English body-snatchers, Dr. Allen hadn't been alone in his assessment of Brock's obsessive personality. And all this was before the sensational trial that had rocked the medical community.

But what disturbed Dr. Allen more than anything else as he had tossed uneasily in bed was an incident now vague in his memory that had occurred shortly after Diana's birth. He had come upon Brock sitting alone in the cafeteria reading an obscure medical journal and had been rather surprised to discover that the article was about the life of Dr. Aureliano Urrutia, Sr., the Mexican exile who had moved to San Antonio and performed the first surgical separation of Siamese twins in 1922. Dr. Allen would never forget how Brock had so heatedly argued that they also deserved a place in the scholarly journals alongside Dr. Urrutia. He had explained to Brock that their operation had failed to keep both girls alive, yet the young intern had gone right on insisting that technique, not results, was the key to medical innovation. The memory of that odd conversation made Dr. Allen nervous. And over and over the same thought tumbled around in his mind—this was the man who had carried Diana's sister from the operating room.

By the time daylight began to come through his windows, all thought of sleep was gone, and Dr. Allen had decided on a course of action. He got up, shaved, dressed, made himself a cup of coffee, left a note for his receptionist-nurse to cancel all appointments and take the day off. He was at Scribner's when it opened. But Diana wasn't there.

After a rather disturbing conversation with the store manager, who told him of the upheaval Diana had caused the day before, when her fiancé had stormed in looking so upset, it became apparent that she wasn't going to be in that day at all.

At first, Dr. Allen thought of calling Tom at the bank, but the girl had obviously had a falling out with her fiancé, and besides, the young man had seemed awfully peculiar. No, this should remain in the family. It would be no use calling Diana's apartment, either. Even if she answered, it would be too easy for her to put him off over the phone. He would go over there. He would see for himself.

✦✦✦

The air in the living room where Diana sat was stale and heavy, suggestive of windows that were hardly ever opened. Twenty years ago one might have described the place as elegant, but the leather furniture had long since cracked, and the arms of the red velvet couch had worn through. A friend might still have deemed the room shabby-genteel. Anyone else would have called it just plain shabby.

Mrs. Regan, an elderly, but, as Diana had learned, spirited woman, who looked like the cook in a Rembrandt painting, came out of the kitchen, bearing a tea tray.

"I hope lemon's all right," Mrs. Regan chirped, "because I've run out of milk."

"Lemon will be fine," Diana replied, smiling politely. She wanted the amenities to be over. She had hit the jackpot on her first try. He was the right Franklin Fleming, he was alive, and he was somewhere in this house. Mrs. Regan had been looking after him for years and was more than willing to talk about the dreadful thing that had happened to her dear Mr. Fleming.

"You're some kind of newspaper person, aren't you?" Mrs. Regan asked as she sat down.

"Actually, I'm doing some research on Dr. Brock's court case," Diana said, trying to stay within the bounds of truth.

"All your research will just tell you what I said years ago," Mrs. Regan replied, obviously eager to talk to any willing listener. "That man should have gotten the electric chair for what he did. Mr. Fleming wasn't the only one, either, you know."

"How many others were there?"

"Who's to say? A lot of patients didn't want to talk—didn't want the publicity. But you can guess how many operations a surgeon must go through in five years at a hospital. Every one of them offering a potential victim."

"Victim?" Diana said.

"Victim." Mrs. Regan repeated. "And he got worse toward the end, too, you know. Telling patients there were things wrong with them that weren't, so he could experiment. Like they were guinea pigs instead of human beings."

Diana heard the sound of air wheezing through a rusty pipe. It was a cross between a low moan and a guttural croak and her eyes traveled in its direction to a darkened corner of the room she hadn't noticed before, half-expecting to see some huge, froglike creature crouching on the floor.

Instead she saw a thin old man, with skin like wrinkled parchment, sitting in a wheelchair. He was impeccably dressed in a blue suit, white shirt, and bright-red tie, with a pink carnation pinned to his lapel. He was so still and silent that for a moment Diana thought one of those life-like George Segal plaster sculptures had somehow found its way into the living room.

"Now you can see what happened to poor Mr. Fleming," Mrs. Regan piped up. "Dr. Brock damaged a nerve in his spinal column."

From the thin, blue lips of the old man Diana heard the blood-chilling wheezing come again.

Mrs. Regan smiled at her. "That's just Mr. Fleming's way of telling you he'd like to show you his scar. He understands everything we're saying. It's just that he can't express himself the way we do."

Then Mrs. Regan was out of her chair, beckoning Diana to follow. "Come on. He likes having visitors."

Hesitantly Diana got up and walked over to the figure in the wheelchair. Mrs. Regan tilted the old man's head down as if it were filled with sawdust and pointed to the back of his neck.

"See," she said, gesturing, "there it is. At the end of his scar. Dr. Brock's mark, his signature."

In the dim light Diana had to bend over close to get a good look. She saw three thin, puckered lines at the base of the old man's neck. They looked almost like a sergeant's chevrons turned on their side: ⟩⟩⟩

"Can you see it? Brock left this on all his patients," Mrs. Regan explained, "like an artist signing a painting."

"Yes, I see it," Diana said. Indeed, she couldn't stop looking at it. Not for what it was, but for what it meant: Dr. Brock was a man who took pride in his handiwork.

"It's a mathematical symbol," Mrs. Regan continued. "It means, 'greater than what went before.' That monster thought he was making improvements."

"But that doesn't make any sense!" Diana gasped.

"I told you, the man had a deranged mind. That's why I say he should have been electrocuted. Then he wouldn't be walking the streets as free as you and me."

The words echoed through Diana's mind. She didn't

know whether to be frightened or elated. "He's not in prison?" she asked. "The newspaper said he was convicted."

"The man jumped bail. He never spent a single day in jail. Not in his whole life."

"I didn't know that," Diana said. "They never got him?" The emotions she felt were causing her to come unraveled, ask foolish questions. She was afraid she'd blow her cover. Surely anyone researching the court case would have access to an important piece of information like that.

Mr. Fleming made one of his noises again, a staccato grunt of surprising intensity. Astonishingly, Mrs. Regan knew just what it meant.

"Mr. Fleming would like you to see his Christmas cards," she said, and went over to a table, where she opened a drawer and took out a stack of envelopes. "They're from Dr. Brock. He sends one every year. As if we had to be reminded."

Diana examined the stack of mail in her hand.

"There's no return address on any of these," she remarked.

For twenty-two years Mrs. Regan had been mulling over that very fact. "That's right, but they're all postmarked New York City, if you'll notice. Not that it'll do you any good. You wouldn't be the first person who tried to find that man."

Diana opened the envelopes. The cards were all identical: a jolly red Santa with a dark-haired, wide-eyed little girl sitting on his lap and a text that read, "Thinking of You." They were signed "Sincerely, Doc Brock."

Dr. Allen rang Diana's doorbell for a very long time before he decided that she wasn't going to answer. But that didn't mean she wasn't there.

Diana had not been acting in a rational manner. For all he knew, she could be in her apartment wielding a carving knife just in case he decided to knock the door down.

But he had a better idea than that. He knew there was a gate out back, leading to the garden, from where he could at least see through the glass doors. So he walked around to the back of the building and slipped in through the unlocked gate.

Dr. Allen had all he could do to keep down his breakfast. What he saw astonished and sickened him. The glass doors to the garden had been smashed to bits, as if someone had taken a baseball bat to them. Lying near the doors was what he at first thought was a small fur throw-rug. It wasn't until he stood directly over it that he recognized it for what it was—a small puppy, its fur matted with pasty, darkened blood. He had seen a lot of blood in his life, but he had to look away.

Through the shattered remains of the glass doors his eyes probed the apartment for Diana.

He refused to believe what his eyes told him, so he went inside for a closer look. Whoever had last been in these rooms had obviously operated with a single principle in mind: absolutely nothing must be allowed to remain intact.

The furniture had been torn apart, the rugs had been ripped, the paintings slashed, the appliances smashed. The floor was littered with rubble, as if a wrecking ball had swept through the room before the tenants had been notified that they had to move out.

Near the remains of what had been an expensive tape deck, the old man carefully stooped to pick up a photograph lying in the mess on the floor. It was a picture of Diana. One of her legs was missing, carefully cut off at the thigh. It was a piece of madness that baffled him. His eyes settled on Diana's porcelain ballerina collection, now in a tangled heap on the mantel. Each of the figurines had a leg missing, too.

Dr. Allen shook his head in disbelief. He found it impossible to fathom the workings of a mind that would wreak such destruction.

Could it be Diana? Had the new information about her birth so overwhelmed her with self-hate that she would foul her nest in such a dreadful manner?

His eye lit on an oriental fabric print that remained hanging on the wall, even though it had been slashed repeatedly. Through the vents cut into the silk material he could see that the plaster behind it was strangely discolored. He pulled the print to the floor.

On the wall in front of him the outline of a human body was still unmistakably clear, despite all the scraping and washing that had tried to remove it. Without his glasses Dr. Allen could barely make out the words RE-MEMBER ME scrawled above the figure.

Then he saw something between the legs of the figure. At first he thought it might be a crack in the wall, but then he noticed it was too regular a design for that. It was a marking, all right, and it had been scratched into the plaster. He had to get down on his knees to study it more closely. Then he saw what it was.

The doctor shuddered involuntarily as he traced the scratching with his fingers: three arrows, one inside the next. ⟩⟩⟩

He thought he knew that mark. He thought he knew what it meant. And what was far worse, he thought he knew who had made it.

Diana left Mr. Fleming's house as soon as she was decently able to do so. When she got back onto the street, she took several deep breaths, not just because the room had been so close and stuffy but because she felt she had left a house of the dead to reenter the world of the living.

And Mr. Fleming might as well have been dead after

what Brock had done to him. Diana decided she would rather be dead than live like that, confined to a wheelchair, as easily manipulated as a puppet.

She was alive, though, and whole, and she was going to stay that way. Notwithstanding what she had seen and her present fatigue, her determination to find Brock hadn't changed.

Diana had to go to three pay phones before she found one that worked. She felt relieved that there was indeed a Lewis Nelson, attorney-at-law, listed in the phone directory. When she tried his office, he answered the telephone.

That was her first hint that things were not as they should be with Mr. Nelson. He answered the phone himself. He didn't even have a secretary.

The second was his eagerness to talk to her. She had thought he might be reticent, unwilling to discuss the matter. She couldn't have been more wrong. In fact, he sounded as though he had nothing else to do. She had a feeling that hers was his first phone call in weeks.

His evasiveness when she offered to come to his office was also suspect. He suggested, then insisted, that they meet in a bar. More discreet, he said, but she couldn't imagine what he meant by that.

Nevertheless, by one thirty in the afternoon, Diana was sitting at a table in a crowded midtown pub, sipping a coke, because the last thing she needed was to get drunk or have her faculties at anything less than their best.

The bar was packed. It seemed to lead a double life: a business-lunch restaurant during the day, turning into a singles bar at night. Right now it appeared to be about midway through its transformation, with men at tables deeply preoccupied with facts and figures and men at the bar trying to hustle girls.

Diana knew it was Nelson the minute he came in. He

was middle-aged and overweight, his face was ruddy and sweating, and he wore a seersucker suit, white shirt, and narrow black tie that screamed "I Like Ike" all the way across the room. Just her luck to find somebody who was lost in a time warp.

She would have gone over to him, but she wouldn't have been able to make her way through the crowd. Instead she watched him work his way along the bar, bobbing up and down like a volleyball player, questioning unattached women as he went.

He elbowed past one drinker at the bar, who immediately turned nasty: "Watch it, would ya?"

"Cram it up your ass, buddy," the stocky, turnip-faced lawyer said harshly, in a voice that carried all the way across the room.

Great, Diana thought. The smooth, suave professional type.

Then Nelson saw her. Sitting alone. Minding her own business. Not looking to get picked up. Well, at least he had some kind of instinct. He made his way across the bar to her table and pointed a chubby finger in her direction. "You. You're Diana Stewart."

"Mr. Nelson?" Diana asked.

He sat down and mopped the sweat from his brow with a fraying handkerchief. "I knew it was you," Nelson chuckled. "I said to myself, 'Lewis, if you're having any kind of luck at all, the prettiest girl in this place is going to be waiting to meet you.'"

"I want to thank you," Diana said. "It's very kind of you to see me on such short notice."

The lawyer spread his beefy arms expansively in a kind of we're-all-in-this-thing-together gesture. "You're looking for Brock, I'm looking for Brock. He still owes me eight grand from 1958, and that's like twenty-five thousand of today's dollars."

He clamped a fat hand on the wrist of a passing waiter.

"Double whiskey sour," he said, "and another of whatever this little lady's having."

Nelson turned his attention back to Diana.

"So what's got you looking for that whackoff, anyway?" He hesitated for a moment, then seemed to think better of his question. "No, don't tell me. I don't want to know." Fear of being involved with Brock was palpable in his eyes.

"You were his attorney, weren't you?" Diana asked.

Nelson sighed wearily. There was a lifetime of regret in it. "For my sins, I was," he said. "Worst mistake I ever made. There I was, a young fella, just starting out. I take on Doc Brock's case, and before I know it, every certifiable maniac in the city's campin' in my outer office, waitin' for me to defend him. Try and help one coconut, and bam"—he clapped his hammy hands together—"all the others start droppin' out of the trees. I couldn't get a straight client after that to save my soul. It might of rubbed off on me, too, for all I know."

As if to emphasize his point, he made a grotesque, rubber-lipped face, and then laughed.

"Just a joke," he chortled. "Didn't mean to scare you."

Diana gave him a polite smile to let him know everything was all right. It was a necessary lie. But she was getting good at lying. All she wanted was information, and she was becoming increasingly less selective about how she got it.

"You were his lawyer, then. Do you think Brock was guilty?" Diana asked.

For the first time Nelson looked at her as though she might not be as intelligent as he was. "Come on, lady," he said, in a tone of voice that made the unspoken obvious. "Who's kidding who? This guy was like one of those car nuts, always tinkerin'. Except with him, it was people."

As casually as possible Diana popped the question she

had come there to ask. "Has anyone heard from him since the trial?"

Nelson shook his head. "Not a word. Skipped bail and disappeared, just like that." He snapped his fingers to punctuate his words.

This was the answer Diana had feared, but she was not prepared to dismiss the matter so easily. "He must have some family. A wife, a sister, someone."

She looked into Nelson's empty face. Maybe he wants money, she thought. Maybe he doesn't want to give away information for free.

"I *have* to find him," Diana said, putting a world of unspoken innuendo into the remark. If he wanted the other thing, she thought, it served her purpose to let him believe she would give it to him.

And for a moment Nelson was interested. She could see that. He was hungry in every way a man can be hungry. He could practically taste the ripe fruit that was sitting in front of him. Diana watched him consider lying to her, but whatever it was that had once made him go into the legal profession prevailed.

"Look, honey, I'm leveling with you," he said. "There's not a soul alive who can tell you where to find that man. And me, I'd be the last person on earth he'd let know where he was. I'd be honor-bound to turn him in, you see, as an officer of the court."

"I see," Diana said, hope draining from her eyes.

But then she had one last thought. They said everyone had his price. Diana wasn't positive this was true, but she was sure Lewis Nelson had his. She just hadn't found it yet. She gave it one last try. "Mr. Nelson, why did you agree to see me, if you didn't have anything to tell me?"

He smiled again, that same self-satisfied grin he thought was so ingratiating. "It isn't every day in the week that a pretty girl offers to buy me a drink."

Then his face got serious, even concerned, and he leaned forward with sudden intensity. "You are buying, aren't you?"

Well, Diana thought sadly, at least I know his price. A free drink.

She got rid of Nelson as quickly as she could. For his part, he would have kept her there all afternoon, drinking her liquor and practicing his smile. But she pleaded an urgent appointment and ended the meeting.

It was only after Diana left the bar that the full force of the situation hit her. She had exhausted her leads. She had nowhere else to go.

In quiet desperation she walked around midtown, not looking in the store windows, not even fully conscious of where she was heading.

But something in her had chosen a destination, because before too long she found herself walking through the Columbus Circle entrance to Central Park. The park made her feel better. She had always considered it one of the seven wonders of the Western world. The Colossus of Rhodes had nothing on Central Park. Here in New York City, where real estate was possibly at a higher premium than anywhere else in the world, they had still managed to keep this great expanse of land free, well tended, and, in the daytime at least, reasonably safe.

Most of all she enjoyed the animals. Not the ones in the Zoo, although they were nice enough, but what she really liked seeing was all the dogs set free to play.

That made her think of Taffy again, which she didn't want to do. What had her sister done to the poor little animal?

For that matter, what had her sister done to her? Not for the first time Diana thought about what had happened in Dr. Allen's office. Yes, the old man might have failed her last night, but from the moment she was born—from before she was born, actually—he had shown her nothing but kindness, generosity, and concern. And how had she repaid him? By sticking a letter-opener against his throat and frightening the poor old man half to death. She was lucky he hadn't gotten another heart attack. And beyond that, there was something she hardly dared to let herself think about. What if he hadn't gotten out of her way? How far would she have gone?

She flashed back to that moment, to the obsession she had felt about the contents of the file cabinet, to the excitement that had welled up within her when she had touched the thin blade to the old man's fleshy throat. Diana was sure she would have cut him. Perhaps she was more like her sister than she dared to admit.

A group of dogs playing together, exulting in their momentary freedom, caught her attention, and she sat down on a grassy knoll to watch them.

Two of the dogs, a cute little cocker and a small dachshund, saw her and came bounding up the hill, mouths open and tails wagging, to see who she was.

Diana wished that people could be half as perceptive as dogs. Dogs knew right away that she was okay, that she didn't mean any harm. Dogs! Supposedly dumb animals. So why did people, intelligent people who had known her for years, accuse her of the vilest things imaginable?

She picked up a stick lying on the grass beside her and tossed it down the hill. The dachshund went scuttling happily off after it. He picked it up in his teeth and proudly brought it over to her. "You're a well-trained little rascal, aren't you?" Diana said halfheartedly.

The dog rubbed his head against her leg and nestled his nose in her lap. Diana patted his side. She took the stick from his mouth, and tossed it down the hill again.

Again the dog scampered after it and again he brought it back. But this time he wouldn't drop it. Diana pulled at the stick, and with a gleam in his eye the dachshund growled playfully and pulled back. This tug-of-war was obviously going to last a while. The animal leaned down on his haunches and dug his paws into the grass.

Then Diana noticed something near the center of the dog's back. A hairless, oval-shaped pink patch. Poor baby. Had he been injured recently? She smoothed the dog's hair aside to get a closer look.

And gasped.

Midway down the dachshund's spine, exactly as they had appeared on the base of Mr. Fleming's puppetlike neck, were three arrows one within the other: ⟩⟩⟩

Dr. Brock: his mark!

Diana reached for the dachshund's dog tag. Brock's dog would carry Brock's address.

"Spike!" somebody shouted, the voice barely noticeable above the sounds of the park.

And then the dachshund wasn't beneath her hand anymore. The animal whirled and scampered off happily in the direction of the call. Far in the distance, perhaps four hundred yards away, a bearded man with a baseball cap pulled down over his eyes started off in the direction of the park's Fifth Avenue exit.

"Brock," Diana thought.

Instantly she was on her feet in pursuit of the dog and his master. She had been awake all night, and her legs felt as though someone had strapped bricks to them. For a moment she was able to keep pace, and the sixty yards separating her and the animal narrowed. The dog beelined across the grassy field, virtually disappearing in a tangle of children and strollers out for a good time. Her lungs heaved for air, her breathing became labored and painful, and Diana began to lose ground. She called after the man, but her cries were lost in the din of the afternoon's activity. She cursed her body forward through the blistering heat. To have such a godsend dropped into her lap and then to have it whisked away again was something she simply would not allow to happen. Sidestepping a small child, Diana barreled over his mother, sending the woman sprawling onto a dirt walkway. Just ninety yards away, Diana could see the bearded man at the Fifth Avenue exit.

Barking wildly, the dachshund reached his master and leaped up, eager to see him. The man scooped the animal into his arms, dropped it into a small wicker carrier, and waited for an approaching bus.

Please, God, Diana thought, running on feet that were starting to send shafts of pain through her shins, let me get there before that bus does.

But she didn't. The bus stopped, and the doors opened. Pouring on what little speed she could, Diana made a last, desperate effort to catch the vehicle. The bearded man climbed up the steps, and the doors closed behind him, leaving Diana a mere ten yards away.

The bus pulled out from the curb, but Diana's feet kept going. Fifth Avenue traffic got fiercely congested. Maybe she could still catch it.

At Seventy-first Street the bus stopped at a red light. Diana weaved her way through the last cars and trucks and pounded frantically on the door.

"Let me in!" she yelled. "Please!"

She hoped she had enough strength left to be heard.

Mercifully, the driver noticed her and opened the doors. She climbed aboard just as the light changed again, and the bus moved forward.

"Thank you," Diana panted to the driver, who returned a weary nod.

She rummaged through her purse and pulled out a dollar bill. "Can you change a dollar?" she asked, still wheezing for breath. The driver pointed to a sign on the side of the chrome fare box. "I'm not allowed to make change."

"That's all I've got."

"I'm sorry, lady. I'm not allowed."

Diana glanced toward the rear of the bus, where the bearded man was sitting with the dog in his lap. She was going to talk to that man. She had had enough bureaucracy to last her the rest of her life.

"Here," she said, stuffing the dollar bill into the coin box. "This is all I have. Keep the change." And she walked toward the rear of the bus before the driver could say anything.

Sitting herself down next to the bearded man, the dog's pink scar loomed out at her only inches away. It was Brock's sign, all right.

The dachshund's owner took off his baseball cap and ran a hand through his hair. Diana was taken aback. She had expected a middle-aged doctor of around fifty. This man couldn't be over thirty, thirty-five at the very most.

She broke the ice with the only thing that came to mind. "Cute little dog. How old is he?"

The young man looked at her, deciding whether or not he wanted to answer. He liked what he saw and he flashed her a grin.

"Two and a half," he said, then paused for a moment before adding, "Spike would like to know how old you are."

Diana returned the smile with one of her own. "Tell Spike I'm too old for him."

"That's okay, he likes older women."

This was not the direction Diana wanted the conversation to take. The bus stopped to let some people off. It was time to get down to business. "Looks like he had a little operation," Diana said, pointing at the dog's scar.

The young man nodded proudly. "Picked a fight with a German Shepherd and needed a little patching up. Didn't even realize he was outweighed. Spike's small, but he's feisty." His implication was obvious: just like me.

Diana decided she'd better deflect that one, too. "Sounds like my little dog," she said, convincing herself she was invoking Taffy's name in a good cause. "I'm new in the city and I was wondering if you could tell me the name of your vet."

The young man saw another opening. "You're new in town, huh? Where are you from?"

"Chicago," Diana lied, hoping she hadn't picked his hometown.

"Oh, yeah? You just get in?"

Jesus, Diana thought. This guy must have gotten his training at fraternity dances. "I got in last week and I really need the name of a good vet," she repeated.

But the young man was equally persistent. "You like New York? What part of the city are you living in?"

"Upper East Side. Is that where your vet is?"

"I don't know any vet up there," the young man answered.

"Well, where is your vet?" Diana said flatly, trying not to let her exasperation show. "Who operated on Spike?"

"A doctor down in the East Village, on Bartholomew Street."

Diana pressed her advantage. "Who? What's his name?"

"Dr. Gavin," the young man said.

Diana was thrown off base, but only for an instant. Of course, it made sense. Brock wouldn't be using his own name. She asked for the spelling to make sure: "G-A-V-I-N?"

"I'm not sure. I-N or E-N. One of those."

"And he operated on Spike?"

The young man sighed. He was getting tired of this.

"Yeah," he replied. "Did a good job, too."

Diana's heart practically leaped into her mouth. She had found her man.

and by the nails for. He had hoped to clear the
from her garbled, cut-off call. Now it
she had left an emergency. Did he have a...

...you have to keep calling the place...

17

The answering-service girls were having a rough time
of it. Working here was like working in a fire station.
Sometimes they could just sit there, gossiping or doing
their fingernails, but other times it seemed that everyone
in Manhattan was dialing their clients.

It was like that now. The switchboard was flashing
like a slot machine that had suddenly decided to pay off
once and for all. There were four operators on duty:
Lucille, a black woman, whose huge frame and bulbous
breasts seemed to be held together by a skintight pink
blouse; Noreen, a Haitian girl with a thick French
accent and a fishnet to flatten her hair; and two Marias
from Puerto Rico. The women were jacking in and
out of lines as fast as they could, trying to keep the
messages decently straight.

"Hello, Dr. Steven's office. Will you hold, please?"
one of the Marias asked, trying to answer two calls at
once.

The pandemonium was taking its toll on Noreen, and
her accent was getting thicker. "I'm sorry. Dis is just
an ansoring serveece. I don't know where Monsieur
Butler can be reached." She disconnected the caller.
"Asshole," she mumbled into the dead line.

"Dr. Steven's office," Lucille snapped, and then caught
herself in error. "Lordy, I'm sorry, Miller Associates."

One of the Marias plugged into another line. "Dr.
Allen's residence. I'm sorry, this is his answering service."

Damn, Diana thought. She needed Dr. Allen right now,

and he wasn't there. She had rushed to the nearest phone booth after getting off the bus. "I have to speak to him," she said. "It's an emergency. Did he leave a number where he can be reached?"

"Have you tried his office?" asked the voice on the line.

"I tried. No one's there."

"In an emergency," said the woman, beginning to flip through her notebook, "you can contact Dr. . . ."—there was a pause, and Diana shifted nervously in the phone booth—"Dr. Kopelman at 246-7700."

"No. I have to talk to Dr. Allen himself as soon as possible. I'm going to leave a message. Okay? Will you make sure he gets it?"

"Just a moment, please," said the voice, and put Diana on hold before she could get another word in.

Diana inserted another dime and stood waiting. Finally the woman came back on the line. "Dr. Allen's residence."

"I just spoke to you a second ago," Diana protested.

"What's the message, please?"

"Tell Dr. Allen that Diana Stewart called and—"

The voice interrupted her. "Does he have your number?"

"Yes, he does, but I'm not home. Just tell him I've located Dr. Brock. He's living on Bartholomew Street and has changed his name to Gavin."

The voice was considerably behind Diana in absorbing all this information. "B-R-O-C-K?" it asked.

"That's right," Diana said, "on Bartholomew Street. I'm going there now. Tell Dr. Allen to meet me there and tell him it's important."

Diana waited to be asked how to spell Gavin, but instead the voice said, "I'll tell him," and hung up on her.

Diana stood in the phone both, hoping that her decision to tell Dr. Allen was the right one. Certainly she couldn't just go down there alone without anyone knowing. She had to trust somebody, and she was running out of candidates.

Bartholomew Street didn't exactly bolster Diana's confidence. Even the cab driver looked oddly at her when she told him where she wanted to go and he repeated the street name to make sure he had heard right.

Bartholomew Street was what the whites who had left the inner cities thought all urban America would look like in a very few years. It was a row of rundown, dilapidated two-family dwellings, which had, no doubt, been a very pleasant middle-class neighborhood twenty years before. Now broken and boarded-up windows dotted the buildings like bandages on a wounded man. Trash, apparently not picked up for weeks, overflowed its containers and spilled onto the street. There were no children; there was no noise. Dogs and cats roamed the street, but not the kind of dogs and cats Diana wanted to take home or cuddle. They were lean, bony, and half-wild; they looked like the sole survivors of a holocaust.

Slowly the taxi cruised the deserted street as Diana searched the doorways and windows for some evidence of a Dr. Gavin. Surely a veterinarian's office would have some sort of sign or shingle visible from the curb. But five blocks later the cab had covered the street from one end to the other, and Diana wasn't so convinced. Instructing the driver to slow to a mere crawl, she sent the car back up the same five blocks, getting out from time to time for a closer inspection of the mailboxes and makeshift nameplates. Finally she spotted the painted wood plaque she was looking for and pointed it out to the driver. Reluctantly he pulled over to the curb.

"You sure you want to get out here, lady?" he asked.

"Yes, thank you," Diana replied, and paid him.

As she got out of the cab, the driver tried again. "I'm willing to wait."

"No, it's okay. I'll be fine."

Still, her palms were sweating when the cab pulled away and left her alone on the deserted street. The cab-driver had seemed genuinely concerned for her well-being. A stranger. It gave her confidence for what she had to do.

She walked up the steps to the door of the two-story brick house. A small wooden sign by the bell read, "J. Gavin, Veterinarian." She half-expected to see his trade-mark etched there as well.

It took every bit of her courage to ring the doorbell. She waited a long time, but there was no answer. Some-where inside her, she was relieved. At least she had tried. She had done her best, and there was nobody in the house. She would just have to come back, that's all. Maybe with Dr. Allen, when there was more day-light.

Diana turned and was starting down the steps when she heard the unmistakable sound of a door being opened, behind her.

She only thought it took all her courage to ring the doorbell. It took even more to turn around. But she did. And saw a short, chunky man, with wavy black hair starting to go gray, puffy cheeks, a sallow complexion that hinted of inner turmoil, and the most piercing dark eyes she had ever seen. His clothes told her that his lack of concern for what anyone thought of him was ex-ceeded only by the contempt he felt for himself. He stared at her with an intensity that unnerved her.

Diana knew she was looking at Raymond Brock.

"Are you Dr. Gavin?" she asked.

"That's right, Joel Gavin," the man said. He spoke in a low, uninflected voice. It wasn't that he mumbled; rather, he seemed out of practice talking to people.

"I'm Diana Stewart."

She looked for a reaction—a flicker of interest, if nothing else—but got only a continuation of the blank stare. She had a feeling that if she just stood there, not saying a word, Raymond Brock or Joel Gavin or whatever he wanted to call himself would just stand there and continue to stare at her until she finally went away.

"I thought you might recognize the name," Diana said finally, matching Joel's gaze.

"No," he said, in that same uninflected voice, "but please come in. Perhaps you can tell me why I should."

For a fleeting moment she struggled with an urge to bolt for the street. She had to remind herself that she was not dealing with some omnipotent, evil power but rather with a seedy, middle-aged man who was inviting her into his equally seedy home. He looked in very bad shape. She thought she might even be strong enough to deal with him physically, if it came to that.

Except for his eyes.

Which caused her one more moment of alarm that she might be doing the wrongest thing possible. Then the door closed behind her. The musty smell of the foyer was nearly enough to make her gag. The smell wasn't foul, merely old and closeted. Old enough to be dead.

The man gestured toward a door as grandly as if princely riches lay behind it. The wide, authoritative sweep of his arm was strangely at odds with everything else about him. Perhaps it was merely a matter of his being inside again, on his own turf.

"In here, please." His voice was firm.

Diana followed the direction of his gesture and found herself not inside a princely palace but inside the dim, dirty office of a self-appointed veterinarian. Stacks of old medical books littered the floor. A well-worn couch was piled high with manila folders chock-full of what seemed like hundreds of pages of handwritten notes. Obviously the man was not overburdened with visitors; the dust was undisturbed.

Then she saw the cages, an entire wall of them, filled

with dirty, sloppily bandaged creatures that seemed to hobble and slink far more than any illness or captivity would account for. Diana had to look away.

The former Dr. Brock took a seat behind his cluttered desk. Diana noticed the fishbowl sitting on top of it. There were three goldfish swimming around inside. Even the water seemed dusty.

Joel gestured grandly again, this time at a ratty armchair that faced his desk. "Please sit down."

Diana did, and felt the springs give way beneath her.

Joel simply sat there, studying her, waiting for her to say whatever it was she had come to say.

Diana plunged right into it. "The last time you saw me, Doctor, was twenty-six years ago. You were the assisting physician at my birth. It was a Siamese birth. I thought you might remember."

Only now did Joel's eyes show interest. "January 26, 1955," he said. "The only conjoined twins ever born at Gotham Hospital."

"Then you do remember." There was hope in her voice.

"Of course I remember," Joel said icily. "Twins you see a lot of. But Siamese a doctor's lucky to get once in a lifetime. You see, they occur but once in every hundred thousand births. Did you know that?"

"No," Diana answered. "Apparently it's not something people like to talk about." She hesitated, then continued. "Which I suppose is one of the reasons I'm here. I was told by Dr. Walter Allen that you were the person who took my sister's body to Autopsy."

"So what?" Joel replied, picking up a container of fish food and sprinkling some of the contents into the bowl. "Does Wally know you're here?"

"No, he doesn't," Diana said quickly. "I only came here because I thought you'd be able to tell me what happened to my sister after the operation."

The doctor tapped the fishbowl, making the goldfish

dart in all directions. "Diana Lynn Stewart . . . How did you ever find old Doc Brock?"

Diana's throat tightened. This man couldn't have remembered her middle name after all these years. "No one else knows you're here," she assured him, wondering if he could sense the lie. "I haven't told anyone."

"Not even young Johnson?"

And how did he know that? "Look," Diana declared, stumbling over the words, "I just want to know where my sister is. I don't care about who you are or what you did."

Joel searched her eyes, trying to read them. "That's good," he said, " 'cause I don't, either."

"Please, Doctor, I need your help. I know my sister didn't die."

"Is that an accusation?"

This obviously wasn't getting her anywhere. Their eyes locked, and she went for broke. "You kept her alive, didn't you?" Diana said, with quiet conviction.

He appeared almost wistful. "They could have saved her, but they didn't. Don't you believe an old doctor? She's dead."

Diana took a deep, shaky breath. "Then where is the autopsy report? Where is her death certificate? Where is she buried?"

"How should I remember? That was more than twenty-five years ago!"

Diana's frustration spilled out of her mouth.

"You're lying to me! She's alive, and you know it."

Joel pounded his desk in rage. Veins popped out on his forehead. "Look, Miss Know-it-all, we're not up there on East Eighty-second Street! I don't have to listen to your crap down here! Not in my home I don't. Down here I piss on little know-it-alls like you."

The man was losing control, and for the first time Diana understood what he was capable of. Her face drained of color.

Joel sensed his advantage. "You're sure you didn't tell anyone you were coming here?"

"Nobody. Nobody at a—"

The instant she said it, she knew it was a mistake. A terrible mistake.

Joel was already on his feet, moving out from behind his desk. As Diana started to rise, he pushed her back down into the chair. "All right, you wise-ass bitch, just wait here. I'll get your sister's goddamned death certificate."

And before Diana had time to react, he was out of the office, closing the door behind him.

Quickly Diana ticked off her alternatives. She could make a dash for the street and risk infuriating Brock further. Or maybe it was better just to wait him out, humor him, go along with his story, and leave quietly— if he would let her. She wondered what the hell he could be doing out there. She knew damned well he hadn't gone to get a death certificate.

Her eyes darted around the room, jumping from the paper-strewn desk to the cluttered couch and finally coming to rest on the bookshelf. An old, yellowed copy of *Gray's Anatomy* was there, as were several other tattered medical reference books: *Six Problems in Simian Endocrinology; Procédure Chirurgical à l'Hôpital de Paris, 1857; Aspects of Tissue Implantation in the Post-Natal Infant; Experiments in Surgical Procedure—a thesis by Hans Ulrich, University of Hamburg, 1942.*

Diana didn't want to see any more titles like the last one. Her eyes veered away to the animal cages.

A sickly rabbit munched on some wilted lettuce. A gerbil scratched his nose. A cat with matted fur stared out at her. She wondered what kind of people could possibly bring their sick pets to a man like Brock in a place like this.

Her eyes wandered back to the gerbil. He appeared to be the healthiest of the bunch. Something tubular and bonelike protruded from under the animal's belly. He scratched at the thing as if trying to play with it.

Diana moved in for a closer look. It wasn't a bone. And it wasn't a toy. It was a small white porcelain ballerina's leg. Broken off at the thigh.

Diana had to call on every last bit of self-control to keep from screaming.

Her eyes darted to the cat again. On the floor of the cat's cage near its water bowl lay a broken flesh-colored ballerina's leg.

And in the cage next to the cat's, a pigeon with a bandaged wing. Standing on a broken blue china leg. She could have reached out and touched it.

For an instant the implications were too much for Diana to grasp, and then the full meaning of the broken legs burst in on her.

She knew who had broken those legs.

And now Diana knew what she had to do. She was going to get the hell out of that house while she still could. But panic rose from the pit of her stomach, almost paralyzing her, and she moaned softly, trying to keep it down.

She tightened her muscles, drew in her breath, and moved quietly across the room. If she could get into the hallway, she could find her way to the street.

She clutched the doorknob and turned it. It moved a quarter of an inch and stopped. She turned it again as hard as she could. It still wouldn't give. Tears welled up in her eyes, blurring her vision.

She rushed to the window and threw back the curtains. Heavy steel security bars criss-crossed the glass, which was so dirty that she could barely see through it. Diana wondered if there were bars on the windows of every room in the place or if Brock had brought her in here specifically because of them.

Outside in the hallway, the squawking, screeching

cacophony of animal sounds that Diana had been hearing since she entered the building began to get louder. It sounded as though something was agitating the animals, maybe even hurting them.

Her eyes searched the room, desperately looking for some kind of weapon. Anything to stagger him with when he opened the door. A small pair of scissors lay on the desk; they looked too small and blunt for what she had to do. On the bookshelf behind the desk was a delicate glass paperweight. She grabbed it and rolled it around in her palm. No way. Even if she got close enough to bring it down on his head, it seemed too flimsy to do any harm. Her eyes flew over the books, the hundreds of books that filled the office. For a long moment she toyed with the idea of finding the heaviest one she could and hammering it into his face.

That's when she noticed the ammonia bottle standing on the windowsill. Diana knew it would be her best shot. At least it gave her the element of surprise.

She grabbed the goldfish bowl off the desk, clamped her hand over the top, and using her fingers to keep the fish in, drained the water onto the floor behind the couch. She unscrewed the cap of the ammonia bottle and poured the contents into the bowl. The fish wriggled frantically to the surface.

Quickly she placed the fishbowl back on the desk. Before she could even sit down, the door to the office flew open in a burst.

Joel stood there calmly, smiling at her.

✦✦✦

Dr. Allen leaned the full weight of his body against a cold metal cabinet in Gotham Hospital's Inactive File Room. His mind erupted with unanswered questions. Why had Diana's apartment been ravaged? Had his deranged colleague found her at home? Had Diana put up a fight? If she was harmed, he'd never forgive himself. It was his fault, plain and simple. Had Diana ever lied to him even once in her life? Then why hadn't he believed her? He found the answer within himself. He had changed. He had allowed the city to corrupt him, to make him suspicious and cynical. He had become as callous and bankrupt as Manhattan itself. His thoughts kept returning to the Hippocratic Oath, and in a painful moment of self-recrimination he realized that he had forsaken it years ago in the pursuit of moneyed patients and an apartment with a view. Now Dr. Allen prayed that he would not be too late.

After stopping at Diana's home, he had returned again to the bookstore, then hurried to the hospital. From the nurse at the main reception desk he had learned that a girl answering to Diana's description had been there early that morning.

The broken door on the eighth floor left no doubt. Brock's empty file left no clues. But had Diana come to the same dead end? She could be anywhere now. She could need help. Maybe she was even trying to reach him.

It was a possibility. It was enough of a possibility for him to go to a phone booth and dial his answering service.

The phone rang five times before it was picked up. "Dr. Allen's residence."

"Hello, this is Dr. Allen. Have there been any messages for me?"

"We've got a whole stack of messages for you today, Doctor."

"Just tell me if a Diana Stewart called."

There was a long pause as the operator flipped through the message slips. "Yes, indeedy, I have it right here, Diana Stewart. She left a message for you that she has located Dr. Brock and that you should meet her at his office. I think, on . . . it looks like Bartholomew Street.

240

And she says it's important," the operator added, in a tone of voice that implied she knew better.

"Is that all she said?" His frail heart pounded harder against the walls of his chest. "Isn't there a street number?"

"That's all she's got written down here."

"Who took that message?"

"Maria Sanchez did, but she's left already. She'll be back tomorrow. Should I have her call you then?"

"No, that's all right, thank you." Dr. Allen hung up.

He realized that he was sweating and took out a handkerchief and wiped his brow. He was an old man and not cut out for this sort of thing.

He patted his pockets nervously. He had remembered to bring it, hadn't he? He ran his hands up his seersucker sport jacket. There it was, small and hard and secure. His hand reached into his trouser pocket and dug out an ammunition clip. Then, looking to see that no one was watching, he turned toward the wall and from his inside breast pocket pulled out a small handgun. It had been kept in a drawer for twenty years—when you're a doctor in Manhattan, you never know. The gun had not been fired since those two rounds of practice shots such a long time ago. He was shaking as he snapped in the clip. What if he actually had to use this thing? But he decided he would rather walk unarmed into a lion's cage than go see Brock unprotected.

Out on Sixth Avenue he tried to get a cab. One came to a stop on the other side of the street, and he rushed across to get it to an accompaniment of rude shouts and honking horns. A young Wall Street type beat him to it—some upstart banker, who obviously had no respect for seniority. Dr. Allen stood on the curb, feeling like a failure. How could he help Diana when he couldn't even get a cab?

A sudden, sharp stab of pain cut across his chest. The sweat popped out on his forehead again. His heart.

It did that to him every so often. Maybe it was anxiety, but he couldn't be sure. It might be the angina acting up again. This was no time to go keeling over in the street.

The pain stabbed at his chest once more, hard enough to make him want to sink to his knees. He reached into his pocket and took out the little vial of nitroglycerin pills that he was never without. He dropped one in his mouth and swallowed hard. His throat was so dry that he could hardly get it down, but then he felt better.

He looked down the street again. The light changed, and the traffic surged forward. There wasn't an empty cab in sight.

Joel presented Diana with a document the likes of which she had never seen before: an official death certificate of the State of New York. The man who called himself Dr. Gavin lounged in his desk chair, watching her carefully.

The name and date on the certificate were clear and unmistakable: Laurian Stewart. January 26, 1955.

"Are you convinced?" Joel's lips barely moved.

"I believe you." Diana wasn't convinced and she didn't sound it either.

"Are you sure it's right, Diana?"

She looked up at him. He seemed to be almost laughing at her.

"Well, it's got the signature and stamp."

"I could have faked that," he shrugged, an awful grin spreading across his pasty face.

"I think I'd like to leave now," she said, as firmly as she could.

His hand reached for the fish powder. "So soon?"

She knew for certain now that he was toying with her. Her stomach knotted, and she could feel her breath coming shallow. She let her eyes flick over to the goldfish bowl. The fish were dead, floating belly-up on the surface of the clear liquid. They couldn't have been more than a foot away from him.

"You can't keep me here, you know," Diana stammered.

Joel leaned toward her. "Am I keeping you here, Diana?"

He had her flapping around uselessly like a butterfly in a jar. He was really enjoying himself now.

Then she saw his nostrils flare. Sharply he sniffed the air. The ammonia smell climbed deep into his sinuses.

"I swear I won't tell anyone that you live here." She was begging now, but it was too late.

His eyes lit on the dead fish, and in a second Diana was up and on her feet. Quick as an adder, Joel's hand snapped across the desk and grabbed her wrist.

That was what the ammonia was for.

With her free hand Diana seized the goldfish bowl and hurled the liquid in his face.

A painful shriek filled his mouth, and his chair shot back, hitting the wall. Letting go of her arm, he clawed at his eyes, blinded and tortured by the dreadful chemical.

Diana made a dash for the door. This time, the knob turned for her. She opened it . . .

. . . and screamed.

There in the doorway, eyes alight, mouth agape, teeth bared, and panting like a crazed beast, was the girl who looked so much like her. Laurie's arms were raised high over her head, her hands clutching a metal animal cage with its bottom removed.

Diana tried sidestepping the oncoming attack, but the cage slammed down over her head as Laurie's dreadful cry screeched off the walls. "THE CUNT IS MINE! CUT THE TRUNKUS!"

The force of the blow sent Diana tumbling backward

into the office. She seized hold of a long metal floor lamp and thrust it out viciously, keeping the mad girl at bay.

Freeing her head of the metal cage and swinging the lamp like a baseball bat, Diana tried maneuvering her sister away from the door. Laurie held her ground obstinately, using her arms to parry the blows. Then Diana realized where her sister would be most vulnerable. With one quick step she lunged forward, planting the metal lamp-pole squarely into the prosthetic leg. With an awful crack the plastic split, and the artificial limb snapped cleanly at midcalf, severing the cables and pressure pumps that gave it life.

For a second Laurie hung in the air, then her body crashed to the floor, sending a rush of breath hissing through her teeth.

Diana bolted for the open door. Laurie rolled onto her side and gripped her hands tightly around her sister's ankle. Laurie's fingers were like ice clamps. Diana kicked at them frantically, smashing her heel across the girl's knuckles. Unable to free herself, she began dragging her frenzied sister across the floor.

Then what felt like a ton of flesh landed on her back, and immediately afterward the flimsy glass paperweight slammed into her skull. The ton of flesh was Joel, and Diana was unconscious even before his weight bore her to the floor.

Dr. Allen hadn't taken the subway in years, but after losing three more cabs to the younger and more aggressive, he decided that the subway was the only way he was ever going to make it to Bartholomew Street. When he finally found a station at Lexington and Fifty-first Street, he learned that the subway, like so many other things in this world, had changed completely. It now cost almost four times as much, and the simple A, B, and D letters he remembered had apparently been gone so long that the attendant at the token booth didn't even know what they were. Twice Dr. Allen had to change trains to get downtown. At Bleecker Street he managed to get a seat next to the window. As the subway passed through station after station, the spraypainted scrawl of New York's graffiti galleries flickered to life in the headlights of the train. Dr. Allen read words that in his day would not have been spoken among the closest of friends, let alone written in public places.

Finally, gasping for breath and clutching an aching side, he emerged into the hot night air of a neighborhood whose condition and smell sickened him. The pain slashed across his chest again. He had no breath. His eyes blurred. He collapsed, sweaty and shaking, against the side of a decrepit building. He had thought the ache in his side was from climbing the subway stairs, but it was obviously not.

This had never happened to him before, to feel the pain again after taking a pill. He felt exhausted, inadequate. He wondered if he would die right here on this dismal street.

He couldn't. He had to find Diana. He took another nitroglycerin pill and waited till the shaking stopped. It took a long time.

Diana snapped her eyes open to the shrill squeak of the operating table as it rolled unsteadily down the rutted corridor. Her very first thought was that she had been taken to a hospital. A crisp white surgical smock draped her nude body, and out of the corner of her eye she could see that whoever was pushing the table to wherever it was going was similarly smocked in starched hospital whites.

Diana stared upward at the fluorescent lights, trying to blink away her clouded vision. She was lying flat on her back, but the ceiling was so low that she could prac-

245

tically reach up and touch it. Hospital ceilings weren't supposed to be built that way, nor were they supposed to be peeling like this one.

Something was terribly wrong.

You didn't hear frenzied screaming like this in proper hospitals, either. Twisting her head from side to side, Diana saw row after row of wire-mesh cages piled high along the walls, one atop another. But the cages didn't hold any ordinary animals. Instead they were filled with creatures from the pages of old art books, animals that might have been created by the fevered imagination of Hieronymous Bosch. The beasts in here, too, were born of a thousand unholy nightmares: a small piglet feebly standing on the legs of a cat, a creature with the head of a dachshund and the body of a monkey connected by a neck swathed in blood-soaked bandages, a duck frantically trying to lift its head off the cage floor and onto its rabbitlike torso.

Diana tried to scream as loud as she could. All that came out was a muffled whimper.

She twisted and turned on the moving table, her neck straining, her eyes bulging in horror. It wasn't any use. With devilish thoroughness they had strapped her down at the ankles and wrists, and her arms had been roped to her sides.

And then she remembered exactly where she was and tried to scream again. The gag choked back what little sound she made.

At the end of the corridor the moving table banged through two white swinging doors and rolled quickly into what Diana could tell, with one quick glance that shriveled her soul, was an operating room.

Dr. Allen was limping badly by the time he reached the corner of Bartholomew Street. In the darkness under the shattered street lights it was impossible to tell how far down the street stretched or how many buildings could be concealing Diana. Her message hadn't left a house number, and there was no Dr. Brock listed anywhere in Manhattan.

He would just have to start from the beginning; it was the only way. He would hit every house ten times, if that's what it took. The first dilapidated brownstone was only a few yards away, and he staggered weakly up the steps and knocked on the door. In a moment a fat woman in a T-shirt appeared in the doorway. Dr. Allen struggled to describe the man he was looking for. He tried to imagine how that tormented face would have decayed over the last twenty-two years. Had the teeth finally yellowed from all those cigars? Had that unruly mop of jet-black hair bothered to turn gray or had it simply fallen out? And how had Brock wrinkled? Where were the small crevices dug by a lifetime of defeat and desolation? For certain, there'd be few laugh lines on a man like that.

The fat woman listened, but claimed she had only moved in a week ago, and she didn't know of no Brock. She disappeared back behind the door.

Then a dreadful thought flashed through Dr. Allen's mind. Maybe Diana had given him the wrong street, or worse, maybe his answering service had copied it down incorrectly. It wouldn't have been the first time. He cursed the Maria who had taken the message. That was the problem with this stinking city; nobody gave a damn anymore.

Wearily Dr. Allen trudged down the street to knock on the next door.

The two girls lay on separate tables, but once again they were side by side in the middle of an operating room, almost as they had begun more than twenty-five years ago. Laurie was on one of the tables, her eyes aglow with anticipation. Diana was strapped to the other, the gag stifling her muffled pleas.

The choking sounds were annoying Laurie, ruining her fun.

"Shut up!" Laurie screamed at her. "Joel, tell her to shut up."

Diana persisted, her muted cries getting louder.

Joel stopped his preparation of the IV equipment and turned to Diana, rubbing the sting from his ammonia reddened eyes. "She's right, you know. It's pointless trying to talk. Anyway, I know what you want to tell me. But don't you think it's been unfair for Laurie all these years?"

And with that he turned his back on the girls again. Striking a wooden match, he lit a Bunsen burner, sending the hot gas flames leaping into the air. With a slight turn of the nozzle, he adjusted the gas flow downward and carefully placed a beaker of water over the fire. The steady hiss of the burner punctuated the silence of the room as the flames lapped gently at the calibrated glass container.

Diana watched as he dipped two gleaming surgical knives into the boiling water. He let them sit for a moment, then meticulously wiped them dry. Diana bit into her gag, trying desperately to make her pleas heard.

"She's making them noises again. I'm gonna pull out her tongue," Laurie barked, her eyes hungry with expectation. She waited for a reaction from Joel, but he was too busy lining up his knives. Laurie reached out and stuck her finger deep into Diana's ear. Frantically Diana jerked her head away, and that got Joel's attention.

"Stop poking her, Laurie!" he scolded.

"Well, then let me help you," Laurie pouted. She felt left out.

"Just sit still, I'm almost ready." He rummaged through a drawer for a one-and-a-half-inch hypodermic needle, a Monojet, if he could find one. Finally settling for a one-inch job, he attached it to a syringe and aspirated one hundred milligrams of a pentobarbital sodium solution into the empty cartridge. Just enough, thought Joel, to keep her nice and groggy for thirty-five minutes. Then for the operation itself he would use halothane gas to put her out completely.

Laurie clapped her hands together in delight. In another moment, the hypodermic was ready and filled with a clear yellow liquid. Joel showed it to Diana. "This won't hurt. It's just a little pre-op cocktail. It'll relax your muscles, help you sleep."

He soaked a cotton swab with alcohol and dabbed Diana's arm with it. She fought against the straps. Once he stuck that needle into her, it would be all over. She would be even more helpless than she was now.

But her thrashing was useless. The needle slid easily into her arm.

Laurie giggled. "She's scared of you, Joel. But I'm not. You wouldn't hurt me, would you, Joel?"

Joel changed the needle and filled the syringe a second time. He turned to Laurie, the complete professional, a dedicated doctor doing once more what he had been trained for.

"Lie still now," he instructed her.

Laurie lay down on the operating table and Joel swabbed her arm with alcohol.

"Close your eyes, Laurie."

"I'm not going to."

"Come on," he said gently. "You know how upset you get."

Laurie squeezed her eyes shut and took the injection. Immediately, she looked up at him.

"It's not working, fishface. I'm not sleepy yet. You won't cut me until I'm asleep, will you?"

Joel pulled a sheet up to her neck, as though he was tucking her into bed. "No," he said softly, "I won't operate until you're asleep."

On the other table, Diana listened through a growing blur. She heard the tenderness in the doctor's voice and knew what it meant. It was the voice of a man who would do anything for a woman, anything she wanted.

And Diana knew exactly what her sister wanted.

Nervously Joel examined the intricate equipment and tools that surrounded the table, checking to make sure that the life-support systems were working as they should, that the knives and sponges were within easy reach. Satisfied, he flicked on the high-intensity surgical lamps, flooding the operating tables with stark white light. He was about to do the most important thing he had ever done in his life. A genius on the threshold of greatness.

Diana lay quietly on the operating table, eyes wide open, fighting desperately with all her will to retain consciousness. The pentobarbital was pounding its way deep into her skull. She felt the sheet fall off her left leg.

Slowly Joel stroked her thigh, making little concentric circles with a small alcohol-soaked sponge, carefully disinfecting the tense, subtly muscled leg. He rubbed her skin with a delicate caress, all the while speaking quietly to her.

"In a way, Diana, you've grown to be a woman in front of my own eyes. Do you know that this leg is actually the only part of your body that I'm not completely familiar with?"

Even in her panic and drug-induced torpor, Diana knew that something was wrong with what he was saying. Was Brock in his madness confusing her with her sister?

Then that thought was jolted out of her mind by the sharp ring of the doorbell cutting through the clinic. Diana's heart leaped. Dr. Allen had come for her! He had gotten her message.

But Joel kept on working and talking, seemingly oblivious to the interruption. "Do you know the true meaning of the word 'identical,' Diana? I know things about your body that I'm sure you don't even remember any more. You lost your first baby-tooth at the age of five years and three months. You hear better with your left ear than you do with your right. You menstruated early, at the age of eleven years and eighteen weeks. You were young, it must have embarrassed you. Your hair grows six-tenths of an inch per month, a little faster during the summer. Your bladder is unusually small, which is why you have to get up at least once a night to relieve yourself."

The doorbell rang again, and this time Joel looked up briefly before resuming his biological litany.

"You had twenty/twenty vision until the age of fifteen. Now you're slightly nearsighted, twenty/forty, if my memory is correct. You have a lovely birthmark on your left forearm, measuring three-eighths of an inch at its widest point." He lifted the sheet to see if the birthmark was there. When he saw it, he grinned. "Score another point for good old Doc Brock. And, Diana, you're slightly diabetic—I bet you didn't even know that."

His tone darkened ominously. "But despite your shared physiognomy, Diana, the girl lying next to you is a cheated version of yourself. From the day you were born, there was never any question which of you had been smiled upon."

Then he fell silent, remembering how fragile the minuscule body had been, how feebly Laurie's heart had beaten. It was a miracle that he had even heard her whimper, seen the almost imperceptible movement of her tiny chest. If he hadn't been alone, if he had been another hundred feet further down the hospital corridor, the infant would have been transferred directly to Autopsy. Instead the first hint of life had sent him darting into a deserted emergency room. He had filled a syringe with a life-sustaining stimulant and injected it into her sticklike arm, while gently massaging the tiny heart.

And when he knew that the crippled baby was going to live, he felt an elation he had never experienced before or since. In that moment he understood something of the Chinese saying, If you save a life, you are responsible for it.

No one had cared whether the little body lived or died. Certainly not the surgeons who had so carelessly left her for dead. Joel could see no reason to tell anyone that the child had survived. It was he who had saved it, now it was his. He would keep it and care for it and love it and it would love him back.

Even as the memories bubbled in Joel's mind, the surgeon in him took over again.

With a red wax pencil he drew a thin line across the swell of Diana's thigh. She felt the pressure against her skin, and it shook her mind back to wakefulness. Joel saw her muscles tighten, the ripple in her quadriceps, infusing his voice with confidence:

"No one's accusing you of theft, Diana, but whatever was there to take was taken by you. You left the hospital swaddled softly in blankets. That one over there," he said, nodding in Laurie's direction, "left the hospital hidden by me in a plastic basin piled high with dirty linen. You went home to a cozy cradle and a loving breast; my little Laurie spent the first weeks of her life in a one-room apartment, sucking oxygen from a tube."

Diana thought he sounded as though he blamed her for all of it, including his one-room apartment.

"At five years of age, Diana, you were running across a school yard playing hopscotch with your friends. Laurie was crawling until the age of eight. But that didn't matter, she was content where she was. She may not have laughed as much as you or slept as peacefully, but in her own way she was happy. So you see, Diana, while I'm sure all your books would tell you that I am to blame for the infection in Laurie's mind, I must take issue. It is you who have created the ache in her heart.

It is through your eyes that she now sees herself. It's on your legs that she came running home to me."

Then the doorbell rang again, longer and more insistently than before. God, please, let it keep ringing, Diana thought. She could see Joel glance up and glare in its direction. It was rattling him. "Did you know," he mumbled, trying to shut out the distraction, "that an infant's heart at birth is no bigger than a fully grown duck's?"

He tossed the cotton swabbing into an aluminum disposal unit and with careful deliberation chose a scalpel from the row of knives that were laid out on a table next to him. He held it over the flame of the Bunsen burner, turning it from one side to the other, testing the blade against the calloused skin of his thumb.

The doorbell sounded again, long and hard this time, for at least thirty seconds. Joel looked up, frustration clouding his eyes. What he was about to do required every bit of concentration he could muster. There could be no interruptions—no barking dogs, no yakking patients, and no ringing doorbells. Complete silence, that's what he needed.

He returned the scalpel to its place on the table and pulled the white sheet back over Diana's leg. He switched off the surgical lights and headed for the hallway. At the swinging doors he stepped back and shook a finger at Diana. "Not a peep from you. Remember, I can always take off a little more."

Diana dug her ankles and wrists into the coarse straps that bound her, praying that the pain would keep her awake. If she had any chance at all, it was now, while he was gone.

Outside in the swampy evening air, a disheartened Dr. Allen pressed the buzzer one more time. He looked again at the wooden plaque. J. Gavin, Veterinarian. What was a vet doing in this lifeless neighborhood? It had to be one of those government-subsidized situations, or a practice passed on from father to son. The old man wondered if he had stayed in his childhood neighborhood in Queens, might he not be living today on a street much like this. Still, if anyone in this godforsaken place knew where Brock was, it would be another doctor, even if he was only a vet. He'd wait a moment more.

Diana could hear the shuffle of Joel's footsteps punctuating the silence, echoing down the hall. For a second she relaxed her body, but this only allowed the stiffness to rush through her torso, filling her arms and legs with aching cramps. Panicky, she jerked her left ankle hard against the straps. The operating table made a shrill squeak, but her foot reacted with only the slightest tingle. The straps had cut off the circulation in her limbs; she could hardly feel anything. Or was that the effect of the injection? She didn't know. Again she jerked her leg, harder this time, and the table responded, jumping a half-inch off the floor and landing with a backbreaking jolt.

Then in a burst she vented her fury, raging against her bondage, bucking her body desperately atop the metal cot, which sounded its protests with groans and squeals. Angrily she snapped her weight to one side, and for a split second the table reared in the air before crashing back on all four legs. That was it!

Rolling her shoulders from side to side, Diana began shifting her weight rhythmically from one edge of the table to the other. Slowly the table started rocking, gathering momentum, lifting the two right-hand wheels off the floor and then the two left. If she could make the table topple over and stick her left knee out before it hit the ground—maybe a broken leg would delay the operation.

As the table swung back and forth, the screws holding it together started to loosen and rattle. Then, breaking the rhythmic sway, Diana jerked her pelvis upward against the straps and heard the table groan against the strain. She felt the rope around her right ankle give a little, and with a bone-crushing tug she yanked her foot free.

Thank God. At least that was something. She shuddered to think of what Brock might do to her if he came back and found her like this.

She looked over at the other operating table. Her sister slept peacefully under the drug. Then Diana saw something else. On the rollaway cart between the two tables a row of gleaming surgical knives was neatly laid out for the dreadful thing that Brock planned to do. They were practically next to her head. If only her arm had been free, she could have grabbed one and cut herself loose. With her liberated foot she scratched frantically at the cords binding her other ankle, but it was useless. Maybe . . . No, it seemed impossible.

Flexing her right leg, Diana extended it sideways toward the cart. The knives seemed miles away. To reach them her foot would have to travel at least one hundred and sixty degrees. The *jambe à la main.* How many times had Madame Margot told her, "Your ligaments are too tight and your muscles too short." There was no way she'd be able to complete the arc. Her body just wasn't built for that.

Like the big hand on a clock, her right·leg moved past the quarter-hour. Diana's toes, as prehensile as a monkey's, reached out hopelessly toward the knives. Already she could feel the muscles bunching in her thigh, pulling painfully at her groin. And she was still at least a foot away.

Extend! she told herself, forcing her leg out further, feeling the tendons tear away from the bones. Every fraction of an inch was a battle against the torture and the limitations of her body. Why hadn't she practiced more, why wasn't she built differently? The thoughts whirled through her mind. She groaned with the exertion, gulping for air, her lips silently reciting the only prayer she could remember. "Holy Mary, full of grace, blessed art thou among women and blessed is the fruit of thy womb, Jesus." The momentary distraction seemed to crowd out the pain, allowing the ligaments to loosen and the muscles to stretch. Her leg inched out further, shortening the gap.

Small, muffled moans escaped from beneath her gag, and her face contorted with agony. The sweat-drenched smock clung to her body. Further, goddamn you! she yelled to herself.

Then the tip of her big toe touched something cold and hung there precariously. The metal cart! Slowly Diana hooked her toes tightly around the cart's edge. With a quick tug she tried to pull it toward her. That's when she heard a tearing noise inside her thigh—a stacatto like ripping, and then a short, quick snap. Diana couldn't tell if she had torn a tendon or a muscle, or if she'd ever walk again. An excruciating pain rocketed through her body and roared into her head. It felt as though a little man with a hammer was trying to smash his way out of her skull. Convulsively she bit down into her swollen lower lip, piercing through raw nerve, but her foot managed to keep hold. With a tiny jerk the cart rolled forward ever so slightly.

Her toes crawled up onto the metallic surface and grabbed the first small scalpel. She winced in pain as the blade cut through her skin, sending dark-red droplets of blood dripping onto the white cloth. Diana ignored the pain, tightening her toes around the blade still further. Then barely breathing, she raised the instrument carefully off its tray. One inch, then another, still she held it.

Moving her leg ever so deliberately, she brought the knife back across the narrow space toward her body. Halfway across, she felt it slipping, greased by her own blood, which was now trickling onto the floor. One moment she had the scalpel and the next moment she didn't. She couldn't stop it. It clattered to the floor with a metallic rattle that she was sure could be heard all the way to Central Park.

Diana choked back tears of defeat. He'll kill me now, she thought. Even if he wasn't going to kill me before, he'll kill me now.

Joel looked through the curtains in his office window, trying to see who was at the door. Whoever it was had his back to him. The doorbell rang again. For the fifth time! What the hell was going on? Who was out there? His hand scratched at his forehead where the ammonia had eaten into his skin. Moving into the foyer, he glanced down the corridor at the closed white doors of the operating room.

Behind them Diana had her toes wrapped securely around another scalpel. She gripped it as firmly as she could, disregarding the deep cuts it was making in her flesh, using the pain to keep awake. She bent her knee again, bringing the knife across her waist and over to her left side.

For a moment her whole body shook with the strain as the knife hovered just above her wrist. Then cautiously she inched it down onto her rope bonds. With agonizing slowness and infinite care, Diana began to slice through the straps that bound her arms to the table. One after another the strands of filament popped loose from the thick rope, cut free by the razor-sharp edge of the surgical instrument.

Then the knife stopped, caught in the coarse hemp. It wouldn't budge. Diana jerked it sideways with her toes.

But much too quickly. The knife skidded free of the rope, slicing cleanly across the palm of her hand. The pain forced a muffled shriek from her exhausted body, and this time she couldn't stop the tears that streamed down her cheeks.

Still clutching the blood-wet scalpel, her right foot hung limply over the side of the table. Already it had ceased to feel like a part of her.

Joel opened the front door just a crack and peeked outside. He recognized his visitor right away. He was a doddering old fool now instead of a young fool, but it was Allen, all right. There was no mistaking him. The girl must have told him where she was going. The bitch. Who else would be coming down here looking for him?

Joel braced his foot against the open door and moved back into the shadows. In a high-pitched voice he spoke to his ex-colleague in the Spanish he had picked up during fourteen years in the neighborhood.

"*Quién es, por favor?*"

"I'd like to speak to Dr. Gavin," the old man answered.

"*Señor Gavin no está en casa.*"

"Will he be back soon?"

"*Señor Gavin está en New Jersey.*"

"Can he be reached by telephone?"

"*No es posible, señor,*" Joel snapped back.

Dr. Allen moved around to the side, trying to get a good look at the face he was speaking to, but Joel saw him coming and angled his body further back into the shadows.

Dr. Allen mimed holding a telephone receiver to his ear. "Can I make a phone call? Please let me in."

"*Señor Gavin no está en casa. Está en New Jersey.*"

And with that, Joel slammed the door in the old doctor's face.

For a moment, when she heard Dr. Allen's voice Diana thought she was imagining it. She was only able to catch every other word, yet that was assurance enough that the doctor had come to help her.

She worked furiously while the two men talked, all the while quietly blessing Dr. Allen for caring when

258

no one else did. She might die under Brock's knife, but at least she knew now that someone would mourn.

The pentobarbital Diana had taken in the arm was pulsing through her body with relentless assault. It was blurring her mind, slowing her reflexes. Her temples throbbed from the effort of merely keeping awake. She stared ahead, unblinking, frightened that if she closed her eyes, she would not have the strength to open those tiny flaps of skin again. The last thing she remembered hearing was a single set of footsteps hurrying back down the hall.

Joel entered the operating room and looked around. The two girls slept quietly under the effect of the drug. Their breathing was light and regular.

Not his. His was coming faster now. He could scarcely contain his excitement. Allen's interruption had only served to key him up to a higher pitch, and the anticipation had his nerves on edge.

He had waited so long for this. At first he hadn't wanted to do it, but finally Laurie had wheedled and cajoled and shamed him into it, as he supposed he had always known she would. At least he felt prepared in every way possible. He had had more than enough time to study and practice and perfect his technique.

Of course, a lot depended on the degree of musculature and circulatory development that he would uncover in that shriveled stump of hers, but there was every chance that in three short months his little baby would be walking—or at least limping—on two beautifully chiseled legs. Fleshy legs. Tanned legs. Legs that could wrap themselves around your back and draw you deeper inside.

Pulse pounding with excitement, Joel switched on the surgical lamps and stepped between the two operating tables. He pulled the rolling metal cart that bore his surgical knives up beside him, and checked them again, to make sure. He could leave nothing to chance. With quivering fingers his hand slid over the stainless-steel instruments, drawing confidence from their very touch. The knives were all there, neatly in a row, just as he had left them.

He stood motionless and sucked in a deep breath to try to calm himself down. He was ready now. He hesitated one final moment, teasing himself with anticipation. Then he took a step closer to where Diana lay sleeping and gently lifted the sheet back to expose her left leg.

But there was no leg, only a withered stump.

For an instant Joel thought he had gone insane.

He ripped the sheet off the sleeping body.

It was Laurie!

His jaw hung slack.

He stood there in shock.

It took a fraction of a second for reality to penetrate his stunned consciousness. The bodies had been switched. Danger signals crowded into his brain.

He whirled around to look behind him . . .

. . . and a jet of white-hot flame blasted his face.

Diana sprang off the operating table, her hands desperately clutching the Bunsen burner, her mouth clenched in a grim line. Again she aimed the weapon, using it like a blowtorch to hit Joel full in the mouth with another jet of burning gas. The strength of his scream shattered his own eardrums.

His hair ignited like a bale of hay, and his face glowed orange like a hot coal. With a cry of rage that shook the room, he lurched backward against the rollaway cart, the heat tearing at his eyes.

His hands groped for the surgical knives, raking the table with charred fingers, then seizing the instruments in both knotted fists. Pain had driven reason from him, but instinct remained, and, like Diana's, his instinct was for survival. And the way to survive was to destroy.

Take the knives and cut to pieces the thing that was hurting him.

He staggered forward blindly searching for Diana, slicing the knives through the air in a shapeless arc. He would know when he found her. He would hear the scream and feel the soft skin rip beneath the blades.

Diana flattened herself against the wall, watching helplessly as the howling mass of black, molten flesh reeled towards her, the deadly knives carving away the narrowing space that separated them.

She battled against her every impulse, keeping the screams bottled up in her throat. The blowtorch was useless now. The sputter at the end of the last explosion of flame had been enough to tell her it was empty.

Joel's knives pushed in closer, searching, begging, demanding her body. Already Diana could feel the waves of air from his swinging arms buffeting her face. For a millisecond she was incapable of moving; she felt rooted to the floor, a fascinated witness to her own destruction. Then Joel lurched forward, and she dropped to her knees as the knives slashed above her head, scraping across the tiled wall like a thousand pieces of chalk squeaking on a blackboard. His foot touched hers, and immediately he knew he had her trapped and ready to be slaughtered. He pointed his face down toward the floor and opened his eyes as wide as he could, the two small orbs glowing bright with fire. Whether he could actually see anything at all Diana would never know, but with a sudden shriek of death Joel raised both arms high overhead, ready to plunge the scalpels into her skull.

Diana could see them streaking for her head even as she pulled her buttocks up tight against slippery tile. She wanted to use the wall as a springboard. She was counting on whatever strength was left in her dance-hardened legs. Shifting her weight to the balls of her feet and doubling herself over for maximum leverage, she shot off the wall like a sprinter leaving the blocks, lunging forward at Joel's belly, ramming the mountain of flesh with her sweat-soaked head.

Joel's gut collapsed under the impact of the blow, and he exploded backward like a man shot out of a cannon. He reached out spasmodically to cushion his fall, toppling onto the table where Laurie still lay unconscious under the effect of the drug. The knives in his fist thudded into Laurie's chest like darts into a cork board.

Hurtled across the room by her own momentum, Diana lay sprawled on her stomach, her vision obscured by an overturned table. But she heard a dull, wet, smacking sound that sickened her. Getting to her knees, she saw Joel slumped across the body of the strange, deformed girl he had loved and devoted his life to. The flames began to envelop his torso and arms, sending a putrid yellow smoke curling upward into the air. His features had shriveled and were soldered together by the searing heat. He seemed to stare back at her through the two black holes that were once his eyes.

Dragging herself to her feet, Diana approached the two corpses and steadied herself against the table where her sister lay bleeding from the carnage in her chest. Diana couldn't believe that they were dead and she was alive, that she had won.

But she had. That thought registered. And following it came another. If she wanted to stay alive, she had to get out of there. Already the operating table was smoldering, threatening to erupt into flames. The building was old and dilapidated. In a minute it would be tinder.

Diana turned to leave. She hadn't taken a step when, like a corpse jolted to life, Laurie sprang bolt upright on the operating table with a howling, cheated scream that went rocketing off the walls. Her fingers stretched clawlike around her sister's neck, a garish grin spreading across her face. Diana let loose with a cry of her own. She could feel the gates of hell closing behind her. Flailing furiously at the rapacious hands, Diana eluded their grasp and went racing for the swinging doors. Laurie's head listed limply to the side, the smile of anticipation still frozen on her face. The bony fingers relaxed their grip on the smoky air, and her body toppled to the cold cement floor.

And then somehow Diana was outside, standing alone on the empty street. Blinking the tears from her eyes, nauseous, still fighting off the drug. But she was alive! Alive! She wanted to laugh and cry and shout and scream all at once. She breathed in deeply. Even the air smelled good.

And then suddenly there were sirens and flashing lights. A police car skidded to a halt at the edge of the sidewalk, and another came in right behind it. Uniformed policemen piled out, guns drawn, running toward her and then past her into Brock's house. One spoke to her. She nodded, not understanding, not able to say anything. And he, too, was gone.

Only then did she notice Dr. Allen climbing out of the back seat of the first cruiser, smiling at her, holding his arms wide for her.

Diana found herself smiling back at him. At life. At everything. Not happy yet, but with a giddy, almost delirious sensation somewhere inside her. Diana had never believed in fate and she didn't intend to begin now. Yet in a strange way she felt that something had awakened her past and for some reason she had been tested. She had passed the test, she knew that. Just as she knew that there were others in her life who hadn't. Like Tom. Yes, especially Tom. But that was behind her now.

Then her gaze lifted over the squalid street and settled on the shimmering red and white lights of the automobiles cruising the Bowery far in the distance. Caught in the waves of heat floating up from the pavement, the little specks of light seemed to blur into a single glow, like so many fireflies trapped in a jar. To Diana it looked like a giant lantern searching for her in the blackness, beckoning her back to humanity.

She wanted to go. Dr. Allen would help her. She started down the street, faltering at first, then more firmly. And in an instant she was running toward him.

On her own two legs.

About the Authors

Paul Jason and Jeffrey Sager were born in New York City and Boston, respectively. They met as freshmen roommates at Harvard College and attended the Harvard Business School together. *Entangled* is their first novel, and they are currently working on a second collaboration.

More Bestsellers From SIGNET